WHO KILLED BUSTER SPARKLE?

John W. Bateman

Attention schools and businesses: for discounted copies on large orders, please contact the publisher directly.

For information contact:
Unsolicited Press
Portland, Oregon
www.unsolicitedpress.com
orders@unsolicitedpress.com
619-354-8005

Cover Design: Divian L. Conner
Editor: Bekah Stogner

ISBN: 978-1-947021-79-2

Gratitude...

For comedian, writer, friend, accidental mentor Bob Smith, whose stubborn, humorous, contrary, inspiring, bullheaded approach to life, writing, and persisting taught me to keep writing and moving forward. No matter what. Especially when it came to Buster and Peaches.

For Mike Albo, Dimitri Anastasopoulos, Kirsten Bakis, Chris Bram, Michael Carroll, Rob Conant, Donnetta Graves (best conversation over mac & cheese that this writer has ever had), Christie Jimenez, James Hannaham (coach), John Norris, T.K. Lee, Mark Oliver, Eddie Sarfaty, Chris Shirley, Court Stroud, Kathleen Warnock, Michael Zam. For advice, manuscript notes, feedback, wit, and patience.

For Chris Arruda, Steven Bidwell, Brad Carpenter, Christine Clemmer, Divian Conner, Joe Cote, Joe Harrell, Livy & Katy Haskell, Sara Jimenez, Marie Josey, Myung Mi Kim, Gideon Lester, Christine Mayers, Rich Morris, Edwin Pabon, Dave Rimple, Draper Shreeve, Tony Valenzuela. Suellen. For encouragement, example, and mojo.

For Heather & Tim Miller, cause if you'd never had kids, then Buster Sparkle might not have been born.

For all the wonderful, weird, exceedingly talented friends who share their creative grounds where this story would (eventually) sprout. For Woogee Bae, Hunter Capps, Shayna Israel, Nate Moore, Mika Stanton. For Marti Gould Cummings and drag coffee.

For Tuesdays at Nine in NYC, the Yale Writers' Conference, the Author Secret Society, the Department of English Innovative Writing Program at University of

Buffalo, Glitterwolf Magazine. LP 183. For CRUX Climbing, who showed me how to understand, how to trust, and that there are no binaries.

For the Brown University Literary Arts Program Waitlist: the best thing I've never gotten.

For the team of honchos at Unsolicited Press, who didn't care that I didn't have an agent and helped give Buster and Peaches life between covers.

For my family who didn't try to commit me (as far as I know) when I announced that I'd quit my job in NYC and headed to grad school for writing.

Contents

For Kate, Henri, and Tee
Be you. Be true.

CHAPTER ONE

Buster Sparkle decided that life as a ghost was unspectacularly dull. Especially with partial amnesia.

Buster knew, though, that he now missed people. Fishing had become a cruel taunt. When Buster first conjured a pole and a can of worms, he thought that surely he'd made it to heaven (although he'd never really quite believed in it when he was alive). Except he realized that those apparitions offered nothing for live fish. Buster still hadn't even figured out how to "go bump in the night."

Invisible and isolated. If God existed, this must have been designed as punishment for transgressions in a life that Buster remembered only in pieces. Bored, Buster now wandered the quiet streets of Clover, Mississippi, searching for nothing, hoping for something, oblivious to everything. Except a few stray cats, which hissed and ran before he even had time to muster up a good *Scram!*

So, even without hope of actually meeting the pale, fleshy woman who rocked on the porch of #3 Raspberry Lane, Buster approached the rotting gate. A dewy, cracked walk led to the wooden-plank steps of the home. The thick air felt no different to Buster than if he had drawn an actual breath. Yet, as a ghost, Buster's existence was as complete as blurred fragments of a dream. He remembered a few things, but could not recall when he had last spoken to a living person who spoke back. Still, he decided to watch this woman sip coffee on the Spartan porch, barely sheltered from the steamy morning. It far exceeded another failed attempt to go fishing, and, now that he couldn't talk to anyone, people actually interested him.

A simple construction of boards and paint, #3 Raspberry Lane was well kept and orderly, like a storefront without merchandise. It wore chips and bends like fine wrinkles, most certainly having seen a decade or two more than the white woman who rocked on its porch. Buster waited and stared across a sparse, well-groomed square of grass that faded into a wilting stand of flowers. The ground looked dry despite the dew, though spring was not yet a memory and August droughts were three months away.

Even the weather in Mississippi could be oppressive.

He paused at a mailbox, opened and waiting for a delivery. It rose from a spray of dead grass. The smashed body of a dirt-encrusted whiskey bottle jutted from the muddy clay in the drainage ditch: a fence post of regret. On the side of the mailbox, in reflective letters, Buster read "J. Cotton." Below, in handwritten cursive ink:"AKA Pe♥ches."

The woman had stopped rocking. A pink bathrobe covered her broad shoulders as she looked up from her reading.

Buster turned to walk.

"Well, are you just gonna stare, or you gonna say hello?" she asked.

Buster continued walking.

"I'm talking to you," she said behind him. The woman's voice had an unanticipated deep tone.

Buster stopped mid-step. *She sounds like a man*, he thought.

"Yes, you. Didn't your momma teach you that it's not polite to stare?"

Wait. She can't be talking to me. His ephemeral throat closed, and he swallowed. Buster had not been acknowledged by anyone for a frustratingly ambiguous amount of time. Still, the accusatorial greeting from a white person echoed as familiar as guilt for skipping church. He turned and faced the house again. The woman had already stepped down from the glossy boards of the porch to the cracked walk and now headed in his direction. Her skin shone brightly in the sun.

"I get all kinda crazy boys on the down low staring at me. Ain't none of you learn how to properly say hi?"

Holy shit, he thought. Clearly, this woman could see him. "Um, I..." Buster stammered.

"You what? Can't use manners?"

"I'm... I'm sorry. I just," stunned to be in a conversation with a living person, he started, then stopped. *Why the hell am I apologizing?* he wondered.

"You just what? I had a bad show last night and, now, some fella is staring me down while I'm trying to say my morning prayers and have my coffee," she said.

This woman was not happy.

"I didn't know you could see me," Buster blurted in defense. He could have simply walked away, but this conversation terrified and excited him.

She raised an eyebrow. "Do what?"

"Look, I didn't mean no disrespect, but I didn't know you could..."

"Are you high?" She wrinkled her forehead.

"No ma'am. I'm-" He stopped. *Might as well,* he thought. "Here. Touch me."

"Oh, hell no," She put her finger up, not so subtly hiding a Louisville Slugger behind her with her other hand.

Buster flinched.

"I am done with closet cases asking me to 'touch you' and then getting all outta shape when you think a buddy mighta seen you." Her grip on the wooden bat tightened.

Dammit, put that away, he thought, then asked, "What are you talkin about?"

"Yeeees," she drew out. "I know your type." She moved side to side and planted one end of the bat onto the ground. "All macho and rough until you get a glimpse of Peaches Juba Lee, and then you not so straight," her voice pitched high. Her hand rested on her hip, and traced one side of her mouth with her finger. "Top, my ass," she muttered.

"Wait, what? Straight? What in the — what are you talking about? I'm a ghost, woman. I'm dead!"

Peaches cackled so hard that she started to cough, and then bent over to catch her breath. "Whooo, Boy! A ghost. That is a new one, I must say. I never had a gentleman caller try to claim he's dead." Her voice dropped. "Although...

some of 'em might as well have been once we got the music on." She stuck her finger straight up and pointed it toward the ground.

"Ma'am. I ain't got a damn clue what you think I'm doing here. I was walkin'," He paused. *It's the only way*, he thought, as unpleasant as he knew it would be. "My name is Buster Sparkle." Buster extended his leathered hand toward her.

"Well. Hello, Mr. Sparkle," as she extended her large pinkish hand for Buster's. "I'm Peaches, I'm..."

The moment their hands touched, or, at least should have touched, she shrieked, and both of them jerked back. As her hand briefly passed through his, Buster felt a surge of nausea followed by flashes of people and places. What stood out in that collection of moments, however, when Peaches briefly possessed him, is that Buster immediately realized that there was much more to Peaches than the way she appeared.

Buster wrestled with the new image of Peaches in his head as she stumbled backwards toward her house, continuing to stare at him. "Oh, Lord no! I am not ready to go! Peaches Juba Lee ain't ready to meet baby Jesus! Not today. I been a good—" she took another breath. "I already prayed about that summer in N'Orleans!"

Buster swaggered briefly. He felt Peaches in that momentary pass—a surge of fragments and memories from Peaches like bits of shells washing on a shore. It wasn't what Buster saw from her outside, but what he couldn't see, yet felt, from their momentary contact. And it confused him.

"Please Lord, don't take me now," she stammered as she shuffled backwards to the house.

"I'm not, I ain't," Buster swallowed. "I'm a ghost."

Peaches headed swiftly for the porch, choking the words, "A-maa-zin grace... how sweet the sound." Her voice dropped to baritone, "That saaaaved a wretch..." she gasped.

Buster turned away, then back, and finally walked through the open gate and up to the house. She couldn't hurt him, and he needed to know why she could see him. Peaches had picked up a Bible by her rocking chair and held it against her chest as she finally caught her breath and belted, "LIKE ME."

"Good grief. I ain't gonna hurt you," said Buster as he stepped onto the porch. "All I wanna do is fish, and you the first person—"

"No!" Peaches put her hand up, palm out. "You cannot... come into my house!"

And with that command, Buster felt neither hot nor cold, but in between. Something, like a rope tied through his stomach and attached to his belly button, yanked him from the house into the yard thirty feet away.

Peaches stopped sobbing.

Buster looked at his hands and feet and back at her. "How did—"

She just stared.

Buster tried to take a step forward, but he couldn't. Like a spoon stirring molasses, the harder he moved, the more difficult it became. He stepped back with ease.

"I... I..." he tried to speak.

Peaches looked at him with wonder.

"I just hadn't met nobody who could... see me," Buster said. The air grew thicker, and Buster stepped toward the street, as if a tide pushed him away from the house.

"You—you stay out there! Don't conjure up a demon whilst I figure out something to do."

"I can't come to you!" shouted Buster. "You ain't gotta worry about that. Besides, there ain't nothing to do."

"You aren't taking me home to baby Jesus?" asked Peaches.

"Nope. I—"

She smacked the Bible on a small table next to her rocker. "Then why the hell not?! I done all my prayers, all my Sunday schoolin', I took our Lord as my..."

"I ain't takin you nowhere else, neither," interrupted Buster. "I just wanna talk to you!"

"Oh." She paused and adjusted her housecoat. "Am I

dead?"

"Not as far as I kin tell," said Buster.

"But you are," she said.

"I think we got that cleared up."

"Why are you here?" she asked.

He shrugged. "Just walkin' today."

"Walkin' where?" Peaches asked.

"To town, I guess," answered Buster.

"To town? To do what?"

"Nuthin'. Don't wanna fish. Too hot, anyway," he said.

"Fishin?! You a ghost. Since when do ghosts fish?" she asked.

"Hold on a minute. Since when do men look like women?"

"Huh." Peaches put her hand on her left hip. "A sassy one, too," she said.

"Look. I didn't mean to scare you. I been a ghost for a while now. And you the first person I've met that can see me, and I wanna know why."

Peaches looked at him. "Why you reckon that is?"

"I'm just as surprised as you," said Buster. Both stared at each other without a word before he asked, "Can you see other ghosts?"

"Not 'til you sauntered up like a closeted peeping Tom."

"Do what?"

"So. A ghost. Why can I see you?" asked Peaches.

"I don't know—"

"What do you mean you don't—" she interrupted.

"Wait a minute. How 'bout I ask you some questions?" Buster sparred back.

"Lord have mercy," she said softly.

"Like, why you dressed as a woman?" Buster asked.

"What in the hell kinda question is that? I'm the first person who can see you and you wanna ask about my clothes?!"

"Cause I know you a man."

14

Peaches crossed her arms. "Where you from, Mr. Sparkle?"

He paused at being called by his formal name by this white woman—or man—or both. "Clover. I grew up just outside town," he said. "At least, I'm pretty sure of that."

"And we never met?" she asked.

"Not that I can recall," he answered.

"Well. Let. Me. Keep. It. Simple. Yes, you right. If, by man, you simply mean what's between my legs."

Buster shuffled and looked at his feet.

"Now, don't get bashful. You asked cause you seem to already know."

"But ain't that what makes..." Buster stopped himself.

Peaches tilted her head and looked at Buster down her nose. "Ain't that what?" she repeated.

Buster shifted. He wanted to know. "Why?"

"Why do I wear a woman's housecoat? Cause I want to. Cause I can. Cause it feels right." She spoke louder each time.

"But you a man."

"Huh. You a ghost, trying to go fishing. Why?" Peaches sparred back.

"Cause I want to," he answered.

"Okay then, we settled. For now." Peaches kept her arms crossed and stood firmly with her back to the house. She eyed her Bible.

"But that... that just don't seem normal. You prolly the only man in Clover wearing a dress," said Buster.

Peaches smacked her lips together and made a loud POP! She then took the middle finger of her left hand and wiped her left eyebrow. "Let's talk about *normal*. Cause you, being dead an all, havin' this conversation... is totally normal. I *must* be crazy because here I am, continuing in this discussion, when instead I should be asking you why the *hell* I can see you. All you seem to be is the ghost of Not-Christmas-Forgetfulness."

Buster remained silent.

Peaches sighed. "I might as well let you off the hook on

15

this one, seeing how I'm still talking. Some might call me a 'drag queen' although that's different. That's only what I do for a living. That doesn't describe how I feel on the inside. And yes, I was born a 'man' if you are so worried about whether I have a penis. But I got the soul of a woman. Now, that may be a bit much to handle for a dead man who just wants to walk to town, but your confusion ain't my issue."

Neither spoke for a few seconds. Buster looked away.

"Wait a second. How do you fish anyway? Can you pick stuff up?" Peaches put her hands on her hips. "Cause if you aren't all in my head, I got a zipper on a dress I need help--"

"Not exactly."

"Really? You telling me you going fishing, but can't pick up a fishing pole. Well isn't that like going to the hardware store to buy orange juice?"

"Huh?"

Peaches shook her head. Neither spoke.

"I'm waiting—are you gonna stand there like you hit a ball through my window without apologizing?" asked Peaches.

"Apologize? For what?"

She sighed. "Clearly you didn't get out much," said Peaches.

"Like I said, hadn't really talked to anybody in as long as I can remember, and I... well, it's kinda," Buster stopped and pointed at the mailbox, "Who's J. Cotton?"

"Me. That's my birth name," said Peaches.

"What is it?"

"Jasper. Jasper Cotton."

"Jasper, it's nice to meet you," said Buster. "I'm sorry I scared you. You the first person that kin see me. Only person, I reckon."

She rolled her eyes. "Close enough, I guess. I'm sorry, too. Come to think of it, my baseball bat probably made you as nervous as when I see 'em coming for me. But you can call me Peaches, Mr. Sparkle. That's just for the mail."

"Well, if you say so, although..." he didn't want to

finish the sentence and admit to this woman, or man, that he couldn't call a man by that name. He shook his head. "Call me Buster." He turned and glanced down the road for town.

"Busta," Peaches called out.

He looked back at her over his shoulder.

"You really alone? Can't even see other ghosts?" she asked.

"Hadn't seen another yet."

"Is that right," she said.

"Just me," he started walking.

"Wait!" called Peaches. "Don't leave me just yet; get back here! I got other questions for you. What's it like being dead? Am I gonna start hearing voices? Are my walls gonna start bleeding?"

Buster shook his head. Not ready to leave, certainly not ready to stay, Buster needed some time to sort through what just happened.

"Fine, then! Go on out and *not fish*." Her voice fading, Peaches called after him, "Mighty lonely to be the only one in a little town like Clover."

CHAPTER TWO

Buster stared at the mirrored surface of the pond. If Jasper could see him, then would a fish eventually bite? Maybe his fishing pole might appear real at some point? At least, that's what he wanted to believe as he sat on the neglected levee of the forgotten pond surrounded by a cluster of young pine. Buster couldn't remember much about this pool of dank water, except that he simply *knew* he'd been coming here before he was a ghost. Didn't he? It must have been his fishing spot before this existence, but the memory was fuzzy and distant.

With no luck or response from below the water, Buster left the levee and followed an old cow path barely making its claim against a growing thicket of blackberry and honeysuckle. His house sat atop a small rise above a field on the other side of a fencerow. Buster referred to the old house as "his," although Sally and Earl lived there, too. Maybe the house wasn't actually his, and he'd simply woken up there one morning. But he didn't recall whether his life had been composed of random circumstances, and random in death sounded absurd.

Invisibility carried a price that Buster no longer wanted to pay. If Jasper could see him, perhaps someone else would, too.

Buster walked up the porch steps and sat on a spindle chair. In the nearby swing, Sally balanced a checkbook on her knee and tapped keys on a small calculator. Her mahogany skin glistened warm in the gloaming sundown before she wiped her brow.

"I was invisibly conspicuous to white people and now I'm completely invisible to my own," said Buster as he watched Sally study her numbers and write in the register. The sound of local news on the television came from inside the house like an unwanted guest.

"So why can Jasper see me and you can't?" Buster wondered aloud.

"The regional economy suffers another setback as a local nursery closes its doors, losing half its stock to an infestation of a particularly invasive species of ants," said the reporter.

A bottle of beer rested next to Sally on a small table.

"No one knows where these ants originated from, but they are spreading rapidly," announced the television.

Sally clicked her pen and looked at a bank statement. "Dammit, Earl," she muttered. "Can't even keep your beer money tight."

Buster only then noticed that he hadn't seen Earl lately, although it didn't really matter. Sometimes, the details and sequence of events weren't clear, so Buster knew he might not remember, even if Earl had left the house only moments before.

The reporter continued from inside the house. "This particular breed seems similar to the crazy ant, which only recently appeared outside of Texas, where it was first discovered. For a small farming town like Clover, this tiny insect spells big problems."

Buster turned toward the screen door and strained to see the television. "Must be a slow day if all they wanna talk about is bugs." Buster looked back at Sally. "I wish you could see me. Or at least hear me."

Sally scratched off another word, as if trying to cut through the paper. "I am never gonna save up to go to school," she mumbled. "It's like I don't even exist to Earl."

"In related news, a local professor has received another grant for his research into biological ant poisons—" The newscast abruptly stopped after Sally pointed a remote toward the screen door.

"Sally, there's a ghost," said Buster. "This house has a ghost in it."

She put the remote down and sighed. "Maybe I should call Martha," she said as she stood up from the swing and headed for the screen door.

Buster spoke louder and slower, "Your... house... is... haunted," following Sally quickly before the screen swung shut. She headed into the kitchen and picked up the receiver from a telephone sitting on the countertop.

"Boo!" he said.

Sally said nothing as she tapped the phone first.

Buster shook his head. "I gotta go back to Jasper. Maybe he can help me figure out what's going on."

Sally picked up the receiver, started to dial, and then stopped. "Fuckin' bastard," she mumbled. She then walked over to the yellow wall by the door. "What do I do, Nanna?"

Buster looked at Sally, who now touched a faded photograph in a small frame on the wall. He'd never noticed it before. An elderly black woman wearing a short jacket stood on a gravel path in front of a church, clutching a small purse in one hand and an umbrella in the other.

Sally reached for the telephone, picked up the receiver, and dialed.

Buster stared at the picture, but couldn't focus on the figure.

"Martha? It's Sally."

Buster looked at her.

"I'm fine. How're you?"

Buster grumbled.

"I'm fine, I'm telling you," said Sally.

"Then why the hell you call her?" asked Buster.

Sally sighed. "You're right. I just... Earl."

Buster leaned against the wall.

"I don't know Martha, but it just... Well, you know how he is..."

Buster rolled his eyes.

Just then, headlights swept the house, briefly flashing the living room, and Buster heard the sound of tires crunching on gravel.

"Martha, I think it's him. I gotta go. I don't know what I'd do without you." With that, she hung up the phone and wiped her face. Buster turned and walked into the living room. A truck door slammed shut. Footsteps followed.

Moments later, "Ba-by! I'm home."

"Drunk as a skunk, too," said Buster.

Sally walked past Buster toward the front door. She turned on the porch light and latched the screen.

Buster looked over her shoulder. Earl slumped on the porch against a post. A bottle of whiskey sat between his legs, and a barely lit cigarette dangled from his left hand. A lightning bug flickered in the shadow of trees in the yard.

"What in the devil is wrong with you?" demanded Sally.

"Ba-by, I looove you," said Earl. He spit as he spoke.

"Oh, now you gonna sweet talk me?"

"Com 'er."

Sally didn't move.

"Com 'er baby, so I can kiss you."

"Sober up, then you can kiss me."

"Goddangit, I said come HERE." He pounded the bottom of the bottle on the porch. A loose board rattled.

Sally flinched and put her hand on her hip. "Earl, don't talk to me that way."

"Oooo," said Earl as he waved the cigarette in the air. Ashes fell like dust. "Sally don't want Earl to talk like that."

"If you want to kiss an ass, then you should head to the barn before you kiss this lily-white bastard," said Buster.

Earl stopped and stared at Sally. He put one boot on the floor and held onto the post as he stood up and swayed. "My house, I'll do what I want."

"My house," Buster and Sally said together. Buster looked at her and frowned.

"I told you not to come home drunk," added Sally.

"I ain't drunk."

"You drunker than Cooter Brown, Earl." She stammered slightly.

"About as useless, too," muttered Buster.

"Woman, I just had a couple with the boys..."

"Excuse me?! The boys? Who?" Sally did not leave the doorframe, hands on her hips.

21

"Aw, you know...Jimmy and..." Earl slurred, each word dripping into the next like syrup.

"What the hell is on his face?" asked Buster, as he stared at Earl with more disdain. The man looked almost pale green under the porch light.

"Is that lipstick on your cheek?"

Earl wiped his sleeve on his face and looked at it. "Naw, baby, it ain't." He swaggered a step toward the door.

Buster chuckled.

"Right," said Sally, taking a deep breath, "and you ain't about to spend the night on the porch." She turned and shut the door, fumbling quickly with the latch before it clicked with a bright THUNK!

Buster stepped back and watched Sally switch off the porch light and head into the kitchen. He followed and stood at the doorway between the living room and the kitchen, and watched as Sally turned on the faucet and washed a plate.

Moments later BAM! BAM! BAM! from the front door.

Sally dropped a mug. "Dammit!" she cursed as she picked up the piece of a broken handle.

Buster glanced at the front windows through the dim living room.

"Woman!"

Buster then looked back at Sally, who sang softly, "This little light o' mine..."

"Open up!"

Buster looked back toward the front of the house.

"I'm gonna—I'm gonna let it shine..." she continued.

"Open this goddangdoor afore I kick it in!" Earl shouted.

Her voice wavered as she sang louder, "This little light of mine, I'm gonna let it shine..."

"Woman!"

She inhaled before continuing, "Even in my home..."

BAM! BAM! BAM!

Buster walked to the front window and tried to peer through a gap in the curtain.

22

Sally cleared her throat and sang, "...I'm gonna let it shine."

Immediately, the front of the house fell quiet. Earl made no noise. Sally stopped, and Buster heard her gently put a dish in the drying rack. She remained still. The sound of the water faucet filled the otherwise silent house.

Buster tried to look through another window. Nothing but a dark porch and lightning bugs.

The faucet squeaked as Sally turned it off. The old house waited.

Buster couldn't see anything. "Maybe that bastard done passed out," he muttered.

"Please let him pass out," Sally whispered as she stood next to Buster and looked out the window. She carried a skillet in her left hand and turned the porch light back on with her right.

"You too good for him, Sally," said Buster.

"Maybe my brother's right," she said. "Maybe I should move on."

"Smart brother," added Buster.

"But not like he married," she turned back for the kitchen.

Buster looked out the window. The empty porch looked almost yellow in the artificial light.

"Maybe he done gave—"

The bright sound of breaking glass interrupted Buster.

"Earl!" shrieked Sally.

Buster ran into the kitchen. Sally shouted at a small, jagged hole in the dark window above the sink.

"Sonofabitch," he said.

"Woman! Lemme in my house!"

"This ain't your house, Earl. And you ain't coming inside when you talk to me like that!"

"I'm the man a this here house and I'll—"

"Like hell you are!" shouted Buster and Sally together.

This time, Buster turned and stared at Sally. "My house, Sally. Dead or not."

"Woman! I'll show you who wears the pants around here," Earl slurred.

SMACK!

"Right now, seems like Earl can barely keep his pants on," Buster said as Earl tugged on his jeans from behind.

Something hit the side of the house.

SMACK!

"Earl, you white fool, you too drunk to break into a country farm house," said Sally as she set the frying pan on the stovetop.

"I'll fuckin' show you, woman," shouted Earl.

Sally picked up the receiver and hesitated.

"Don't call the cops, Sally, they won't help."

Sally returned it to the cradle.

Buster walked to the kitchen window.

"Oh, ba-by, I'm sorry. Please lemme come inside."

Earl, or at least what looked like Earl, pawed the ground, doubled over on his hands and knees. He retched.

"Ooh, baby..." Earl continued moaning.

"Thank God he's too drunk to come inside," muttered Sally, leaning over the sink to look out the window.

"Is he peein' on himself?" Buster asked.

"Earl! You gonna tuck yourself in?"

"Thank ya honey, I knew you'd..."

The shape collapsed on the ground. "That bastard just passed out," said Buster.

CHAPTER THREE

"Again?" Peaches stared at Buster through the screen door and cooled herself with a red and gold fan.

Buster stood on the porch. The late sun was already behind the trees, giving the house a warm, golden glow. "Jasper, I got nowhere else to go."

Peaches stopped fanning. She breathed deeply, then pushed open the door. "Well, get on up here."

"Thank you," said Buster as he walked into the dim house, a weak A/C groaning against the weight of humidity. A glass pane rattled as it adjusted itself. He followed Peaches down the hallway toward a small room and continued their conversation.

"Jasper, they's makin' too much noise."

"Buster, they live there," said Peaches. She sat on a stool and faced a dresser, looking at her cheek in the mirror.

Buster paused and watched Peaches select a bottle of beige liquid. "I know. But I don't want 'em to."

"You are dead. You have no choice."

Torn between watching her put on makeup and concocting an idea to get back his peace of mind, Buster blurted, "Maybe you can help me scare 'em out."

"Ha! I want no part of that plan. I got better things to do than help a ghost scare a redneck out of his house in the sticks." She smoothed out the base and looked toward Buster in the mirror.

Peaches jerked around suddenly to face Buster. "Don't tell me you a vampire, too! I can't even see your damned reflection. Besides, can't you shut doors and moan like ghosts are supposed to do?"

"No. At least haven't figured it out. Wasn't given a rule book telling me what I can and can't do," responded Buster.

"So, you can't appear in a mirror neither when someone calls your name in the dark three times?"

"Nope. Wait a sec—why don't you try it?"

"No way, no how, and you here anyway! I'm not about to open up some witchy board for the rest of the dead to show up on my porch and ask me to scare away the living," she turned back to the vanity and continued to apply makeup. "But you lived there, right?"

"Yeah. Well, it feels like I did. But I wanna know why you can see me and nobody else can."

"That makes two of us. I don't wanna start seeing other spirits and reading tarot cards." Peaches looked over her shoulder. "Damn, it's spooky to try and talk to you when I can't see you in this here mirror! Besides, I can't afford to lose my mind at this young age," said Peaches.

Buster coughed.

"What?" Peaches then paused and turned to look in the hallway behind Buster. She cleared her throat. "Nugget! Bring mama her hair!" In ten seconds, a thin teenager carrying a blonde wig ran into the room, almost right through Buster.

"Need anything else, Mama Peach?" he asked quietly.

"No, thank you, Carlos, that's all. Get your homework done yet?"

"Not yet, Mama," he stopped mid-step.

"What's your first exam?"

"Trigonometry."

Peaches groaned. "If you need help hemming a dress or singing harmony, let me know. Where's Li'l J today?"

"He had Head Start." Carlos took another step.

"Oh, that's right," said Peaches, as Carlos stopped again and looked at her. "Thank God I'm not the only after-school program he has, or surely your momma and daddy would tar and feather me."

"They think I'm at the library, anyway. Can I go now? I wanna finish before I go home."

"Yes, boo, get on outta here before you catch any more gay," said Peaches.

Carlos ran back as quickly as he'd arrived.

"And don't forget to practice your clarinet for that

audition tape!" cried Peaches after he'd left.

"Who is that kid?" asked Buster.

"That's Carlos. He's one a my nuggets. He and some friends come over after school afore they go home, and I just make sure they do their homework. His little brother Jerome—well, Li'l J—comes too. They come a lot in the summer, too, when their parents are at work."

Buster scratches his chin.

"Just another little gay boy who needs a place to go."

"He ain't got a home?"

Peaches put down the lash she was trying to glue and faced Buster. "Buster, sometimes being bullied at home is worse than being beat up at school."

"Oh," said Buster.

She returned to the mirror. "So, I give them a safe place. Carlos, Li'l J, and all my other nuggets can always stay here if they need it. Some of their parents would run me outta town, cause they think it's my fault their kids are queer. But not everybody admits just how many things about ourselves we don't pick. Not like their parents woke up one day and decided they were gonna be straight. When it comes to religion, folks love to forget that God also made DNA and that we still don't know about all the colors and flavors of the rainbow," Peaches wiped stray lipstick from her mouth before continuing. "So I let 'em stay as much as they need. They just can't drink or smoke or do drugs, and they gotta promise to study, cause that the only way they gonna get outta poverty in Clover, Mississippi."

"So you help them. Their parents really don't like you?"

"Hell no! The only reason some of my nuggets are here is cause their parents work the late shift at the clock factory and don't know they come over. Latchkey kids, we used to be called. They safer here than home alone," said Peaches. "Or, at least more productive."

Buster furrowed his brow. "But you helping. That don't make sense.

"You definitely forgot a lot about being alive," Peaches

27

chuckled nervously. "A big ol' queer in a dress that sings and wishes he was a woman? And now talks to a dead man? Some think I'm gonna send their kids to hell. Some folks just won't believe that God made someone like me, like I'm the mark of Cain. But I try not to let it get me down. Bein' queer and out in the South is another way of being baptized by fire. And fire makes steel stronger. That's what I remind myself when people hate."

"Oh, yeah. Being poor and black in Mississippi wasn't a cakewalk," said Buster. He tried to focus on a specific memory, but it made his eyes itch. *What the hell?*

Finally, Buster added "Why d'you stay, Jasper?"

"Cause Peaches got a career as hostess at the Blue Magnolia. A girl has got to eat. And these kids need people to let 'em know they're loved. Not gonna stand by while someone gets put down for who they are. I did that once long ago and not gonna do it again." She turned suddenly to face Buster again. "Speakin' of, I need another part-time job if you can conjure up one of those for me."

"The blue what?" asked Buster.

"Did you even hear half of what I said?" Peaches deftly returned to a set of eyelashes. "The Blue Mag-nolia. The only gay club for seventy miles around here."

Buster shook his head. "I ain't never heard of it."

"Course not! You think we gonna advertise to all you straight boys anyway? Some of you might come over for batting practice."

"Guess not," shrugged Buster.

"And not the good kind," she muttered softly. "Aside, none a you can dance and you'd just make a mess on our dance floor."

"Can't dance?!"

Peaches looked at Buster out of the corner of her eye. "Can black Casper cut a rug?"

"No, I never had much for dancing. Should I ask if a white Aretha can actually sing?"

"Wait," Peaches turned, one set of eyelashes slightly

askew. "Did you just? You did not throw shade at me. Humph. Maybe you are a little human. I mean. Well. You know."

Buster pointed at some photographs on the mirror. "Who's that?"

"Billie Holiday, silly. Well, when she was young. One of the early divas to walk this earth. Only she ended up flying through it too quick, bless her heart."

"Oh, I think my nanna listened to her."

"Your nanna? So you clearly got a little memory left, boo."

"Some, yeah," said Buster. "But it gets foggy if I think too hard on it. Like trying to focus in the rain. It makes my eye twitch."

"Must be why you think that's your house where Sally and Earl live."

"It IS my house, Jasper."

She turned around to face Buster. "First of all, my name is Peaches, alright? You may think it's yours, but you are dead. And dead men don't own houses. Especially dead black men in Mississippi. Now you gonna have to get outta here before I cast you out, so I can get ready for my show."

Buster stood straight. "Dammit, Jasper, I need your help!"

"Help? To do what? Scare a redneck out of his house in the sticks? You can't expect to ask me for help cause you suddenly find you need a babysitter. Now, I have got to get ready!"

Buster turned and walked down the hall. *Babysitter, my ass*, he thought. Carlos' head peered around a doorframe.

Peaches yelled, "It just kills you to call me Peaches, don't it?"

"I'm already dead, Jasper!" How could he ever call Jasper by a woman's name, even if that's what he—or she—wanted?

"It's a figure of speech!" snapped Peaches as she smacked a table. "GO!" she shouted behind Buster as he approached a closed front door.

"Is Mama alright?" Buster heard a voice behind Carlos.

Two seconds later, Buster stared back at #3 Raspberry Lane. Peaches had cast him out.

"Ornery white fool wants me to call him a woman's name," muttered Buster as he turned and walked through the yard. He scrambled down a washed-out path in the kudzu-covered hillside across the road from Jasper's house. Somehow, he remembered the railroad that sporadically transported goods from the Tombigbee River along the tracks at the bottom of the gully. *Gotta not think so hard*, he thought, as he followed the tracks northeast out of Clover.

Thick vines and briars hung like curtains along the sides of the gully that opened wide as the tracks moved north. "Bet I'll have to walk the whole five miles to my house now, too," said Buster. "I go from one crazy house to another."

Buster wiped his forehead. "Who am I calling crazy? I'm a ghost that sweats, can't fly, and can't possess nothing."

He approached a bend in the tracks near his house on Old West Point Road, not quite certain how long it had taken. Sometimes, walking and showing up somewhere just happened, and others, it required effort. This afternoon seemed no different than when he was alive, and Buster seemed to have walked the entire distance. He could hear the shouting before he set foot on his—or what he thought had been his—property.

"Earl! Get your ass off the couch and come help me," shrieked Sally, her voice schoolteacher-sharp.

"Woman! Can't you see I'm listenin' to the game?" Earl slurred.

Buster walked up the short, gravel drive under the shade of two pecan trees. "Damn, I hope he's not drunk again."

"You can listen to the game just as easily in here in the kitchen as you can there in your chair."

There was a moment's pause.

"Earl!" she screamed.

As Buster stepped onto the porch, he suddenly found himself standing in the small living room. "Now, why didn't that happen an hour ago?" he asked. As usual, neither Earl nor Sally heard him.

Earl sat in a recliner by a fan, listening to a radio that sat on top of a dark television. Sally was not in sight.

Something flew through Buster's head and bounced at Earl's feet, knocking over three empty beer cans. Buster sneezed and tasted tomato.

"What the-?" Earl grumbled as he kicked a rotten fruit with his foot.

"What did you call me?" asked Sally.

"I said you f-"

Crack! The radio popped as the announcer shouted, "And the BEARS get another man on base as the Missi-..."

"Dammit! Get it togethuh, boys!" Earl turned and shouted at the radio as he hammered his fist on the top of the silent television.

Buster peeked into the kitchen and faced a thick, pungent odor. Sally stood in front of a basket of large tomatoes. Next to her were three piles: half washed, some peeled, another pile cut. Empty mason jars formed a line on the counter. Although his mouth no longer watered with hunger, Buster tasted the warm acidity as if he'd bitten into one.

Sally turned face-to-face with Buster and, before he could back away, walked right through him.

Zzzzzt! The buzz of a mosquito rang sharply in his ears as Buster shook with a small pop. In a flash, anger swelled and passed through him.

He groaned and put his hands to his head and breathed deeply. "People ain't supposed to possess ghosts," he said. "At least Sally ain't so bad."

The arguing continued in the other room. Buster leaned against the doorframe while he rubbed his ears. One thing had proven itself false, at least for Buster. Other than when he just appeared in a room, he couldn't walk through walls.

The ringing stopped, but not until the front screen door cracked sharply when it hit the jamb. Buster felt another pop as Sally stormed back through him. His skin tingled hotly.

"Dammit," winced Buster, as he doubled over and held onto the kitchen counter. Sally's anger, doubt, and jealousy buzzed through him like hot tequila, as he wondered whether Earl nailed that redheaded, white tramp from the liquor store.

He shuddered and shook his head. "So that's where Earl buys his cheap, cracker beer," mumbled Buster. He felt nauseous and sweaty, and his ears swelled with pressure.

Sally stomped around the kitchen, collecting scraps in a brown paper bag. "Damn drafty house," she said before she closed a window over the sink. Sally turned toward Buster.

He reached for the wall and stepped away from her.

Sally left the kitchen and headed to the front, and shouted out the front door, "Tell that nasty skank that she's got it coming if I catch her with you."

Buster shook his head as the buzzing began to subside. He could hear Sally sobbing in the adjacent room.

"I gotta lay down," said Buster. Slightly dizzy, he headed for the back of the house. Buster turned into the hallway and took an immediate right into a room that he considered his, although there was nothing to suggest this as true other than an emphatic speculation that he once lived in this house. A bed, pushed up against a wall, stood next to a sewing machine.

"A hangover is better 'n this." He put his hand on his head and rubbed. The room was dark and not too warm. Exhausted, Buster fell onto the bed.

It creaked.

"What the-?" Buster jumped up.

Sally stopped sobbing. Buster's heart pounded as a radio commercial drifted from the front room. Standing perfectly still, Buster whispered, "I just made a noise. A real noise." He looked at the chain hanging in front of him from the ceiling fan. He swatted at it and missed. Or, it missed him. His hand should've sent the chain flying wildly, but it dangled, steady and straight. Buster braced his stance on the wooden floor to take another swing.

Creak! Buster looked at his feet. He felt the board beneath him move. "I'll be damned..."

"Who's there?" Sally shrieked from the kitchen.

A smirk crept across Buster's face.

"Earl! You'd better not be messin' w' me!"

Buster put all his weight on his left foot, then his right and then jumped back to his left again. The board quietly shifted under his weight clearly and unmistakably, unlike other times when he thought things were moving, but they didn't. He shifted again. A faint creak loosened itself from the plank and echoed down the hall. Pounding footsteps followed, along with the flick of a light switch.

"Earl!" Sally peered through the door with a large, wooden rolling pin.

Buster stood in the bright light of the room. He jumped and stomped and kicked his feet on the floorboards. Not a sound—at least not a real one. Not even the hint of one.

"Dammit!" Buster shouted before he attempted to shove the desk against the wall. Nothing moved. Nothing.

Sally sighed. "These open windows is like livin' in a barn," she said, entering the room.

Buster sat on the bed to avoid contact. As Sally closed the window, Buster saw her red face and puffy eyes, and said, "That was your memory from the store, wasn't it? You saw Earl flirt with that woman. Cause I ain't never been there."

He leaned his back against the wall. "I ain't gonna try an' scare you again today, Sally."

"I didn't want to grow up to live like this," she whispered calmly before turning around. She cocked her head to the side and looked at the bed. "Huh. Almost looks like—" She then pulled the covers to straighten them, lifting Buster in the process.

He continued to watch Sally as she turned and flicked the light switch, leaving Buster alone in the dark of a house that he no longer owned, even if he now possessed it.

CHAPTER FOUR

"Welcome back, I guess," said Peaches, as she eyed Buster coming up the walk. She reached over and patted her hand on the seat of the empty rocker next to her.

"All they do is fight," said Buster.

"Don't bring it here." Peaches cleared her throat. "And before you get started talking about your I-gotta-jackass-in-my-house problems, let's talk about me for a minute. Why can I see you? Are you some ghost of twisted Christmas that's here to tell me how I'm gonna die or something? Cause if so, I don't wanna know. I'd rather be surprised when I drop dead in the shower from cancer of the hair follicles cause of hairspray and glitter. If it's diabetes, bring it on, because I am not about to give up my red velvet doughnuts. Just make sure I look good when they load me in the casket."

Buster exhaled. "Jasper, if I knew that, then maybe I'd know what happened to me."

"There you go again."

"Fine. It ain't about me, even though I'm the dead one."

"That's not what I meant, boo. Yes, you're dead and I am sorry. Cause life is for living, not wandering around trying to figure what went wrong. But I'm serious. I don't believe in accidents." She drank from a sweating glass of pink lemonade. "Why exactly are you here on my porch?"

"Cause I'm tired of this, Jasper! You see me. I don't have no place else to go where I can talk to somebody, and finally, I meet you and can talk to you."

She put the glass back on the table beside her and wiped the back of her neck with her damp hand. "Thought you were a loner."

"I was," said Buster. He sat in the rocker. "I don't like it anymore. I miss fishing. I want to know what else I'm missing. What I can't remember. Maybe you can help. You help those kids. Your nuggets. Maybe you can help me."

Peaches looked at the beaded boards above the porch. "Guess that haint blue don't work quite like they always said. I have lived near two cemeteries my entire life, and never thought about ghosts or spirits. Now, one shows up and asks for my help. To haunt a house that MIGHT be his."

Buster looked into the sunny yard. "Trust me that asking for help from you don't come easy."

"So, you lonely?"

"I guess. But more than that. Why am I in this house? You right – is it or was it mine? I don't know if I knew Sally and Earl or am supposed to know them, or what."

"Any pictures of you in that farmhouse?"

"Hadn't seen any," said Buster.

"Well, no telling," Peaches took another drink. "That Sally oughta leave that boy."

"And the sky is blue. Why do you think she stays?"

"Ha!" Peaches laughed hard and coughed before dropping her voice, "There's old Herman out on his porch," she nodded toward a neighbor's house. "He's one curious coot."

"Hey, honey boo, how are you?" Peaches spoke loudly, waved, and flashed a big white smile. A wrinkled, half-bent man shuffled quickly for his door. "He don't like for me to notice him," Peaches whispered to Buster. "But he notices a lot. He thinks he might catch something. So, I smile bright and pretty and love my neighbor anyway!" She turned back to Buster. "She stay because she don't know better."

"What's that mean?"

"People stay put when they shouldn't cause they don't believe somethin' else is out there waiting. Maybe like you." Peaches paused as her chair tipped back further.

"Humph," said Buster. "How do I believe in somethin else when I don't understand now?"

"So, yes, she don't know something—maybe some*one*—else is waiting for her. She think it's all—what's his name?"

"Earl."

"Earl and small town Clover where no one's different cause different will get you fired, and workin' at a job she prolly hates, but thinking it'll change any day, too. Maybe if she cooks right or keeps the house clean or does something JUST RIGHT, then he'll change. She thinks she can MAKE it work. She got Earl-on-the-brain is what she got."

"Do what?" Buster turned and looked at Peaches.

"Co-depen-dency, boo. Where you can't wipe your own ass."

The two sat quietly. A lawn mower sputtered softly in the distance. The sweet, faint watermelon scent of fresh cut grass lingered and a firefly blinked yellow-green under a chinaberry tree.

"Wonder when my li'l nuggets gonna be done with dinner."

"Gimme a nudge, Jasper," said Buster as he tried to rock the chair.

Peaches raised half of an eyebrow and looked at Buster from the corner of her eye.

"Please," he added.

Peaches tipped his rocker with her foot and mumbled. "Lord hep me if a dead straight man ain't trying to—"

"Excuse me?" interjected Buster.

"I said civil rights."

"Psssh. Watch who you talking to," said Buster. "I may be a little forgetful, but I am not ignorant. I did live through desegregation. Too bad that's not what I forgot."

Peaches flapped her fan. "I can't take much more a this heat. Sun already going down and it's still 98. Why didn't I move up North when I was young?"

"You and me both. Least you can do something about it now."

"So can you, Busta." Peaches turned and looked at him square in the eyes. "Help yourself move on to the next place, I mean. And don't roll those ghost eyes at me, cause I am not somebody that you wanna sass. I will cut you."

"You can't even touch me," said Buster.

36

"Don't," said Peaches as she put up her hand, palm facing Buster. "Well, color me purple, cause I gotta broke nail."

Buster turned away and watched a partially-rusted pickup truck drive slowly in front of Peaches' house.

"So, let's find out why you dead, Buster," said Peaches. "Maybe that'll help you. Do you remember where you worked? Bet I could find something out there."

"Maybe. But Jasper, you can't just go gallivantin' around and pretend you know me," said Buster.

"And why the hell not?" asked Peaches.

"Cause."

"Cause WHAT?"

"Well, you know."

Peaches cocked her head. "No. I don't. 'Splain it to me."

"Cause, well." Buster shuffled on his feet. He really didn't want to say what he thought. Peaches would simply cast him off the porch again.

"Well, go on and say it. You thinking it." She paused. "You damn fool."

Buster scratched his head.

"What — you worried they gonna think you're queer, too? You're dead, Buster. 'Sides, I wasn't planning on telling anybody I knew you. Not that I would now. I kinda liked you. Maybe. Not so sure right now."

Buster shifted in the rocker and watched a butterfly hover momentarily above his hand before flapping to a wilted flower on a nearby bush. "So how do you plan on finding out 'bout me without asking?"

"You let me figure that out," she said, watching the monarch. Suddenly, her voice pitched higher, "How long you been dead? You musta got struck in the head."

"Why does that matter?" he asked.

"Well, you ain't supposed to be here. Something's off. I never heard of a ghost with amnesia."

"You know any other ghosts?"

"Hush."

"Maybe I am supposed to be here. You don't know that."

"Oh, that's just lazy talk, like folks that don't want to change. You don't even know how you died," said Peaches. "I aim to find out."

"How?"

"I'll figure it out."

Buster laughed skeptically. "You gonna get yourself killed."

Peaches raised her eyebrows and cast a sideways glance. "And what, be dead like you?"

"Ha. That would be something."

She abruptly faced Buster. "Why can't you participate in your own rapture?"

"Say what?"

"I mean, why don't you wanna figure out how you died so you kin move on?" She stopped rocking momentarily. "Ooo, maybe you were murdered!" She rocked again. "Maybe it was a hate crime!"

"Well, don't sound excited!" said Buster.

"Buster, all you seem to want is to fish and kick that couple out of a house that you don't belong in. What did you do when you was alive? Didn't you get enough fishing done then?"

"Fishing was my favorite thing — what in the hell's wrong with that?"

"You didn't have a girlfriend?" Peaches asked.

"Nope. Not that I remember."

"Humph." Peaches paused. "Boyf—"

"NAW," said Buster loudly.

"Well, don't shrivel your pickle. It's not that big a deal. Did you ever get lonesome?"

"You know, I didn't much like being around folks," he said. "Not then, anyway."

"That's getting us somewhere, at least. For a man that didn't like people, you got what you wanted: invisible to ev'rybody. 'Cept now, you don't seem to like it very much."

"Seems that way, I guess."

"You guess? You GUESS?" Peaches flapped her fan shut. "Buster, what in th- who...I mean. You see any other ghosts running around?" Peaches extended one of her thick arms toward the road. A truck without a muffler roared by as it headed north away from town.

"I already done told you I ain't seen no ghosts."

"And no one else sees you besides a Mississippi queen. Don't you see you are outta place? Something isn't right. And it's not gonna right itself til you figure it out."

"I know I'm outta place. Now it sounds like you are singing my tune," said Buster.

She fanned herself rapidly. "You are a ghost for a reason, Buster, just like the Grande Old Dame upstairs put me in Clover, Mississippi. You are not MOVING ON until you get off your butt and help yourself move on."

At that moment, the sound of feet on cement was followed by a backpack and a couple of sweating bodies.

"There's Willie!" smiled Peaches. "And my Shay-shay!"

"Hi, Mama Peach!" cried Willie. "Movie night?"

"Right on time! Where are the others?"

"Just behind me—Carlos wanted to buy Li'l J some Skittles." Willie stopped at the steps and wiped his forehead.

"What are you doin out here? It's too hot."

"Just rocking 'til my nuggets showed, Shayla, and the house cooled off. The girls will be here shortly."

"Who are the girls?" asked Buster, as he quickly got out of the rocker before Willie plopped into it.

"Don't get comfortable," said Peaches to Willie as she stood. "The 'squitos will eat us up if we stay out here."

Peaches ushered them through the front door. Peaches headed for the A/C unit as the other two sat in the living room. Within minutes, other feet, some light and rapid, others measured and spiked by heels, walked up the steps.

"Knock knock!" said a soft voice.

"Hey, Stella baby, come on in," said Peaches, returning from the kitchen with glasses and some lemonade. "You, too, nuggets."

A spiky woman opened the screened door. "Need help with that pitcher?" Stella smiled as she walked behind Peaches into the living room. Two more kids followed, one Buster recognized as Carlos.

"If she do need help with a pitcher, no doubt she'll call a catcher like you," teased another voice from the porch.

"Rest assured that I won't be calling *you*, Lucy," answered Peaches.

"Sugar, I'm not on stage today. *Mike* will do," said Lucy-Mike. "Or fabulous. I'll take either."

"Pick one already!" said Stella.

"I have!" insisted Mike-Lucy.

"What?" asked Stella.

"Genderfuk!"

Stella sighed. "What the hell is that?"

"WHO. And I am sitting right in front of you!" demanded Lucy-Mike.

"ENOUGH," shouted Peaches. "There's room for everybody... guy, gal, or go-between. Not everyone's gay, not everyone's drag, and not everyone's trans. Just look at me!"

Buster scratched his head and looked at Peaches.

"Drag or no drag, Mike or Lucy, you still the same sassy shade queen as always," said Peaches.

Willie snickered.

Jerome looked up, "What's so funny?"

"I hope you put an extra cup a sugar in there. I wanna feel that diabe-tease comin," said Lucy-Mike.

Peaches clacked her tongue and looked at her, before asking loudly, "So what movie y'all wanna see?"

"*Priscilla!*" shouted Jerome.

"*Paris!*" said Willie.

"*Rocky Horror!*" Shayla nodded.

"*Breakfast Club!*" said Carlos.

The room quieted and turns to Carlos. Buster watched, somewhat bewildered at this strange mix in Jasper's house. He could not place any memory — or even the fuzzy hint of one — that compared to the fellowship unfolding in front of him. He wanted more. Something opened and immediately began filling an absence Buster felt for the first time his memory allowed.

Peaches raised an eyebrow. "Whatever you want to be, you be," she said. "But we will not be watching Miss Molly on my clock, bless her heart." Willie extended a fist toward Shayla, who accepted.

"Thank God," said Shayla.

"Don't call Her unless you need Her, little nugget," said Peaches as she rested the lemonade on the coffee table. "Who feels like popcorn?"

"Is anybody else coming over, Mama Peaches?" asked Jerome.

"Yeah, Mama, who else is gonna join us?"

Peaches paused and looked at six pairs of eyes, then glanced at Buster. "I'll see if we can't drum up a couple more, but it might just be us. You nuggets got to be home before dark and it's already after six. Some of your parents don't want you here with me."

"It's okay, Mama, we got it all worked out," said Willie.

Peaches stopped. "Oh?"

"I'm stayin' with Carlos and Jerome. They stayin' with me."

"And you know my mama don't mind me staying with you, Mama Peaches," said Shayla.

Stella looked at Peaches, "Sound like they *have* got it all worked out, Peaches."

"You nuggets gonna be the death a me. I don't want Department of Human Services ringing my doorbell!"

"You got nothing to worry about," said Stella, "We are all here, so it ain't like nobody gonna accuse you of anything."

"Right," groaned Lucy-Mike. "Nothing but passing the queer."

Shayla spoke up. "I was gay when I was five, Mama. Long before I met you."

"For real?" said Jerome.

"Yup," said Willie. "She knew she wanted to work at Homo Depot before that."

Shayla punched Willie.

"Damn, son, why you doing that?" he said as he looked at Shayla.

"Well if your greatest ambition is to be a sales clerk at Abercrombie & *Bitch*, then I guess you can say that. Just cause I'm into women doesn't mean I'm gonna work at a hardware store."

"You tell 'em, girl. You ain't about that life," said Lucy-Mike.

Peaches popped Lucy-Mike on the head.

"What?"

"What did I say about using that kind of lingo around my nuggets?"

"What lingo?"

"These kids need to learn functional English so they can leave Clover. Don't encourage that talk in my house."

Lucy-Mike rolled his eyes. "Because we all speak the Queen's white English here in Missi-ssipp-i?"

Shayla answered Jerome. "Some folks know they are gay from the time they leave kindergarten. Others figure it out."

"I wish I was gay," said Jerome. "Then, I could marry Miss Stella!"

"Aw, you just the precious little angel," smiled Stella, as she leaned forward from her chair and hugged Jerome sitting near the floor. "But it don't work like that for me."

Buster shook his head. "Jasper, what's he mean?"

Peaches smiled and glanced from Buster to Jerome. "It's okay, boo, you'll have plenty of options when you get older. Miss Stella's queer, alright, but not gay. She was just born the wrong gender. So, being gay wouldn't quite work. Besides, you probably couldn't marry her anyway. The county clerk in Clover still refuses to give gays marriage licenses."

"Unless they married to sister Clementine down at the

42

Lafayette Baptist Church. Cause that man she married is on the down-low," said Lucy-Mike.

"Wait. So. God just put Miss Stella in the wrong body!" proclaimed Li'l J.

"Doll, you are more precious than anything I've ever seen," said Stella. She leaned forward to Lucy. "Hush up. Who told you?"

Lucy smirked, "A little bird."

Stella exaggerated a gasp.

"What the hell is the down-low?" asked Buster. "I understand maybe half a what they're saying."

"Enough, Ladies! We are not gonna be shady cunts in my house! Oh dear Lordy, Li'l J, don't listen to Mama Peaches right now."

Jerome leaned to Shayla, "What's a *cunt,* Shay-Shay?"

Shayla, beet red and choking, shook her head. Willie rolled onto the floor, snorting and laughing through tears at the same time.

"Mmmkay!" Peaches said loudly, and strutted over to the television. "Here we go. What's the vote on *Priscilla, Queen of the Desert?*"

Jerome flung his hand, giddy with smiles. His confidence evaporated as he looked around and realized his lone vote. Buster felt a peculiar desire to raise his hand, even though he had no idea why or what movie Li'l J wanted to watch.

Stella patted his head, "It's okay, Li'l J, you keep your hand up. Every vote counts."

"That's right, little buddy," nodded Buster.

"*Rocky Horror?*" asked Peaches.

No hands.

Lucy huffed.

"*Paris is Burning!*" said Willie.

Five hands went up.

"I don't know, I dunno," Peaches shook her head. "I don't know if that's quite right for movie night yet."

Lucy blurted out, "Girl, you gonna have to let these

nuggets understand where we came from so we don't go back."

Peaches sighed.

Willie asked, "Why do you not wanna watch, Mama?"

"She met Venus and some of the other girls on a trip to New York City a long, *long* time ago," said Stella.

"Not that long ago!" said Peaches.

"Bless that poor little tranny's heart," said Lucy.

"Don't say that word!" said Stella.

"I can say it if I wanna own it!" cried Lucy.

"It's not yours to own! Not in front of me!" shouted Stella.

"We can take it back!"

"Enough!" shouted Peaches. "Lord, how many children do I have in this room tonight?"

Like a mouse pausing on a kitchen run, Jerome asked, "You went to New York City? My brother is gonna go there one day!"

Peaches remained focused on Lucy.

"Whew, girl, don't give me shade," said Lucy, "We just wanna watch a movie."

"We'll watch a movie. But let me read you now. That poor little *tranny* went the way so many of us is lucky we didn't go. Do not disrespect anybody in my house who died cause they's greatest crime is being true to themselves. And if Stella doesn't like that word, then don't use it around her. In fact, don't use it behind her back, either. Unless you walk that path, it's not your word to take back."

"Well, maybe I'm not the only one who hears you preach—maybe that's your next calling," teased Buster.

"Easy, Mama," said Lucy. "Who's disrespecting?"

"Easy, nothing." Peaches turned to the small pairs of eyes now focused in wonder. Peaches glanced at Buster briefly.

"Ahem. As long as we are talking movies," said Stella, "how are these kids gonna be themselves if they don't know how hard some of us fought to have it in the first place?"

Carlos looked at Peaches. "Pleeaase, Mama?"

She looked at Willie, Jerome, and Shayla. "Okay. We'll watch it."

Jerome moved closer to Stella as Willie and Shayla gave a high five to each other. Carlos and Lucy snapped their fingers. Stella tousled Jerome's head.

As if stuck in a memory somewhere else, Peaches added, "Y'all gonna be safe in my house."

CHAPTER FIVE

Buster made a bend along Old West Point Road and headed up the grassy hill for the house. Peaches hadn't been home earlier that morning, so Buster walked Clover's main drag hoping for some recognition, some sign that he wasn't entirely invisible. Yet, nothing. Not at the diner where wrinkled men played games of checkers whose excitement rivaled that of a boiling pot. Not at the corner service station that still had a "Full Service" pump and a pile of car parts behind a fence. Maybe a strange look from a cat, but then again, what cat doesn't stare, dart, and run unpredictably?

Earl's truck sat on the gravel outside of the house, where Buster felt like it never belonged. Buster walked up the steps and paused at the open screen door. Few sounds, other than a radio, made it from inside the house.

Immediately, Buster stood in the living room as if he'd never left.

"The gift I can't figure out how to control," mumbled Buster. The radio by Earl's chair crackled as a talk show played. A black heel rested between beer cans next to Earl's chair. Buster walked over to look closer and bent over. The radio whistled, then popped, and the talk program faded in static.

"That's new," he muttered at the radio.

He rose and the static softened back into a talk show. He heard laughter in the back.

Buster tried to kick the black shoe, but missed. "I can't walk through a wall, and I can't kick a woman's shoe. But a person can give me the heebie-jeebies, and I'll randomly show up inside this house. Of all the ghost powers to have, I got the worst ones." He walked to the hall that led to the back of the house.

Buster passed Sally's sewing room on the right, where he'd previously managed to make a noise. He turned left in the darkness and saw a closed bedroom door.

More laughter.

Something akin to anger surged within, and Buster took two steps toward the closed door into the darkness of the hall.

Creak! The bedroom door opened slightly.

In the sliver of light that sliced the dark hallway, Buster stared eye to eye with a woman, straddling Earl, wearing nothing but a bra. She suddenly grabbed a sheet and pulled it around her.

"You dirty bastard," muttered Buster.

"Earl! I think Sally's home!"

"Naw, baaaaaby," he slurred, "She ain't done at the college til 6 tonight."

Late afternoon sun reflected in the woman's fire red hair. She pulled herself off Earl, who remained flat on the bed.

"What, baby?"

"Earl! Someone's there!"

"Damn right," said Buster.

Earl fumbled to the edge of the bed and rose, completely naked. He stepped for the door and opened it wider. Earl swayed lightly. Light from the room bounced from the wisp of cigarette smoke that filled the small hallway.

Buster stepped back against the wall to avoid possession by Earl. That was the last thing Buster wanted. He saw the redhead, whose hair now looked more orange, pull on a pair of jeans. Earl peered into the hallway, bracing himself on the door, and snorted a "sonofabitch."

Earl smelled of beer and stale cigarettes and perfume that hinted of glass cleaner.

"Naw, baby, ain't nobody here."

"I heard something."

"Prolly just a ghost," snickered Earl.

"You gonna find out," grumbled Buster.

"You drunk fool, I told you we should notta done this today," said the redhead.

"C'mon, baby, it's just a breeze."

"Ain't no fucking breeze in July in Mississippi, Earl. Sally's gonna catch us. I gotta feeling."

"I gotta feeling too. Come back to bed."

"I'm done. If you ain't gonna take me back to the liquor store, then I'll walk back."

Buster muttered, "So you the girl!"

"I'm serious, Earl. I got a funny feeling. I gotta git home afore Sally comes busting up in here."

"Aw, baby, you know she ain't nuthin..."

Instantly, Buster boiled. Buster's arms tingled as if an electric current pulsed through them. Buster took one step, and with a full kick, planted his foot firmly on the door. It swung into the brightly lit room, knob bouncing into the wall. In that moment, the entire house shivered and its shadows flickered.

The redhead shrieked.

Buster stood motionless in the hallway as the tingle surged back up his arms, through his torso, and into his legs. He looked at his hands and feet, wondering if they might turn to flesh and blood.

Moments later, Buster heard footsteps on the dry gravel outside the house.

"Baaby, come back, it's just the damn wind," Earl shouted while leaning through an open window.

Behind Earl's shouts, Buster heard something else, like an echo, except the echo wasn't Earl's protests. Very clearly, yet softly, a mouse scurried in the attic, a distant afternoon thunderstorm clapped, a heartbeat pounded in a chest, and Sally whispered while driving home, "I can do this. I can make this work."

The shadows stopped flickering as Earl stormed from the room past Buster in the hallway. Buster heard Earl somewhere in the kitchen, fumbling through the refrigerator. A beer can opened. A moment later, the radio turned up and another can knocked over.

Must be in his chair, thought Buster.

"Fuck!" yelled Earl. Buster heard an empty can hit a wall.

A moment later, the refrigerator opened again, followed by another fizzy crack of an opened beer. "Damn woman ain't got no right," Earl said to no one. "Fucking wind."

Buster focused on the door he'd previously moved. It stood wide open. A patch of late afternoon sun fell across the bedroom into the hallway near Buster's feet. Buster put his hand on the doorknob. It felt real. It even felt moveable. He closed his eyes, squeezed and turned the knob. Sure enough, it felt like it moved, but when Buster opened his eyes, only his hand had moved.

"How did I kick the damn door?" he whispered. And then laughed. As if he needed to whisper.

Buster retraced his steps – surely there was something that made the difference, that creaked the floorboard and allowed him to kick the door.

"It can't be luck," he said.

Buster walked into Earl's bedroom and stood in the sunlight to savor the surge of tangibility. Covers spilled onto the floor. The strong warmth of the sun felt real. He began to sweat, just like a living person. Buster wiped his brow and felt the water on his hands. He held his hand in the sunbeam to let the sweat reflect the light. It glistened and refracted as the bead formed a drip on his fingers. The bead grew into a droplet the size of a ladybug. The droplet bulged and pulled itself away from his fingers, taking flight. A brief moment after it left Buster's fingers, the droplet vanished. It never existed.

Buster turned back for the dark hallway, where the sunbeam now reached across the room and through the door like a melon slice. Buster leaned on one foot, then the other, trying to put pressure on the bare floorboards.

Nothing.

How had he made the sound in the dark hallway? *Wait a minute*, thought Buster. He walked into the other bedroom where he'd scared Sally. Other than ambient light from outside the east-facing window, it was almost as dim as the hallway.

He stood in the middle of the floor, where the boards might be weakest. Buster took a breath, and counted, "One... two... three." With that, Buster leaned onto his left, then back to his right. Undeniably, the board *felt* like it moved, but Buster could see it didn't.

The radio from the living room popped on with static as the public radio tuned in. "Welcome to Classics Hour," sounded a voice.

"Damn that uppity shit!" yelled Earl, as he moved to change stations but hit the volume instead.

"How in the hell am I supposed to do anything as a freakin' ghost if I can't do nothin!" Buster grumbled. With that, he spun and threw a fist at the wall behind him. Instead of hitting a wall, however, Buster hit a small, framed picture of Sally riding a horse in a green pasture.

Buster's fist landed. As expected, Buster felt the simulated crack of glass. Then he saw something else, a tiny shard, ever so slim, popped out of the frame. Silently, it fell, but it wasn't the falling that mattered. The sliver did not vanish, but hit the floor. Buster had actually broken something. Something tangible.

The radio popped off.

Stunned, Buster left his fist firmly planted in the small picture, the glass now shattered in a tiny spider web of magnanimous proportions. His mind racing, Buster removed his fist, hoping this new reality wasn't another ghostly hallucination. The glass cracked again, this time releasing two, then five, then twenty shards as the glass popped into a hundred little pieces that clicked and tinkled as they fell. The picture itself swung loosely, then dropped five feet to the floor, sending glass everywhere.

Buster stood solid, looking at his fist, as the rest of the glass fell from his fingers. Immediately following, Buster heard empty beer cans knocking around and boom! Boom! Boom! as Earl left his recliner and bounded into the dark room.

"What the fu-?" said Earl.

Buster smiled and stared at Earl, who looked from the floor to the wall to the empty room to the wall again. Buster grinned with nervous excitement as the connection between himself and the world of the living grew ever so slightly. The shattered photo was enough for him. Even though it might not tell Earl that he wasn't alone, it meant one clear thing: Buster could move real objects. And that was going to be a very useful thing.

*****

"Jasper! I did it!" Buster paced at the steps of the porch as he waited anxiously for Peaches.

"Jasper?" he turned and took two steps to the left and back. "You home, Jasper?" The sound of a door closing, followed by heavy footsteps, came from within the house.

Buster stopped.

The screen door squawked opened. "Lord, have mercy," said Peaches as she stood in the door frame. "I'd say look at what the cat drug in, but I'm not sure what kinda cat would bring you home. Can't you find someone else to haunt?"

Distracted, Buster stared. Peaches wore a heavy pink bathrobe, hand on her hip.

"Is that paint on your face?"

"Really? That's what you need to ask me this very minute?"

"No. Jasper, you gotta let me in. I finally did it!"

"Oh, I do? Just cause you did something? Can't you tell I'm busy?"

"Doing what?"

"Excuse me?! Is that your business? I'm a busy girl trying to work and feed myself, and instead, I got a ghost running around trying to tell me he did... something. I am not letting you in my house until you tell me what's got you all fired up early this morning."

Buster's knee shook with excitement. "I done broke

something at the house!"

She paused and raised an eyebrow. "Lord, you just like a child," said Peaches, as she threw her hand up off her hip. "Well, get on up here before you let the 'squitos in. I may be able cast you out, but not them little devils."

The invisible barrier around Peaches' house relented, and Buster walked easily up the steps onto the porch. "I knew you'd wanna know. This means something!"

"I'd bust your butt if I could and knew it would help," said Peaches as Buster followed her into the house.

He remained in the doorway as Peaches took a seat on an old couch.

"Well, boo, you just gonna stand there? I ain't got all day."

Buster walked to a worn, velvet-covered chair opposite of Peaches and sat down.

Peaches straightened a nightgown across her broad shoulders and stared at Buster.

Buster's right knee rapidly bobbed up and down. He shook his head, "I broke a picture. Just like I was living flesh an blood."

"Well, that's dandy. You broke something."

"I slammed a door shut, too," he added. *Why isn't he excited about this?*

Peaches covered her mouth as she yawned. "Boo, that's great, but I don't see no hurry to run over here like you seen a ghost—what's so funny?"

Buster tried to hold back a grin. "Like I seen a what?"

"Like you seen a gho—," Peaches bit her lip. She stifled a laugh. "Funny, boo. For a dead straight man. So, when did this happen?"

Buster told her about the previous afternoon: finding Earl with another woman, slamming the door in the darkness, breaking the picture.

"That dirty fool!" said Peaches. "He got him one woman and can't keep his pecker in his pants for her?"

"Yeah, yeah, he's a playa, but *Jasper...* I *moved* stuff."

"Buster, that's great, but Earl is one fine mess."

Buster's forehead wrinkled. "Why are we talking about Earl?"

"Why aren't you concerned about Sally?"

"I—I don't know, but that's not the point."

"Maybe it is. Great you moved something, Buster, but life isn't all about you. Maybe being dead isn't, either."

"Me being dead IS about me."

"Ha! So why you invisible to everybody but me? Something is wrong in your house. If it's yours. And not just you being a ghost, cause that isn't right neither. Sally has a low-down, good-for-nothing pimp living with her. Fix it. That man is low cotton. Move Earl's ass outta that house."

"What do you think I've been tryin to do?!"

"But leave Sally alone."

"Why you so worried about Sally?" asked Buster. "I mean, maybe I can get my house back—"

"And do what with it, Buster? You dead. You got to stop worrying 'bout yourself. Maybe you got to fix what's wrong right where you are."

Buster didn't speak.

"So you shut the damn door and broke a picture and made a noise. But what you gonna do with that, child? Just live alone in a dark empty house, fish for fish that don't bite, and stay a ghost where you don't belong? Buster, maybe you got it backwards. You can do something but don't let it be for yourself. Get that nasty Earl outta that house afore he really tear up little Sally."

Buster remained quiet.

"Don't look it me like that."

"Like what."

"All poor puppy dog."

"Why are you so mean, Jasper?"

"Mean? You haven't seen me mean, boo. I'm just honest."

Buster listened to the air conditioner rattle. Maybe Peaches had a point. But what?

53

"So let's figure out what you gonna do now that you know how to move stuff."

"I didn't say I knew how," said Buster. "I just did it. But it's gotta be in the dark."

"Then, maybe you can go bump in the night after all. We can find out. No doubt you can do it again. You just got to get the Good Lord's help to bring it out. And don't roll your eyes at me when I mention Her name."

"Jasper, you more confusing than a rambling preacher to a hungry congregation. First a lecture on moving on, now God's involved. You gay. How can you believe in God when..."

"When what, Buster?"

"When." He paused, "When the preacher say that isn't right."

"Oooh, so you gonna have a li'l Bible study with Peaches? You gonna tell me God is gonna smite me cause I ain't living a certain way because a preacher said it? Do you think black folks is Cain? Cursed by God cause that's what white churches once told everybody?"

"Jesus, Jasper. I am not trying to start an argument with you. I don't know how we even got on this subject."

"Then what you wanna talk to me about?"

"I came to tell you I moved something," he said.

"Then why you preaching?"

"I'm not the one preaching! You brought up God. I'm just asking why you always talking about Him—"

"—Her," Peaches interjected.

"—when all the preachers I ever heard talking about it being wrong."

"Okay, boo. Let's talk. Why you think they say that?" Peaches flapped open a fan.

"Cause it in the Bible," said Buster.

"You ever read the Bible?"

"Well, some."

"Then keep reading. You'll find that little book says a lot, some of which don't make sense. It wrong to eat pork. It wrong to play with animal skin. Like, footballs? Baseballs? It wrong to have two livestock in the same field. It wrong to have clothes made outta wool and cotton. You gotta marry your dead brother's wife. Even if you already got one. So don't start picking pieces you want outta the Bible to judge somebody else, unless you want them to start picking outta the Bible to judge you back. Cause the Bible justified slavery. Segregation. Stoning." Peaches stopped flapping her fan and stood up. "Want me to continue?"

"Look at me. Do I really gotta remind you that you don't need to educate me about slavery, Jim Crow, or burning crosses? I'm not judging." Buster folded his arms. "Can we talk about me now?"

Peaches ignored him. "God made me as I am. That I know. Just like the Lord made you. I can't help it that He made you black and you can't help it that She made me white. I can't change that you straight. Or a ghost. You can't change that I like dresses and sing like Etta James and would rather spend my life as a woman married to a man."

Peaches planted her hand firmly on her hip. "But only the big guy in the sky know what He—or SHE—is doing and don't EVER come around here suggesting that who I am is *wrong* cause some preacher told you that. The good Lord knows my heart. And *that* is how She is gonna look at me."

"Jasper. Good grief, I didn't say you was wrong—"

"Might as well have." Peaches flapped her fan open and sat back down.

"What?! Why are you picking a fight with me?"

Peaches stopped and tilted her head down as she raised her eyebrows, looking at Buster.

"You always start a fight. I just came to tell you I did something and you end up acting like I came after you." Buster stood up. "I don't know why I bother coming."

"Me neither, boo, but here you is, all hot and ready. Ain't nobody coming into mah house to tell me that who I am is wrong."

"Jasper, you fool. I did NOT say that. I just asked the damn question. Not all black folks think white folks is racist. Not all straight folks think gays is wrong. But I do wanna know how you talk about a God that every preacher I ever heard says He don't like you. Cause I wouldn't want that kind of God, just like I don't believe in a God who says slavery is okay."

Peaches turned and looked at a clock on the wall and starting flapping her fan furiously.

"It ain't like I ran up here calling you a bad word or something. You talk about God. And all He done, if He exist, is leave me stuck as a ghost where I can't do nothing. Except today, when I moved something, and I thought you'd be happy for me. You 'spect me to do something for somebody like Sally when I can't do nothing for myself? Why should I listen to you preach? Ain't that the same as you telling me not to listen to some other fool preach about their God?"

Peaches turned to face Buster, "I—" and then stopped.

"So, yeah, I rolled my eyes. Cause I don't know why we are arguing or even what God you talking about. And naw, I don't think God hates nobody. But I ain't gonna listen to ANYBODY who tells me what God wants from me. You said it yourself, ain't nobody else really know 'cept what's in their heart. And if your God exist, then He gonna look at my heart, too, cause that's what He made."

Peaches bit her lip and flapped harder. "You right. I don't know what you gotta do. But you're not where you supposed to be. If all you cared about when you was alive was fishing, then fishing now, as a dead man, is not gonna get you where you supposed to git. The Good Lord only helps those who help themselves. And your lesson is gonna repeat itself 'till you get it. So, now you can move stuff in the dark. Use that to do something good."

"So why are *you* here? Maybe your good Lord forgot about me. Maybe He doesn't like me."

Peaches flapped ferociously and bounced her knee.

Buster leaned against the wall, as he saw sweat drop from Peaches' forehead. She stared directly at him. "DON'T talk to me about being LIKED," she said. "Life ain't about being LIKED."

"Hah. You ain't got to tell me that. But you ain't alone."

Peaches stood up and pointed her folded fan at Buster. "Boo, you got no idea what it's like to be me." With that, she stepped into Buster. "I'm hungry and gotta eat. Now git!"

Instantly his ears buzzed and POP! Buster felt exhausted and nauseous.

Then, he remembered being six years old, standing under a sign that read First Missionary Baptist Church, looking down at saddle browns and pink socks through blurry eyes. Buster saw small, clenched fists between tear drops, and heard children's voices around him singing, "Fag-got, fag-got, Jas-per is a fag-got."

"Please stop," he whispered through choked tears.

"Why, before granddaddy comes and saves you?" teased one girl.

"Only sissies wear pink, you little tick-turd," said a boy.

"Don't call me that! My Nana made me these..."

"You still a faggot crybaby."

Suddenly, Buster felt a strong thick hand grab his arm and yank him from the ground. He felt a pop deep in his shoulder.

"Quit blubbering, Jasper! Don't be a ninny," said a heavy voice.

Buster looked up and saw a burly man with short legs drag Jasper away from the now scattered pack of children.

"Poppa, I didn't do..."

"Stop crying," bellowed the man, who looked ahead as Buster stumble-ran on Jasper's thin legs to keep up.

The buzzing stopped and Buster steadied himself. He stood somewhere outside Clover along the Old West Point Road. Buster wiped his face and felt tears.

Buster suddenly remembered another memory of his own, of two drunk white men stumbling into his grandparents' yard, hurling words that no child should learn except through a history book. *His grandmother grabbed his five-year-old hand and shoved him into a broom closet in the kitchen. "Baby, no matter what, cover your ears and hide under these rags. Not a peep outta you and you can have ice cream before dinner."*

Buster stood on the road, oblivious to the Mississippi heat. He looked up into the clouds, trying to recall the rest of the memory.

"No, Jasper, I don't know what it's like to be you. And you don't know what it's like to be me," he said as a crow flew overhead. For the first time that he could remember, Buster didn't want to go fishing.

CHAPTER SIX

The following day, Buster headed for Raspberry Lane to make some sort of peace—even if it wasn't necessary—with the one living person he knew. "Jasper, I'm gonna go with you," he said from the porch steps.

"Why?"

"Cause. I wanna go. It's doing something."

"Suit yourself," Peaches yawned. "Not like I can keep you away when we're outside my house anyway."

"Maybe I'll remember something."

"That's a start. Better than trying to convince me to haunt your house."

"They was bothering me."

"Like you? Showing up unannounced? Me talking to you like I'm crazy?"

"Fine. Send me away again. But they are in *my* house, Jasper."

"Buster," She looked around before pointing her finger at him, "You may think it's yours, but it ain't. You just living there. Well, being a ghost there 'till you move on."

"Why don't you get to know me before you judge me?" Buster asked.

The tin roof popped in the heat as neither spoke for a moment. "Some people live their whole life wanting to know what the afterlife is like, and all you seem to want is to stay at home or fish, when you could go all kinda places and see all kinda things."

"Like what, Jasper?"

"Hell, I don't know, use your imagination! If you don't wanna solve your murder or something, go snoop around and find out who kilt JFK. Go see famous people. Go someplace you never been. That's what I'd do. Oh, wait, even better, go read me some lottery numbers."

"So now it's about you?" Buster smirked.

"Don't get sassy like me. That's my job. I'm just goin' to the physical plant to apply for work. Not exciting, but you can tag along." Peaches walked down the steps onto the walk wearing a pair of snug jeans and white shirt with the two top buttons opened.

"You goin' like that?"

"Excuse me?"

"Them jeans don't leave much to the imagination."

Peaches looked down and turned to check her front and back. "Are you saying I'm fat?"

"No, Jasper. Never mind. It's fine. At least you ain't... well..."

"What?" she asked.

"You know. Wearing a dress?"

"Lord, Buster, I'm not stupid. I'm a Miss'ippi Queen. I am not about to go to an agriculture college wearing a dress. I already got enough stacked against me."

"So, can I ask you something?" said Buster.

"Oooo, that's always a loaded question - just ask. Let's not get fired up again today. I like you."

"Well, I don't want to upset you or nothing."

Peaches stretched her shoulders back as she walked, "Then ask it like Ms. Ann Landers would."

Buster scratched his head.

"Don't be a dick."

"Oh," he chuckled. "Well," he cleared his throat. "Nothing like that, I don't think. So, you a guy, but you dress like a woman."

"Yes..."

"You're gay, right?"

Peaches stifled a snort. "I like the word 'queer.' It's a little more flexible. Why?"

"I never met a gay before."

"Okay."

"Do you... Do y'all always—"

"—We don't all wear dresses, boo. Most gay men don't dress up like women."

"Oh."

"I'm not typical."

"What's a normal gay man look like?" Buster asked.

"Watch yourself," said Peaches. "Golden rule."

"Huh?"

"What would you say if I asked you what a *normal* black man looked like?"

"I'd think you probably lived in an all-white neighborhood and only spoke to us when we was mowing your yard. We're all different."

"Alright then. Each of us is different, too," she answered, looking at Buster, who opened to speak, then didn't. "Go on," she added.

"But you said you wasn't *typical*. What's that mean?"

"Maybe I should check myself, too. I was born a guy, but sometimes, I don't feel like one. Sometimes, I feel like I was born inside the wrong body. Sometimes, I look at my hands and don't know whose they are. When I was real little, I wanted to grow up and be a momma. I didn't understand it doesn't work that way. At some point, I felt ashamed that I had a penis but didn't want it. I thought, well, maybe I can be happy just bein' gay. I tried that. Then, I'd have dreams that I was a woman, and I never woke up as happy as I was in those dreams. For a long time, all I wanted to do was die and not have these feelings any more. So, for me, it's not really about being *gay*. Who I'm attracted to is different from who I am inside."

A bike whizzed passed.

"So what's it about?"

"You ever hear of gender dysphoria?"

"Say what?"

"Gender dysphoria. When a person doesn't identify with... well, to keep it real simple, *their gender parts...* they have at birth," Peaches answered.

"They don't like bein' a man or a woman?" Buster asked.

"Well... no," said Peaches. "People like me have genetic differences. I'm talking more than X and Y chromosomes and penises and vaginas. Our brains look different. Basically, my brain looks like a woman's brain. Even though I was born with a penis."

"Humph," said Buster, not certain how to continue. The sun had already climbed above the tree line. Buster stepped over a withered worm curled into a question mark. They crossed the street into the open sun.

"Whooo, it's gonna be hot today," Peaches said.

"Think they hiring?"

"Yes, honey. I read the classifieds this week. The physical plant at the college is hiring in housekeeping services."

"How do 'splain bout your other job?" asked Buster.

"I won't have to. I'll tell 'em I'm a hostess—well, I'll probably say *host*—at a nightclub. That's all they need to know and I don't wanna test their understanding when I need work. But most a them don't care 'bout that anyway. They just wanna know if I can clean."

"Really?"

"Buster, are you sure you grew up here?"

"C'mon, Jasper, I may look simple, but I am not stupid. And I do remember a few things. I sure as hell remember what it's like to be black. That don't seem to go away just cause I'm dead. Most white folks around here didn't care to know what black folks could do unless it's mow grass, cook fried chicken or bar-be-que, sing gospel at your funeral, or fold laundry. As long as some colored man came in to sweep the floors and unclog the toilets, a lot of 'em seemed happy. If they even noticed. What I don't know is what they'd say to a white gay man—or what's the word—who dresses like a woman trying to do the same thing."

Peaches said nothing.

"Cat got your tongue?"

"I'm thinking, boo. I never thought about it that way," she said.

"Course not. You's one a them," said Buster.

Peaches stopped under the shade of a magnolia. "Hell,

no."

Dammit, what now? Buster thought to himself.

"One of *them*? You think professors at the college give a shit about a poor white queer like me? Buster, I got news for you. I didn't grow in a big fancy house. As far as I can speculate, none of my family did, neither. I don't even know who my great-granddaddy was. I may look white. But I am not one a *them*."

"That's like a blonde-haired, blue-eyed German saying he wasn't a Nazi. He may not have been, but he wasn't different. And you aren't different. Different is what white folks around here don't like."

"DIFFERENT? You really think I'm not DIFFERENT? Open your eyes, Buster, and take a good look. I wear dresses and sing show tunes. I loved Judy Garland when I was six. Go to the country club and see where my kind is. Nowhere. They won't hire me, unless it's to send their wife flowers or help plan their daughter's wedding. But they'll give black folks jobs to—"

Buster bristled and stepped forward. "Don't go there."

"You right." Peaches cleared her throat. "I am white. At least you have a shot because your skin color, thanks to President Kennedy."

"Did you hear me?" Buster's back straightened. "Is that what you think?! That after four hundred years of chains, black folk got it EASY just cause a president passed a civil rights law? Just keep on crying how bad you got it, fool. You can still fit in. It ain't the same. Women don't lock their doors when you walk by. A room doesn't go quiet when you walk in, with a hundred eyes staring at you. Federal troops took us to school. People were assassinated for helping us. Clover, like most every other Mississippi town with any money, started a white, private, *Christian* school right after the Supreme Court said separate ain't equal. The rest of 'em fled for the hills. See any black teachers or students at that church school? Maybe one or two, every few years."

"I'm a man who likes men and should have been a

woman. Just where do I fit in?" Peaches turned and continued to walk, looking straight ahead.

"No," said Buster, as he stepped ahead of her. "You are NOT done. Lemme ask you, Jasper. Cause I do remember something else from being a kid. Did you watch your nana get raped by drunk white men while a third beat your grandpappy?"

Peaches didn't answer.

"Cause I did. I was five. It was 1964, and all that the white police gave a shit about was that *uppity colored boy* at Ole Miss. Nobody paid no attention to three men who stopped by on account of being nothing but drunk bigots. They beat the shit outta Papa and raped my nana. They didn't know I was hiding in a broom closet, or I'd be dead. Nothing like a little black boy for a couple of Klansmen to beat like a sack of feed. If they hadn't passed out, they'd probably have kilt all of us. Some church people dragged the men back to the road after they passed out, and waited with us in the kitchen until they woke up and left. Ev'rybody was too afraid to call the police and didn't wanna tell them civil rights workers after what happened down in Neshoba. My nana took me to church and then went and drowned herself in the river one week later."

Peaches pursed her lips.

"So, DON'T try to talk to me 'bout you being gay and poor white trash and having it *worse*. That's like saying a rotten orange is worse than a rotten apple. Both stink. We both born in bodies that people gonna say shit about." Buster stepped to the side and motioned for Peaches to continue. "So, be my guest. Go get your job. But don't talk down to me like you all understanding when arguing about different things."

"Did they ever——" Peaches started, then stopped. The two proceeded down the street and turned left onto the main road that passed the Washington Street Cemetery for campus.

Peaches looked toward a small rise in the distance. The

Mississippi heat smothered like a blanket. Buster followed her gaze, and they both stared at a dirty granite confederate soldier, with an arm broken off at the elbow, jutting from the graveyard into the white-blue sky.

Another block, Peaches and Buster crossed between two old brick pillars with a wrought-iron arch above. A sign read: Welcome to the Mississippi Agriculture College. A grove of old trees, some pecan, some oak, greeted visitors through the entrance.

"Jasper."

Something foggy itched in his memory.

"Jasper."

Peaches turned, "What, Buster?"

"I worked here."

"I thought we knew that."

"No, I mean... I think I actually remember."

"Good. Now you might be some help." Immediately, Peaches quit talking as two students rode past on bicycles.

"Crazy faggot," muttered one.

Peaches cleared her throat and tilted her head up slightly as she turned and continued to walk along Washington Street.

Buster watched the biker turn down another street before he ran to catch up with her.

"I mean it, Jasper, I remember something."

"Good. Now stop talking to me when folks are around," said Peaches, staring ahead as if looking for something in the distance.

They walked in silence.

Buster looked over at Peaches, then away. Finally, he said, "Good thing you aren't in a dress."

"Do all dead straight men like to repeat themselves?"

The two approached an enclave of old brick buildings that faced each other across a large lawn. Old cypress trees flanked a path that wound past buildings made of limestone and undistinguished concrete and cement.

Before reaching the enclave of brick and lawn, Peaches

turned and walked along a path that lead north.

"Where's you going?" asked Buster.

"I told you, Buster, the job office. Now, hush."

The two followed a side road that curved toward the basketball coliseum in the distance. A small, one-story limestone glass and brick building, a remnant of 1970's progress, sat under an old cedar tree. A small sign staked the domain out front: MAC Facilities and Human Resources.

Peaches led as Buster followed. The entry to the building smelled of bleached linoleum. Two chairs flanked a small table with a fake plant and stack of magazines. Nothing about the fluorescent blandness of the reception area reminded Buster of anything.

"Less charming than a dentist office," mumbled Buster.

Opposite the unused seating area, a window opened into a work area with three desks. Two desks were covered in papers of sorts, occupied by women. The third desk was neat, clean, and empty, other than a pad of paper and pencil. A plastic nameplate on the empty desk was inscribed with "Supervisor."

"Butch time," said Peaches.

"Good mawnin, ladies," resonated a voice that was not fully Peaches, but not completely divorced from her either. Buster's mouth dropped open as this new Jasper/Peaches persona filled the room.

Before Buster could speak, the very deep and bold Jasper/Peaches put a hand up just out of eyesight of the open window. His/her palm faced Buster.

"My goodness, big fella, and can we help yeeew?" said the woman sitting behind a nameplate that read "Sally Jo."

"Yes, ma'am. My name is Jasper Cotton, and I'm heah about a job I saw listed at the physical plant."

"You sound like a dude, Jasper," said Buster.

Jasper/Peaches ignored him.

"Oh, why sure thing, we'll jist git you fixed up in a jiffy. Just a little paperwork to fill out," continued Sally Jo.

Buster peered into the window. Sally spoke without

leaving her desk and continued to look at Peaches, then looked at other woman and nodded her head. The other woman, Daisy, according to the name plate, smiled briefly, then looked down.

"Can you read an' write?" asked Sally, as she put a finger on her cheek.

"What the hell?" said Buster. "Something ain't right with that woman."

Peaches cleared her throat. "Yes, ma'am," said Jasper/Peaches.

Daisy rose and headed for a door.

"Aw, bless yore sweet li'l heart," Sally added. "Well, not little, but you know what I mean." She flashed a wide toothy grin.

Daisy opened the door slightly and stuck her head through, and then made a motion toward the front counter. She left the door ajar and returned to her desk.

Moments later, a balding, overweight man in a short-sleeved, button-down, sweat-stained shirt appeared in the doorway where the second woman had been. His tie was crooked.

"Well, hello there, *buddy*," he emphasized, "how can I hep you?" As he adjusted his tie, the man smeared mustard on it.

Buster looked at Peaches and wrinkled his eyebrow, "Didn't she just tell him you's here? Why they acting so weird?"

Peaches ignored Buster.

"Yes, sir. I came to see you 'bout the job at the physical plant listed in the paper," cracked Jasper/Peaches. Buster noticed a bead of sweat trickle down his/her temple.

"Jasper," he whispered, "Aw man, it's... you got some makeup on your face."

"Oh," muttered Peaches, as she wiped her face slow and hard as if massaging her jaw. Jasper/Peaches returned quickly and cleared his/her throat.

"Yessir, we got lots a *gentlemen* lookin at that, so if you can fill out this heah application that Sally Jo's givin you, we'll take a look." He put his finger on a folder on the desk and smirked.

"Fat bastard's lying. Just look at him," grumbled Buster, as the sweaty man looked down at an empty folder in his hands. He then put it back on the desk and picked up another one with papers in it and flipped it open, brushing crumbs off his shirt in the process. Jasper/Peaches continued to ignore Buster, forcing a smile through the reception window.

Sally Jo, the younger woman, brought Jasper/Peaches the application form and a pen. "Just lemme know if ya need sumthin, an I'll be right heah, okay?"

"Yes ma'am," and Jasper/Peaches turned and walked to the small sitting area.

"Jasper…

"Hush, boo, I ain't got time," Peaches appeared again in her large, squared frame as she picked a chair in the corner.

Buster peered through the window. "Woman talking to you like you a six-year-old," he grumbled. *Always made me mad*, he thought. The two women muttered softly to each other before resuming other office tasks.

Peaches cleared her throat and focused on the paper.

"Name. Sex. Education. Employment."

"How you gonna answer that?"

Peaches whispered softly. "Nightclub Staff. They'll assume it's at a small honky-tonk, but even some closet boy sees this, he won't say nothing. 'Sides, if I stay general, then they won't ask much for a job like this." Peaches continued writing.

Buster paced.

"Does ev'rybody talk to you like that?"

"Like whut?"

"Like them?" Buster motioned to the window.

"You almost sound like you care, boo," said Peaches, who appeared again, as she looked at Buster.

"I know that tone well. And I still don't much like it."

68

"It's alright. Yeah, some straight folks talk to me like that. Some don't, but they usually aren't bigots or scared. I just let it go."

"Sometimes, when I'd hear that tone, I wanted to burn the place down I was so angry, but being angry got a lotta black men killed," said Buster. "So, I held it back and burned inside. Not sure I am gonna do that now." Buster paced while Peaches completed the application.

The waiting room smelled of bleach, old paint, and stagnation. Captioned photos of the campus, some old, some new, dotted the walls. Most pictures showed large farms, plotted into neat squares and rectangles, resembling a quilt of earth, crops, and irrigation pipes. In one of these photos, behind tall rows of corn, was a small building. Buster stopped and peered more closely at this building.

The caption for the photograph read:
MAC Research Station, also fondly known as The Outhouse, is a small research station where graduate students conduct experiments and research poisons for pesticides and herbicides. Built in 1971.

Buster traced the outline of the building with his finger, feeling the glass. He noticed a small group of figures outside the lab.

"That's on the way to my house," said Buster, as he recognized the patchwork farms he'd walked past countless times before. It had to be his house, if he recognized these nearby farms, didn't it?

"Yes, ma'am, I got my application ready," said Jasper/Peaches as she stood at the reception window.

"Well, aren't you a speedy one?" smiled Sally Jo. "Just leave it right there on the counter. Lemme make a copy of your driver's license before you go."

Buster turned and watched Peaches hand Sally her license through the window. Sally held it up and looked at Jasper/Peaches, then the license, then back.

"I'll be back in just a jiffy; don't you worry one little

bit," she smiled.

"Damn woman annoys me," said Buster. "Wish I could shove those papers off her desk and wipe that fake grin off her face."

Peaches cleared her throat and shot a glance toward Buster. Buster kept quiet and turned back to the photograph of the research station. If what had started was a memory, it passed. Buster touched the picture again, but couldn't recall the thing that had stirred.

"Thank you, ma'am. Y'all have some pretty pictures of the college up here," said Jasper/Peaches.

"Oh, those old thangs? Some of these pictures are from the farms just north of here," said Sally.

"Only been up here for the ball games," said Jasper/Peaches. "Haven't been out to the farms."

Buster turned, "Since when you like football? Or would that have been baseball?"

Peaches dropped a hand down below the window and flipped a middle finger at Buster.

"At's what I thought," answered Buster.

"Well, I'm gonna add this to our pile of applications and we'll be in touch with you just as soon as we make a decision."

"Thank you, Miss. I really hope I get this job. You'll see I'm a hard worker," said Jasper/Peaches.

Sally smiled. "I'm sure you are, honey," she added before turning back to her desk.

Buster watched Peaches as her shoulders dropped. What was left of the Jasper/Peaches persona poured out like air from a deflated balloon. She turned and headed for the door, whispering, "C'mon, boo."

Buster looked at the picture of the Research Station once more before he followed Peaches out into the hot Mississippi summer.

The two walked in silence. Peaches walked slower, and her eyes followed the sidewalk. Buster kept opening his mouth to speak, but couldn't put words together. Peaches was simply no longer Peaches.

After crossing the gates at the edge of the university, Peaches finally broke their silence. "I'm sorry we argued earlier. You were right. I didn't mean to say I had it harder than you, it just came out like that."

"Thank you," said Buster. "I'm so used to hearing people try to tell me that I..."

Peaches put her hand up. "You're right. We both get judged, but it's also different. We can't really compare them; we just gotta listen to understand each other."

A cyclist whizzed quietly passed.

"Wanna know what I remembered?"

Peaches responded similarly, "So what you remember, boo?"

"It's a feeling," answered Buster.

She chuckled. "A feeling? I get that in my leg when a storm's a coming."

"Okay, fine, more than that. Something about that research building in the pictures."

"You mean out by the farms?" asked Peaches.

"You know about that place?"

"Everybody knows about the farms north of the college. In high school, we used to sneak down the dirt roads behind the cornfields to look at stars and drink wine coolers cause we couldn't get beer. I think the store clerk who sold to us was part-blind. Fancy crops and stuff back there. They have one building where all they do is count bugs they find in the dirt."

"That's the one. I think I was there. I mean, not just walking by it, but actually *inside*."

"Good for you, boo," said Peaches, as she put her hands in her pocket.

Buster paused. "Well, if you wanna get rid of me, let's check out that place."

"Not sure I'm ready to get rid of you just yet," she said.

The two continued along Washington Street before turning onto Raspberry Lane. Buster couldn't shake the feeling he had when touching the photograph. If he'd been there as a living person, then surely he could go there as a ghost. Part of him would remember, wouldn't it? Perhaps if he thought about that building long enough, he'd appear there, just like when he sometimes showed up at the farmhouse in the country.

Peaches turned and stopped at her mailbox. "Buster, I gotta take a nap and get ready for my show tonight. You mind leaving me alone for a bit?"

"Alright. I'm gonna head out, maybe head out for that Research Station."

"Be careful," said Peaches.

"Cause I don't wanna go get myself kilt, now do I?" answered Buster.

The furrow on Peaches's forehead relaxed as she smiled gently, "Hush. I have no time for lip from you."

"I'll see you soon," he smiled, as Peaches finally loosened.

"Like I got a choice anyway. Seems like I'll see you until we get you raptured. Now, git, so I can get my beauty sleep for tonight. And I'm sorry for what I said earlier, Buster. I know people judge you, too. Maybe you should come see my show," said Peaches.

"You can stop apologizing, Jasper. Maybe I'll come sometime," said Buster, and he walked away as Peaches headed into her house.

Buster knew that he would pass by the edge of the farms on his walk home. Maybe it would be a short walk through corn, or a longer walk through cotton and maize to find the research station. So far, Buster appeared at places he remembered, like his house, the fishing hole, the cemetery. The rest of getting around, it seemed, required a little more effort. Would thinking about the photograph of the farms be enough for him to show up in the middle of a row of soybeans? How *did* it happen other times? What allowed Buster to appear somewhere he wanted to be? He never *tried* in those instances, at least, not like one tries when learning to ride a bike. Clearly, that sort of trying had not worked with ghostly stuff.

Buster walked. Perhaps walking was the key.

Ten minutes later, Buster headed along the Old West Point Road under the shade of old oaks interrupting an unkempt fence row. He thought about the picture of the research station again. It didn't look big, like other buildings on campus, but maybe that was because the field of corn in front of it was so large.

Buster *wanted* to be at that metal building, but he didn't know exactly how to get to it. He couldn't remember anything about the building, but he *knew* he'd been there.

CHAPTER SEVEN

After two miles of honeysuckle vine, withered gardens, and innumerable dragonflies and gnats, Buster reached vivid, yellow-green rows stretching for the horizon. A green and blue sign marked the boundary of the university farms. The déjà vu familiarity of massive farms wrapped around him like poison ivy, certainly not welcoming, even though this one was owned by a public university rather than inherited by a wealthy white man.

"I've been here," he said.

Buster scanned the horizon for a metal shed, or anything that might resemble the building in the photographs, but the tops of the corn waved like feathers. *Won't know until I try*, he thought. Yet, he cringed at the prospect of walking across the massive farm.

He stepped from the road into the mini-forest and stopped after a few steps down a wide row. Thick, shiny stalks rose above him. The dry summer season had started its slow onslaught elsewhere, yet, here, he tasted the smell of sweetly pungent, irrigated soil. "That college got the money for sure," he said as he inhaled deeply. For a moment, Buster listened to the papery leaves rasp and whisper in the stilted breeze. Insects buzzed their strange language and, in the distance, an engine hummed.

"What stories can you guys tell me?" he mumbled, then added quickly, "Never mind, let's not go there."

He walked further into the deep shade of the endless rows. The buzzing quieted and Buster shivered. "Well, Jasper, you aren't the only one. At least something else knows I exist."

The stalks stood tall, despite the weight of their well-grown ears. Buster almost believed that the plants shifted as he passed down the narrow row, rather than from the faint afternoon breeze.

After a steady walk that included two rabbits, a snake, and more dragonflies, Buster came to the end of the row at a small ditch. It hugged an elevated gravel road that vanished in both directions. To his left rose a tall metal sign inscribed with small numbers and a date. Buster's heart pounded as he realized that, across the road, the building from the photographs rose above the fields, shiny and larger in person.

"Hot damn!" he exclaimed.

Three trucks were parked at the side of the building. In the distance, behind the station, a green tractor turned soil in another expansive field.

Buster stepped out of the curtain of stalks, into the ditch, and onto the farm road.

Behind him, Buster surveyed the field he'd traversed. The corn was simply one section of many, each planted with different crops, like uneven squares on a checkerboard, or a patchwork quilt: the corn he'd just left, sections of cotton, soybeans, more corn, something that looked like maize, and others in the distance. Fields surrounded the building as the center of a farming universe.

He crossed the gravel road for the metal building that looked like a giant half-tube, cut lengthwise. It offered nothing spectacular, other than a nagging feeling that Buster had been there. He continued across another shallow ditch and onto a leveled parking lot. Outside on a post, Buster noticed a bright orange, giant sock of sorts that flapped in the weak summer breeze.

"Now to git inside," said Buster, staring at a weathervane that pointed southwest. "If I been here before, maybe I can just ... pop in."

He crossed the lot and stood at the metal and glass front door. Inside, he saw an open room with desks.

"Boy howdy, Jonny Lee, you see that last sample? That poison flat out kilt them new fire ants eatin' up everything."

Buster faced the voices and saw two college-aged men turn at the corner of the building.

"Shit, did more than that. Plum withered them eggs.

Larvae barely got crawlin' afore they finally died," said Jonny Lee.

"Best poison I ever seen. Queen ate it, kilt the babies as they hatched," said the other guy. "Good thing, too, cause them new ants popping up everywhere is nasty boogers. Worse than crazy ants down in Tex-as."

"Professor Tinsley got him a winner, don't he?" asked Jonny Lee.

"He gonna be able to patent that? I mean, he got all them Brazilians helping him, too."

"Mike, you dumb shit, they ain't from South America. They barely speak Spanish." Jonny Lee spit on the grass. "Go back to hitting balls off the tee box."

"Jonny Lee, you moron, they speak Portu-guese in Brazil. And that's in South America."

"Well, wherever they from, it ain't South America."

"How come you say that?" asked Mike.

"Well they ain't Catholic, for one, like all them Mexicans that hang out at the abandoned Wal-Mart parking lot, waiting on shit farmwork that nobody else will do."

"Fuck if it matters. They right smart and helped old Tinsley brew up one mess a poison."

"Hey, how 'bout a beer when we get outta here today?"

"Sounds good, man. Just gotta pick up my check and then head out."

"Counting bugs again?"

"Fuck, yes. I hate nematodes," said Mike. "I'd rather do anything than count fuckin' worms all day."

"Somebody gotta do it," responded Jonny Lee.

"Psssh. As worthless as the football team was last fall, they oughta send them out here."

"Them boys couldn't even count two touchdowns; you think they can count 'todes?"

Mike laughed.

Buster stepped away from the door as the two approached. Jonny Lee opened, Mike followed, then Buster.

The two headed inside the building, followed by their

invisible guest. The front room wasn't as large as Buster thought, but it had two desks, three phones, and several filing cabinets.

"Hey, Heather," said Mike.

"Hi, boys," smiled the blonde behind the desk. "What are you boys counting today – weevils or nematodes?"

"Neither!" said Jonny. "Just picking up checks."

Wait, thought Buster. *You get paid to count bugs?*

"Don't we ever get just good ol' fashioned hay to haul?" said Mike.

"Or more shit for you to sh—HEY!" sputtered Jonny, as Mike jabbed him with his elbow.

"So, Heather, how about a beer after you get off work?"

Buster groaned with annoyance and both he and Jonny looked at Mike.

"Now, Mike," Heather said, "what would your girlfriend think about you asking me out for a drink?"

"Aw, it ain't nothing," Mike said, as he sat on the edge of Heather's desk. "Just me and Jonny here going. Not like it's a date."

Buster watched Jonny. Jonny looked at Mike and put his hands up and began to walk over to a door that had a small window. *Maybe that's where I need to be,* thought Buster, as he followed Jonny.

"Well, then, Mike, I guess you won't mind if I bring my date tonight," said Heather.

"Oh, that's perfect," said Jonny loudly, suddenly stepping back from the door to rejoin the conversation, "I bet he and Mike would get along real good."

Buster stepped around Jonny and peered through the window. He saw a mostly white, tiled room with long tables, microscopes, and small glass aquariums.

"Oh, well, sure," said Mike as he stood up from the desk.

Jonny approached Mike and clapped his hand on Mike's shoulder. "We'd love to meet your date. Maybe we can shoot pool and talk about bugs and worms and cotton."

In the room on the other side of the small window, Buster could see three people in white coats, on stools at one of the long tables, alternatively hovering over microscopes and writing notes. On the opposite side of the room, two men peered into a large aquarium full of dirt and a few green plants. They pointed toward it with their pens and nodded at each other. At another table, a young woman stood in front of a scale, weighing small glass jars of soil. *What in the hell are they doin'? Bugs, dirt, and fancy lab coats?* Buster asked himself.

Suddenly, the door swung wide open and a short man with perfectly-parted brown hair appeared. Buster stepped back, but a moment too late, as the man walked into and through him. Buster felt a static pop and nausea sweep over him.

"Hi, Professor Tinsley," said Heather.

"Dammit," said Buster. He bent over and rubbed his head as sharp ringing pierced right through him. Buster smelled something that reminded him of sacks of garden fertilizer at the farmers' co-op. His throat burned. This was new.

Chair or department head. So what if fudged I-9 paperwork to get visas...

Buster felt a strange urge to vomit from the semi-putrid smell of rotting eggs; the burning moved from his throat to his body.

Busted my ass. Ants perfect so easy to breed—need tolerance for poisons...

Buster rubbed his belly and looked up at Professor Art Tinsley as he heard fragmented thoughts. Or were these memories? This felt, well, different than when Sally or Peaches possessed him. He tingled as if on fire. Still, Buster heard and felt Tinsley as if the professor spoke aloud. The familiar shrill from human possession followed with dizziness. The nausea passed.

Breed ant.

Create poison.

Save azaleas and cotton.

Who cares how?

Results.

"You got bad juju, buddy," mumbled Buster as he regained his balance.

"Hey, I saw them latest test results you sent around, Professor," said Mike.

"Those were three years in the making, gentlemen," he said and winked at Heather.

"Now ev'rybody's gonna come to you for fire ant poison," said Jonny.

Art Tinsley smiled. "First, it's got to be field tested."

"Fire ant poison? Just pour gas and light a match," said Buster. Still rubbing his head, he looked back through the window into the lab again.

"Them damn pesky critters come back every year," said Mike. "These new ones are really tough."

"The trick is their resistance to poison. Find its genetic weakness and target that."

"You should just breed a bunch of ants until you find a way to kill 'em all," laughed Mike.

The Professor smirked. "Not sure the U.S. Department of Agriculture would think too fondly of that."

Buster noticed that Mike had already turned back to Heather.

"Who's that new boy you got, Professor?" asked Jonny.

"That *new boy* is a fine graduate student. Claudio is his name."

"Right smart, ain't he?" asked Mike, turning away from Heather.

"Yes." Professor Tinsley picked up a folder from Heather's desk. "He'd rather work differential calculus than a pretty coed."

Jonny stifled a laugh. "Where's he from?"

"Brazil—"

Told you, mouthed Mike.

"—Heather, I need you to pull those toxicology reports

from last week, please." Professor Tinsley faced Mike and Jonny, "Boys, you'll have to excuse Heather after you pick up your checks. If you all are finished counting nematodes, then I will see you next week."

"Next week?" Buster muttered. "Must be Friday. I gotta get in there," he said, and turned for the door into the lab.

"Yes, sir," said Jonny.

"See you soon, Heather," said Mike.

Buster heard the two leave the building, but didn't look away from the window into the lab. He had to get inside. Maybe he could wait to follow someone through the door.

With that idea, Buster glimpsed toward the professor. Heather thumbed through files, while Professor Tinsley stood over her shoulder rather closely.

"Hey!" yelled a voice from the lab. Buster heard a muffled POP followed by the sound of breaking glass. Four people ran for one of the aquariums in the back of the room.

The door opened and Professor Tinsley rushed through Buster. The stench of burnt matches once again permeated as Buster leaned against the wall, dizzy. His eyes watered and he heaved. Buster stumbled three steps into the lab as the door slowly closed. He couldn't see, but he heard Tinsley's voice, not in the lab, but in his head. *Just like the crazy ant. Attacks others. Icing ... cake.*

Buster tried to open his eyes as the nausea swirled between fragmented thoughts, but he only heard voices yelling in the lab.

"What on God's Green Earth happened?" someone yelled.

"Watch the broken glass!"

Between shouts in the lab, Buster heard one word, whispered repeatedly, *Reservoir. Reservoir. Reservoir.*

"Get away from the ants!"

"Take him to the emergency shower..."

Buster squinted as the burn grew stronger. The high-pitched ringing in his ears turned into a buzz before his head felt full of cotton, and he broke out in sweats.

"What you mean you fainted?" asked Peaches as she leaned over the mirror, adding an eyelash.

"I fainted, Jasper. And tried to throw up. Just like that. What else does fainting look like?"

"Well, I ain't heard a no ghost faintin'," said Peaches.

"Then call it somethin' else cause after that, I don't remember nothing but wakin' up at home."

"Last time that happened to me, it involved a bottle of poppers, and he was the prison guard and I was the..." Peaches turned from the mirror and looked at Buster, who scratched his head. "Ne'er mind, boo, don't think too hard on that one."

Buster shook his head. He realized that some details, he never needed to know. "Figures."

"So, tell me bout this Professor that gave you the willies," Peaches adjusted her wig.

"Something not right with him," said Buster.

"Tell me something I didn't figure out, boo!"

"Was like my skin was on fire. I never felt that before. And it smelled like a burnt match or something," added Buster. "Plus the stuff I heard in my head."

Peaches stopped and stared at Buster, her hands still clasped against her head. "Has he got horns? You might need to start watching yourself around that one." Peaches paused and leaned over to the door behind Buster. "Nugget? You doin' your school work like mama asked?"

She listened. "Nugget?!", louder this time.

"Yes, Mama Peaches," answered a soft voice. Buster recognized Carlos.

"I gotta make sure my charges don't hear me talking to you too much, neither," said Peaches as she looked Buster, smoothing her lipstick with a finger. "That's one sure way to get me locked up. So, what did you hear when he walked through you?"

"Something about poison, ants, and the reservoir," he said.

"That make any sense to you?"

"I don't know. I need to go back," said Buster. "And I think you need to go too."

"Oh, hell no," said Peaches, as she fluffed some of the hair in the wig. "I am not about to snoop around a lab behind a bunch of corn fields and end up arrested or the victim of a hate crime."

"No, I mean when you start your job, Jasper," said Buster.

"First, I got to get it, and sneaking around campus like a peeping Tom is NOT gonna help me keep it once I do get it."

Buster looked at a black and white photograph taped to the mirror. A black woman sat on a bus in front of a white man. "What would Rosa do?"

"You did *not* just go there." Peaches stood up. "I mean, yes you black and she is your people, but no. You are not gonna pull Ms. Rosa Parks into this and guilt me into anything like you on a crusade for all mistreated ghosts that you don't even know exist."

Buster pleaded, "But she did what she thought was right."

"And so am I, Buster Sparkle. *When* I start that job. Until then, Peaches Juba Lee is gonna keep her night job and is NOT gonna go snooping around someone's office. Especially a Dr. Frankenstein who has ants in his pants, cooks poison, and makes a ghost faint. We gotta be careful around that man."

CHAPTER EIGHT

Peaches rocked on the front porch. "Lord, it's hot. Wish my window unit wasn't out again."

"Wish I could have a beer right now," said Buster.

"Not in my house," said Peaches.

"You don't drink?"

"You ever see me drink?"

"Not yet," he answered.

"Okay, then," Peaches tipped the chair with her foot. "Wait a minute. How's that work — you get hot and feel heat, but can't eat or drink?"

"Pretty much."

"Well, that's just dandy. Ever get hungry?"

"Nope."

"Well, that doesn't make a lick of sense to me."

"Because all the rest of me, being a ghost, makes a whole lotta sense," said Buster.

"You can be funny when you want," Peaches replied, as she rested her head against the back of the rocker and fanned her neck. "Maybe you ain't dead, boo. Maybe that's why you don't see any others or remember a light and a tunnel like they say on all the talk shows. Maybe I'm crazy or you just laid up in the hospital somewhere, waiting to wake up. You sure you're dead?"

Buster shrugged.

She tilted her head to face Buster, half-exhausted, yet half-interested, "So, what's the first thing you remember? After whatever happened that did or didn't kill you?"

"It's kinda blurry," he answered.

"How so?" Peaches wiped her neck with a handkerchief.

"Well, at first, nothing seemed quite right, like a dream that don't really end. Like I kept changing channels on TV and just remembered bits of different shows. Then, the stations slowed down and started to piece together, mostly.

That's how I knew I liked to fish, grew up here outside Clover, that sorta thing." He rubbed his head. "And then I met you."

"Lord, you plum scared the bejesus outta me."

"It's been foggy, mostly. Being a ghost. Everything looked real, but still didn't feel that way. One thing was different, for sure, when I stopped at your house."

"What's that?" she asked.

"You could see me," said Buster.

"Oh, right." Peaches paused before continuing, "Do you remember anything about being alive?"

"Sorta. Maybe. Not cause there ain't a story to remember, it's just the pieces don't quite all fit together yet. It's like I left the room looking for something, but I forgot what, just as I stepped into another room."

"You gotta speak up a little bit," said Peaches. She pulled her shirt away from her body as she fanned down her chest.

"I mean, kinda fuzzy-like. I remember that I remember, but I have a hard time recollecting some stuff."

"Well, I can't imagine a ghost that had never been alive." She fanned her legs. "What's it like now? Sounds like something's changing."

"What's what like?"

"Being dead, silly," she asked. "If that's what you are. I wanna know what it's like! You broke a picture. Can you do other stuff or got any powers? Disappear and reappear when you want?"

"Well. I look real, although nobody else but you can see me. Maybe some cats, crickets, and grasshoppers."

"And butterflies," said Peaches.

"I feel solid, but can't really move stuff, other than the other day. People go through me. That ain't fun. But I feel 'em."

Peaches pointed.

"What?" asked Buster.

"Not just cats and crickets, doll," she said, continuing

to point.

Buster followed her gaze. A butterfly lit briefly on his knee, then fluttered, and tried again. Buster flinched slightly. It tickled when it flapped through him. After a few failed attempts, it flew away.

"And you do look real to me. You also feel a few things, apparently," said Peaches.

"Hah. Yeah, apparently."

"How do you feel people? That different?" Peaches continued.

"Feelings. Thoughts. Sometimes memories. I feel 'em when I cross paths with somebody. That's how I knew you a... man."

"Humph. Well, if you call me that," she muttered. Peaches sat up in the rocker and faced him. "That gotta be some kinda potent, Buster. Be careful who you touch — you might just see something you shouldn't by poking around the wrong body." She pointed a fake fingernail at Buster, "And don't be snooping around in my head, now, ya hear?" She looked at her finger and picked up a file.

"You ain't gotta worry 'bout that, Jasper. I don't like it much when someone's inside me."

Peaches mumbled, "Don't know what you're miss—"

Buster and Peaches made eye contact. "Well, go on, then, what's it like?" she continued.

"You know when someone scuffs their feet on the carpet and then shocks you? Like that to feeling like a waterfall. Sometimes makes me kinda carsick."

She looked at Buster, "A waterfall?"

"Well, at least what I think it feels like to be under a waterfall. A thousand things going through me at once. Except they're thoughts and feelings and stuff."

"Well, that don't sound comfortable," said Peaches, as she started on another nail. "And you still don't remember how you died? If you died."

Buster shook his head and watched a butterfly nearby. The more he thought about his death, the more his memories blurred. He felt a tingle in the back of his neck and looked over his shoulder. Was somebody watching?

"You was there, wasn't you?" laughed Peaches, as she looked up.

Buster shrugged off the feeling. "Yeah, I guess."

"You guess. OF COURSE you was there." Peaches returned to filing a nail. "You have got some kinda special crazy."

"I'm not the one wearing a dress and filing my nails."

Peaches stopped, nail file in mid-stroke, and stared at Buster. "No, ma'am. You did NOT just say that. I am not gonna take smack from a ghost that can't even remember how he died," Peaches stood up. "Get up, Buster. You may not understand me, but if you think I'm crazy, then don't keep coming 'round here bugging me like I'm gonna fix everything for you."

"Easy, Jasper, I'm just foolin' wit you."

"My name. is. PEACHES. You want me to make a joke about segregation?" Peaches stepped toward Buster's chair and pointed her nail file directly at Buster's nose.

"Please, Jasper, don't make me go... I'm sorry..."

"I'm done wit you."

Confused, Buster shook his head and said, "Jasper, I didn't..."

"GIT!"

Immediately, Buster's chest collapsed like a deflated balloon. Yanked from behind his belly button, he was pulled from the chair, off the porch, into the yard, and onto the street in front.

He heard her trailing voice, as if shouted through a tin can on a string, "Don't come around disrespecting me! I got a show tonight and got to pay the rent. I don't need your shade." She stomped into the house, still arguing, voice vanishing. "Ghost or no ghost, I'll be damned if anybody is gonna make fun of me because of the way I dress. I may not look like you but I... c'mon, little nuggets, where are you? Finish your homework? Come help mama... I'm hungry."

Buster stood on the street as the house grew quiet. *What the hell did I say wrong?* He wondered. *I don't understand.* He waited. *Maybe he'll come back out.*

But Peaches didn't come back out, leaving Buster in the middle of a quiet street with unanswered questions. *Why don't I remember dying?* he thought. *And I get a funny feeling about it.* Despite firmly believing he'd been alive, Buster had no real knowledge of his death. But he had to have become a ghost somehow, didn't he? Was he actually dead? *Maybe Peaches is right,* he thought. *I ain't considered that.* It gave him a slight fever.

Buster reached back in his thoughts. He remembered having a house—sort of—and a job—sort of—and then, he didn't have either. He definitely remembered fishing. Didn't he? Focusing was hard and made things fuzzier. Sometimes, he doubted so much, although there wasn't much else to go on. Except maybe fishing, drinking. Maybe a game of checkers. *That's why I like Jasper's porch.* He suddenly remembered playing checkers somewhere on a front porch. He just couldn't remember clearly. It was the uncertainty of a puzzle he couldn't see, but the pieces materialized one at a time.

Still, dead or not, something was wrong. *Jasper is right,* he thought, and, although he'd never really liked people when alive, life in this existence had finally become lonely.

I had family, if I can remember my grandmother. Maybe I'll go to the cemetery and look for my family name. Not like I wanna go home and hear a bunch of fighting.

The longer he thought about the cemetery, the more it intrigued him. Buster looked down the canopied road as a car headed his direction. A chorus of tree frogs filled the early evening air. The roadside dripped with lethargy and humidity. There would've been no point in fishing, cause the fish wouldn't feed in the still, hot air. Not that he could hold an actual pole. So far, fish hadn't actually bitten any sort of ghost-pole he conjured, so it seemed pointless altogether.

The mailbox in front of Peaches' house slumped in the

descending sun, as if strained with exhaustion. A newspaper rested at the end of the walk, still tightly rolled. A two-word headline was visible: "Nursery Closing."

"Now if it just had my obituary, or even how I died, that might be real news," Buster mumbled aloud.

He headed to the corner of Freeman's Cemetery, and stood at its edge along Raspberry Lane. Grasshoppers started like bottle rockets without the grand, declarative final pop. Separated from the road by a drainage ditch rather than a fence, the cemetery looked old and neglected. Full-grown trees sprouted between headstones, some granite and limestone, the rest mostly cement. Buster could survey most of the cemetery from the road: not a fresh grave in sight. If Buster had died, how long ago had it been? His slowly-returning memories and sense of time told him that he was not an old spirit, but he still had no clue whether he'd died one, two, or ten years ago. Newer graves might be a better starting point.

Buster walked for the intersection with Washington Street, the main road that connected downtown Clover with the College. On Washington, toward the College, another gated cemetery had served as the final resting place for Clover's white citizens, long before Mississippi added a star to the flag. Another memory hit Buster: desegregation forced the city of Clover to sell plots to everyone. Unlike Freeman's, the entrance to this cemetery was well-kept, and clearly marked by a weedless iron gate supporting a bronze plaque that read: "Welcome, Friends of Washington Street Cemetery." The letters on the headstones near the front were worn smooth. A few marble markers from the early 1800's rose above Buster's head. They clawed at something in the back of his mind, like an itch furrowed deep in his skin.

"I am not gonna be among these, that's for damn sure," said Buster.

He continued along a path, only half-looking at names while listening to insects jump and buzz. Perhaps he would meet another ghost, although he previously relinquished that idea as fruitful as his grandparents waiting on forty acres and a mule. Not seeing other ghosts seemed to befuddle Peaches as much as it confused Buster.

"*Whaddoyou mean you can't see no other ghosts?*"

"*Just what I said, Jasper. I mean, I just hadn't seen any, so I figure I can't see them.*"

"*And I'm still the only one that sees you?*"

"*Yes.*"

"*Why? That doesn't make sense for me, either. Damn, I wish you'd go get up in someone else's business.*"

"*Not like I picked you.*"

"*And not like I picked having a spirit show up on my porch one day. Just why do you think the good Lord saw fit for me to see you?*"

Buster shrugged.

"*Do you know anything? Always shrugging. Do you even know who kilt you?*"

"*I don't know that I was killed,*" emphasized Buster. "*That was your harebrained idea.*"

"*Well, why else would you be harassing me instead of moving on? People don't just hang around as spirits.*"

"*How do you know?*"

"*Cause I haven't EVER seen a ghost, and I've been living near two cemeteries most of my life. You've got to find out who killed you so you can move on.*"

Buster shook his head. "*And why, Jasper?*"

"*You can't stay a ghost.*"

"*But you don't know that I'm a ghost, or that I can't stay.*"

"*Buster, you are stuck. Ghosts aren't supposed to be here. It's not right.*"

"*Says who? A lot of things aren't right that still happen. Besides, how do you know where ghosts are supposed to be?*"

"*You see any others?*"

"*Naw.*"

"*Okay, then, hush your mouth before I cast you off this here porch.*"

It was a valid point. Neither of them had ever seen another ghost. There must have been a reason he lingered, and Buster's amnesia-like memory seemed peculiar, except that maybe ghosts didn't remember anything or see each other at all. The house he claimed alongside Sally and Earl *felt* like his, but only in the same way that the clothes he wore *felt* like his. The itch almost hurt when he tried to remember. All he'd wanted to do as a ghost was the same thing he remembered doing alive: fish.

"Help me find some graves," he said to a butterfly nearby.

He quickly walked past a few more marble markers marked "C.S.A." and looked into the distance for a newer section of the cemetery. The sun now set lower behind the row of trees, and Buster finally felt a bit of relief.

"I'm dead. Walking in a Mississippi cemetery in the summer looking for a grave. Maybe this is hell," he sighed.

Buster continued among the tombstones. Under footstep, the brown grass sounded like crumpled newspapers. He turned to look behind him. As he expected, he saw no footprints. Old worn headstones, many covered in lichen and oddly angled, looked like bad, giant stone teeth. Further along, crisp, shiny headstones sat closer together and in precise, straight rows. Here, few trees shaded the dry lot. Monotonous, dull, and well-kept under an oppressive Mississippi sun.

Buster wiped away a bead of sweat.

Just ahead, he saw a small mound of fresh gravel, crowned with an ant bed. Buster walked over to the new grave. No headstone marked it, but a small metal plate was spiked into the ground at what would have been its head. He squatted and read aloud: "Mary, infant, one month." A few fake flowers rested on the fresh gravel.

Buster saw another ant mound a few feet away, then another not far from that one. He then realized that he stood like a giant among several, scattered like a city of rounded, brown pyramids.

Ants everywhere.

CHAPTER NINE

Buster tasted pepper as smoke rose from the grease. "Damn, I wish I could eat," he said.

Sally turned away from the range, and faced the window where she'd argued with a very drunk Earl. She gazed for the sky, as if following something in the distance. Buster walked into the kitchen.

"Smells downright tasty, even for a ghost, Sally," he said as he looked out the window. Nothing but grass browning under the August morning sky. "Think we related, Sally? Is that why I'm here?"

The range clicked off behind Buster. Sally lifted bacon from the shiny black skillet. Buster then noticed two plates at the table.

Sally spoke softly.

"Damn, woman, you still with that bastard?" Buster muttered as he stepped back.

Sally spoke louder, this time singing, "*I'm crazy, crazy for feeling so blue...*"

"Oh, good grief," said Buster. He rubbed the back of his neck.

"*I knew you'd love me as long...*"

The telephone rang.

"*... as you wanted...*"

"Hello?" answered Sally, and then promptly hung up the phone.

"Well, that's different," said Buster.

"*And then someday, you'd leave me for somebody new,*" Sally continued singing.

A loud honk came from the drive.

"Here we go again," said Buster.

"Okay, there." Sally stood up and looked at the table, "Ready for two."

Buster stood at the sink and just watched.

A knock at the door.

"I'm comin'!" cried Sally.

Buster moaned, "Why the hell is she so..."

"Heelllooo, shuga! I am jist SO excited that you havin' me over for a proper morning breakfast," said a woman with an accent a mile long. Buster had not heard this one before.

"Who the hell..." he mumbled as he walked into the living room.

"Martha, I'm so happy you came. This is just what I needed."

"You aren't gonna let that cheatin' bastard back in, are ya?" Martha had bright red hair, still in curlers.

"Here, let me take your purse," answered Sally.

"You aren't, are ya?" Martha said louder.

"She loud, but she right," said Buster as he watched Sally purposefully avoid eye contact with Martha.

Martha smacked her lips. "I swear, girl, your brother wouldn't a put up with that bastard here with you."

"Brother?" responded Buster. He glanced around the room looking for family photos. He felt oddly disappointed, yet relieved, that he couldn't see any.

Sally responded, "I know. How are you? Glad you came over, even if it is early."

"Sugar, this ain't early. Early is when your man stops ten seconds after he starts."

"Martha, you hussy!" Sally laughed and clapped her hand over her mouth.

Martha smiled with a faint curtsey. "Welcome to fifteen years of wedded bliss, Sally."

"Well, at least you got there with your man, Martha. I can't even get Earl to stay at home."

"That's cause that sonofabitch don't wanna stay home while he seeks his own level," said Martha. "In places far below you."

"Martha, can we not talk about Earl? Or my brother? I'd just like some company before going to work."

Martha dropped her hands from her hips, "Shuga, you

right, come here." She opened her arms and wrapped them around Sally, and forced out her lower lip. "Losing your brother. Earl turning into a jackass. Moving into this house."

Sally softly said, "It's a lot, but I'll manage."

"Well, now. What other secrets can you share with me?" Buster put his hand out, then pulled back. Maybe this wasn't the time. And it might be too much.

"I know, shuga, I know," said Martha, as she frowned and patted Sally on the back. "Did the college ever say what happened?"

"The coroner said heart failure or something, but I don't know. Not like they gonna put a lot of effort into a black maintenance worker," Sally trembled slightly. "Not sure I want to think of what else it could be."

Buster felt a weakness shoot from his knees into his throat as an unwelcome idea developed. *I can't be her brother. Just can't, there ain't pictures of me anywhere.*

"Curlers, dear, watch the curlers," Martha said.

"Oh, sorry," Sally released Martha and wiped her face. "How about some eggs?"

"Sounds lovely."

The two, followed by Buster, headed into the kitchen.

"You ever go back to the cemetery?" Martha asked as Sally poured coffee.

"Not really." She shifted. "We are going to talk about something else. How about the Clover Festival? Are you gonna make your strawberry jam?

"Oh, Lord, honey, that old thang," Martha laughed. "Sure, why not? Why not go for two blue ribbons instead of one!" she smiled.

"You make good jam, Martha Jo!"

"Well, nothing like your canned ta-maters. You oughta enter those into the contest this year."

Sally looked at Martha. "My brother always liked those."

"Well, what happened to him?" said Buster as he slumped against the wall. *I could find out easy,* he thought, but held back and lowered his hand.

"Oh, Sally, guess what I done heard at the beauty parlor?"

"This better be good, Martha, cause I can't handle no idle sad gossip."

"Lord, child, this isn't idle—this *real* good."

Buster nervously headed for the back of the house, searching for clues.

CHAPTER TEN

"You sure you wasn't a milkman back in the day, Buster? Cause you just like clockwork how you show up at my house." Peaches spoke softly.

This is different, thought Buster. *Has Jasper lost it?* "Why are you whispering?"

"The nuggets are here, boo. I can't just holler at you, or they'll send me off to Whitfield!"

"Oh. Right. Well, now I actually got something to tell you," said Buster.

"This better be more than 'I still can't make a boo!' Cause I got to work tonight," said Peaches.

"Sally had a brother."

Peaches stared at Buster. "Wait. Are you telling me..."

"Nah, can't be me. I looked all over that place for pictures – not a single one of me. What?"

"Get on in here while I put on my face. Sounding more and more to me like that ain't your house," said Peaches, as she opened the screen door and quickly ushered Buster into the house.

"She had a brother. He died at the college, but suspicious like," said Buster. "That's got to be in the news somewhere, don't it? Maybe that's why I see her. Cause I know something."

She put her finger over her mouth as they passed the living room and headed for the small dressing room at the back of the house. Peaches sat at a vanity. "What's his name?" she said quietly, picking up a tube of mascara.

"Dunno."

Peaches held her brush mid-air. "Do what?"

"I don't know his name."

She put the brush back in the tube and began shaking.

"What's so funny?" Buster asked.

"You just too much, boo," she stifled a snort before she

narrated back to Buster. "Oooooo, Peaches! I got a huge scoop for you! The woman who owns the house I'm trying to haunt but can't had a brother who died at the college, but I don't know his name!" She stopped herself. "Okay, I know that it isn't right to laugh, but, Buster, do you know how many people work up at the college?"

He shook his head.

"Let's see. Must be about twenty thousand students. Probably eight hundred professors and coaches and teachers. Another thousand maintenance and crew and secretaries and cafeteria workers and housekeeping and—"

Buster sighed. "Fine. I get it. But hell, Jasper, it's a start."

"Yeah, it is. Start finding out a name. What's Sally's last name?" she asked, picking up her mascara again. "Wait. Don't tell me you hadn't—"

"No, Jasper, I hadn't looked through her mail yet."

"She married to that sonofabitch?"

Buster scratched his chin.

She shook her head. "Well, you make one lousy detective, Buster Sparkle. When a ghost could snoop around just anywhere, you don't seem to wanna get any dish on anything."

"Do you have to point out everything I do wrong, or can you just be little bit excited that I'm finding out stuff that might help you get rid of me?"

"Boo, you are right. And on the right track, but this might take a little bit. And you may wanna go back and be sure you aren't Sally's brother, because right now, I can't picture ol' Buster Sparkle involved in anybody's death but his own. Ornery, yes. Mean spirited, no. Still don't explain why I can see you, but here you are. I don't think I know this Sally, although I might need to meet her and have a word with her about that husband of hers." Peaches threw the end of her scarf around her neck and faced Buster. "Are they even married? Wait, why am I asking you?" She rolled her eyes. "Anywho, I got to head over to The Blue Magnolia. Why don't you come with me?"

Buster bit his lip.

"It's just a bar. Don't look at me like you seen a gho... I mean..." Peaches stopped.

"You kinda funny for a man in a dress," Buster smirked.

"Don't get started wit me," said Peaches.

"Oh lighten up, Jasper. How we gonna get there?"

"We gonna ride in my car."

"Car?! Why in the hell did we walk to campus in the heat the other day?"

"Cause I gotta save my gas money, and I ain't about to walk in my heels all the way out to the bar."

"You wearing heels?

"Yes, now wipe that look off your face and hep me find my keys." Peaches turned to the hallway. "Nugget! You seen my keys?"

Peaches held up her finger to Buster as she waited. "Nugget!?"

"No, Mama, I don't see them," cried a voice from the kitchen.

"I'd lose my head if it wasn't on my neck," she said, while shuffling through a small purse. "Here we go!" Peaches pulled out a set of keys and dangled them in front of Buster.

She spun slightly, flaring out her dress, before heading across the hallway, Buster behind. In a small kitchen, Li'l J worked math problems while Carlos read a paperback.

"I'm almost done, Mama Peaches," said Jerome.

"Oh, that's good, sugar. When your first test?"

"Next week."

"Already?! Well. You ready?" she asked.

"I will be," smiled Li'l J.

"I'm fixin' to head to work; how long you think you gonna be?" asked Peaches.

"Another hour," he mumbled.

"You and your brother get yourself something to eat before you leave, hear me?"

"Yes ma'am," Carlos didn't look up from his book.

Buster noticed a fresh scar on the back of Jerome's

head. He looked at Peaches and pointed at Li'l J.

"Nugget, what's this on your head?" Peaches stood over Jerome.

"It's okay," he shrugged.

"Okay, nothing," Peaches pushed Li'l J's head down and began to inspect the boy's head.

"Ow," said Li'l J, as he tried to shrug Peaches away.

"Nugget, who did this?"

"Nobody," he said.

Carlos looked up at Peaches, then Jerome.

Peaches looked at Buster, as Buster stepped over.

"Is nobody your daddy?"

"No, Mama, just some stupid kid at school," said Li'l J as he shrugged again, pushing back Peaches' hands, and stood up. Buster stepped back.

"Carlos, are you watching out for your little brother?" Peaches asked.

Carlos looked up. "Yes, Mama Peach, but I can't be with him at the elementary school. I told him to go to the teachers."

Li'l J went to the fridge and removed a pitcher of lemonade and returned to the kitchen table.

She bit her lower lip. "I love you nuggets. You are God's children, and don't let anybody make you think different. Watch out for each other. Your power is in each other." She bent over and wrapped her thick arms around Li'l J, who relented and hugged back. "We'll talk later, okay?"

"Love you, too," he said.

"We'll clean up before we leave," said Carlos.

"See you both tomorrow?" asked Peaches.

"I've got band practice tomorrow," answered Carlos.

"Well, I need to round up all you nuggets before too long now that school started. We'll have Willie and Shayla and some others over for a movie night, okay?"

Li'l J smiled. "With popcorn?"

Buster squatted next to him.

"Yes, boo, with popcorn," said Peaches.

Li'l laughed and gave Peaches another hug.

Buster reached his hand out for Li'l and caught Peaches' eye. She shook her head.

"Git—"

"Who you talkin' to, Mama Peaches?" asked Li'l, as Carlos glanced up from his book before returning back to the pages.

Buster pulled back.

"Oh, nothing, just a skeeta flying around here," she said, as she looked at Buster and mouthed the words, "Hell no."

*****

"Imma gonna lay down a rule," said Peaches. She opened the car door on the driver's side and motioned for Buster to crawl through. "And don't be rolling your eyes at me."

She flipped the scarf over her left shoulder before sitting in front of the steering wheel. Peaches closed the door and buckled her seat belt. "Don't be touching my nuggets and getting their secrets."

"But I just wanted..." said Buster.

"I don't give a damn what you want, Buster!" She started the engine. "Not in my house. Not with my nuggets. Go do that on the Professor or something."

"I wanted to know what happened," he argued.

"Buster, when he's ready, he'll talk. Just cause you can read someone's mind don't mean you should. You can't just go around touchin' folks on purpose to be getting' their secrets and shit."

Buster looked out the window. "Fine."

"Fine! Then we agree. You do it, and I will cast you out every time you show up at my house." Peaches gave the engine gas and backed out of driveway.

"Sometimes, you treat me like a child."

"You hadn't seen nothin from Mama Peaches yet."

"Not 'bout to call you 'Mama'," responded Buster.

"Suit me just fine. I already got too many kids running around to worry about. One adult ghost is plenty."

"Why don't you worry about your car a bit more? You got everything in here but a phone book," said Buster.

"Hush," said Peaches. "It's my purse."

"Mighty big purse," he muttered.

After zipping past subdivisions and farmhouses, Peaches turned her brown Hyundai onto an unmarked paved road. Branches from wide trees drooped low and heavy over spotty pavement. Thick curtains of honeysuckle sporadically choked slumping, barbed-wire fences.

"So, what do you do out here?" Buster asked.

"I host a Friday night show. We got a few singers, a few dancers and ... other performers. Sometimes, I tell jokes."

"What's it like?"

"Oh, it's fun. I meet all kinds of folks from all over. Mississippi, Alabama, Tennessee, even queers passing through on their way to L.A. or Atlanta..."

"Naw, I mean the bar. What's it like?"

"The Blue Magnolia? It's a place where everybody's welcome, as long as they don't fight or hate on each other."

Buster tucked one hand under his arm and rubbed his face with the other.

"No need to be nervous. Ain't nobody gonna hurt you. Not like they can see you. It just a bar."

"I ain't never seen a bunch of gays before."

"Ha! Then you don't get out much. We everywhere."

"Really?" Buster asked.

"Here an' queer," Peaches smirked. "Last election, when the Miss'ippi Republican Caucus came to town, we had more pricks in suits than the legislature."

"They know where they was?"

"Course they did! Why else would they be at a bar hidden in the woods singing show tunes?"

Buster looked ahead. "Oh."

"I feel sorry for 'em, actually."

"Who?"

101

"Closet cases. They scared. They don't wanna be themselves, and they don't wanna live the life they got. So they end up lying to ev'rybody, including themselves and God."

Neither spoke.

"Kinda like you," added Peaches.

"I ain't gay," said Buster.

"No shit, Buster. That's not what I mean."

"Then what?"

"You scared. You don't wanna be a ghost, yet you don't wanna do nothing about it."

"Lord, do you ever let a dead man rest in peace? I can't do anything about it, but I'm tryin'! I'd rather be left alone in my house," he said.

"And maybe that's why you still here. Did you live your life when you was alive?"

"Course. I had a job. A house. Fished."

"You suddenly remember all that? Still, that's *existing*. I mean, did you *live*? Did you *participate*?"

Buster folded his arms and stared at Peaches. "Like goin' to a gay bar?"

Peaches snorted and shook her head. The car slowed and approached a tractor crawling as it pulled a trailer of round hay bales that looked like giant cinnamon rolls. "Participate. Fall in love. Sing. Dance. Have a family. Dream about something that you liked? Something special?"

"I don't know what you mean."

Tiny bits of straw swirled through the open windows of the car like dead flower petals.

"I am calling you out on that, Buster Sparkle. When you was little, did you really like something? Was there anything you wanted to be when you grew up?" Peaches pointed to the man on the tractor. "Like this farmer here, maybe he thought he wanted to grow up to be a farmer, too, so he could feed people. So that's what he does."

Buster didn't respond.

"Nothing?"

"Well..." then he stopped.

"You what?"

"It's silly. Nothing, really."

"The only thing that's silly is not bein' ourselves, that part underneath all the B.S. and the fear and the doubt," said Peaches. "Be you, be true. That's what I always say."

As they passed, the farmer waved.

"How much further?" he asked.

"Hold your britches, Busta, we'll get there." She paused, then giggled, "You got ants in your pants?"

Buster didn't flinch and stared blankly at her. "Damn. They pay you for those jokes?"

"Ooooo, my Casper is throwin' shade!" squealed Peaches, as the tractor vanished from view behind them. The car crossed a narrow bridge and turned onto a gravel road.

"Hell, this ain't no different than most juke joints I seen," said Buster.

"Bet you won't be saying that when you see boys two-stepping with each other to Shania Twain."

Buster wrinkled his nose. "Shania? This ain't a country bar, is it?"

"All are welcome. We mix it up. Might as well, cause we don't have a safe place to meet. Not like Oxford or Starkville, anyway. So ev'rybody comes out who wants a drink and a tune and not get hate on," said Peaches. "By the way, you still didn't answer my question, boo. You ain't off the hook."

The gravel road passed a creek before winding through a few pines. The trees parted like a curtain to reveal a metal and cinderblock not-quite-house-not-quite-barn structure surrounded by a few pick-up trucks, an old Cadillac, and a stray dog. A faded blue and white sign near the side of the barn said "the blue magnolia." A neon Budweiser sign flickered under an overhang.

"This it?"

"Naw, boo, this the Piggly Wiggly. We just gonna pick up some milk."

Buster looked at Peaches. "Damn, you can be right

103

smart."

"Well, what you 'spect?"

"I don't know. Guess I thought it'd be pink or somethin'," said Buster.

Peaches snickered.

"What so funny now?" Buster asked.

"Cause the owners had a big fight over whether to paint it pink. Some folks said it'd be too damn obvious it was a gay bar." Peaches parked the car near a back corner of the building.

She continued, "Ain't like we trying to have a Pride Parade out in the woods. In Mississippi. A few of us old enough to remember those civil rights kids who went to Philadelphia and ended up under a levee."

Memories of protests and news reports and KKK marches and Dr. King speeches flickered briefly. Sometimes, Buster's memories didn't want to stay, even when the familiarity remained behind.

"Then, of course, there's the grammar teacher who hated that the name doesn't have capital letters. Like we're a poetry club or something." Peaches stepped out of the car and closed the door. Buster looked at her and held out his hands.

"Sorry, child, I almost forgot you ain't real—I mean, that you ain't alive."

She opened the door. "I gotta crack ma winda," she smiled and waved at another bar patron in the parking lot. "Move over, boo," she whispered as she rolled down the window.

Buster stepped out of the way as Peaches bent over in her dress. Her heels sank into the gravel.

"I got to be more careful when talkin' to you out in public," she continued softly.

"You actually drove wearin' them things?"

"Huh?" Peaches stood up and brushed a few hairs that dangled in front of her face before looking down. "A course, Busta," she whispered, "I ain't gonna drive barefoot. Now, hush, so they don't think I'm cuckoo."

"You mean you ain't, now?" he smirked.

"Don't get funny with me. I'd whip you if it made a damn. Time for Peaches to work!" She smoothed out the wrinkles in her dress and wiped sweat from her brow.

Buster followed Peaches as she sauntered through the grassy edge of the dirt lot, her thick legs balancing on tall spikes that looked as though they could drill for oil with each step. Clearly, Peaches had experience in heels, because she made her way for a side door without losing stride.

"Locked, damn fools," she sputtered. She wiped another bead of sweat from her hairline. Bam! Bam! Bam! Peaches took the bottom of her fist and pounded on the metal door. "Mama Peaches is here; open this door afore I drive through it!"

There was no sound.

"Rodney! You hear me?"

A bolt turned and the door swung open.

"Well, I'm fixin' to melt into a puddle of your next ass whooping if you don't open up and let me cool off," she said.

"Sorry, ma'am," said a boy with a mop.

"Not so fast, Rodney," said Peaches.

"Huh?" Rodney stood motionless, one arm propping a metal door open into a still hot evening, and the other arm holding a wet mop.

There was just enough space for Buster to duck under Rodney's arm and walk behind Peaches.

"I'm good now. Close it, before you let the flies in," Peaches nodded and adjusted her wig.

He obliged. For a brief moment, the dark of the room carried the smell of stale beer and old bleach. Buster heard a ball drop into a pocket of a pool table, indistinguishable laughter, and glasses being washed. *Well, damn. I remember being in a joint like this*, he thought. His eyes took a second to adjust to the light from the room beyond the small hallway.

"Quite nothing like walking into The Blue Magnolia to realize that, as God is my witness, I fucked the wrong man in another life," said Peaches.

Rodney slapped a wet mop on the cement floor.

"Love you too, Mama," said a gruff voice.

"That's cause I help you sell beer, Oscar," said Peaches.

A large room with a long bar opened to Buster's left. Two men sat at the bar, watching a rerun of *The Golden Girls*. Someone at the opposite surveyed a worn but smooth pool table. A disco ball hung right in front of a small stage just ahead.

Peaches sat on a stool nearby, "Oscar, may I have my ginger ale and a cherry?"

She eyed Buster.

"Cherry? Since when has *she* had a cherry?" said a nasally voice in the back.

Oscar stilled a laugh.

"Not since your daddy ask me to top," said Peaches.

"As usual, I'm sure you had to be instructed on what *that* entailed," said the voice, louder. Buster turned, and a thin blonde in a red dress approached Peaches.

"Oh, Lord, already," said Oscar, as he placed a champagne glass in front of Peaches.

"Well, you just take the O, R and Y out of *country,* Jazz Men." The two kissed the air near each other's cheeks, but did not touch.

"You two are gonna play nice, ain't ya?" said Oscar, with one hand on his hip.

"Why, of course! Mama Peaches knows I tease cause I love," said Jazz, as she passed for the other end of the bar.

Peaches rolled her eyes at Buster and turned to Oscar. "I don't see a cold front in the forecast, Oscar, so don't think you have anything to worry about tonight."

Oscar shook his head and returned to cleaning glasses.

Peaches pulled out a bar stool slightly and discreetly patted the seat. "What time you wanting us to start tonight, Oscar?"

"Hell, Peaches, I don't know. It's still light out. Not even eight yet. I'm sure you'll know when to fire up."

Buster shuffled in a circle on his feet before walking over to her.

"What do you people do here?" he asked.

Peaches whispered, "Buster, it's a bar. People drink." She sipped her ginger ale.

"Right."

"Walk around, boo, you won't catch anything."

"It's..."

Peaches looked at him, waiting for him to finish.

"It's nothing, really. Looks like a place I used to drink at," he said, and headed toward the pool table.

"Oscar, when the strippers get here?" asked Peaches.

"The go-go boys? Ah, another hour, I reckon."

Buster turned and made eye contact with Peaches, who flashed a smile. *That fool loves to torment me*, he thought.

"Who you smiling at, Mama Peaches?" asked Jazz Men, as she looked around the mostly empty barroom.

"Nothing, you little hen, just thought I had something in my teeth," Peaches turned back to the bar. "Oscar, honey, Alabama's gotten me so upset, I'm gonna warm up in the back for a bit."

"Oh, hell, that old bit?" cried Jazz Men.

Buster walked for the pool table. Someone lined up pocket shots alone, and someone else threw darts. Two or three near a jukebox, but otherwise, The Blue Magnolia was fairly empty.

"Jazz, I don't want trouble outta you tonight," Oscar said as he counted bottles behind the bar.

"Who, me? Why, I never..."

"...never did learn when to keep your thoughts to yourself. Zippit!" Oscar motioned as if to zip his own mouth. Jazz did not respond. "Tonight is Peaches's night to host. You just sang and look pretty and we'll all be happy."

Jazz relaxed on one foot and smiled, "Okay, sugar, whatever you say."

"Don't forget who counts the money at the end of the night, Jazz Men."

She blew a kiss back in his direction and then proceeded to walk toward the jukebox.

Buster reached out his hand as if to touch her shoulder, but then withdrew quickly. *Might not be worth it*, thought Buster. As he pulled back, he saw a familiar figure in the corner.

Where have I seen you? Buster wondered.

The person clutched a beer, as if protecting it from a passing thief, and then took a quick sip. Buster walked between a few empty chairs toward the corner where the person watched the room. A fairly young man looked up and then back down at his glass mug. He slid the glass in tiny circles on the table and then downed the rest.

Buster sat nearby.

I seen this boy, thought Buster. *But where?*

A heavy, uneven summer tan clouded signs of youth. He looked around the room and back at his now empty beer mug.

"Care for another?"

Buster and the man at the table looked up at Oscar, who'd step from around the bar, beer in hand.

"Oh, thanks," said the man, as he took the mug.

"You look like you seen a ghost, my friend. You okay?" asked Oscar.

"Sure, just waitin' on someone."

"Alright. Hollar if you need something." Oscar turned and wiped down a nearby table before heading back to the bar.

Buster watched the man fidget with his fist in a ball. "C'mon, Jonny, where the fuck are ya?" he mumbled.

"Holy shit — you're Mike. You was at the lab!" said Buster. He turned and looked for Peaches, who was nowhere to be seen. *What the fuck are you doin' here?*

Mike nervously looked at his watch, then drank half his beer and stared at the table. He dropped a metal golf tee.

"Jesus, buddy, slow down," said Buster, as he scanned again for Peaches.

A moment later, someone else walked up to the table. "Dude, you'd better have a good fuckin' reason for draggin' me out here to this shithole." Jonny whispered loudly as he pulled up a chair.

Mike looked around. "Anybody follow ya?"

"What the fuck? No, man, ain't nobody followed me out here. What the fuck is wrong with you?"

Mike drank another sip. "It's the professor."

"Hey, miss, can I get a Bud?" Jonny nodded as Jazz walked by.

"As if," she huffed.

"What the-?" Jonny slapped a palm on the table.

Mike interrupted, "You sure nobody followed you out here?"

"No, man. I told everybody. I shouted *Hey! I'm drivin' out to meet my buddy Mike at that queer bar in the woods.* The announcer on the radio even dedicated a song for you." Jonny sat up straight briefly before leaning in toward Mike. "You ain't messin' with Tina again?"

"Who? No. No! Been 3 months."

"Right," said Jonny.

"I ain't. Listen, I think the professor is up to something."

"Oh, sure. He's probably porking Heather as we speak."

"Fuck you, Jonny, I'm serious."

Jonny turned to look at the bar. "What the fuck does it take to get a beer here?"

"Fuck the goddamn beer, Jonny!" Mike smacked the table, giving Buster a start. Mike hunched over the table and whispered, "I saw the professor spreading ants around the reservoir."

Jonny leaned back and nodded at Oscar. "Look, Mike, I told you that shit your cousin cooks up will make you fucking paranoid. That puts holes in your brain like Swiss cheese. It's already fuckin' up your golf game. Now you seein' bugs everywhere?"

Mike grabbed Jonny's arm. "I saw it. And it don't look

109

like any of the equipment from the farm labs."

Jonny covered a yawn with the back of his fist. "Okay, Mike. Tell me more."

"I seen 'em. I was out there with my girlfriend at the overlook. Saw a truck pull up across the boat ramp near the dock. I didn't think nothing of it, 'cept this dude got out walkin' around without a fishin' pole. Just didn't look right. So, I pulled out my riflescope and saw the professor walking past the dock with a couple of plastic containers. Every hundred feet or so, he dug a little hole and looked like he poured out something."

Jonny quietly stared at Mike. Oscar brought two beers. Mike polished off his and started on the other.

"And what did your girlfriend have to say about you scoping out a dude?"

"She was passed out. We'd smoked a bit and she just fell asleep."

Buster looked at Jonny, who looked at Mike.

"No, it ain't like that, I swear!" said Mike.

"Fine. So how you know it was the professor? How do you know it was ants?"

Mike looked around and leaned over. "Cause I walked down there after he done left."

Jonny checked out Jazz Men. "And?"

"I saw them!"

"What?"

"The ants, you ass. The whole area was crawling!"

Buster shifted in his seat.

"You finish the joint?"

"Ain't you listening? He was dumping ants by the reservoir! That ain't allowed—and them ants will follow that water everywhere."

"Yeah, I know. And the feds probably got a bug in your truck to listen and watch you."

Mike sat still.

"I'm fucking with you, Mike, c'mon. I'm sure there's a explanation for it, and you just too high to see it."

Mike looked at his beer and drank another sip.

"When you last seen Tina?"

"I done told you, Jonny, I ain't done that shit in a month."

"I thought it was three months, Mike."

"I mean it. I'm clean."

"Mike, you haven't stopped long enough. Your brain's already a little rewired."

Mike looked down.

"Or maybe, this part of the Professor's experiment – you ask him? Maybe using ants to test his poison near the reservoir. Maybe he's got permission. He gets all kind of letters from the government. Maybe the Corps of Engineers is letting him work on pest control up there."

Buster noticed that Mike's arm twitched. He looked down and saw his knee shaking.

"You think the Department of Agriculture will let a professor play with ants and just dump 'em out near a fucking reservoir? I ain't got a good feelin' about this Jonny."

What is it with ants, anyway? Buster thought, trying to recall a newscast.

"Talk to Professor Tinsley, buddy. I'm sure he's got a logical explanation. And if something is wrong, go to the cops."

Mike sighed. "I don't think them foreign students is South American. Or Brazilian."

"Okay, Mike," said Jonny.

"You believe me?"

"Look, Mike, you been my best pal since we was eight. I got your back. But you gotta go easy on the drugs."

Mike nodded.

"And why the fuck we at a gay bar, anyway?"

"I don't know. I thought if something bad was goin' down, then no one would be out here."

"You got that right," said Jonny, as he looked over his shoulder as one guy at the bar rubbed his hand on another guy's lower back. "Bunch a queers and dykes."

"And me, dipshit," said Buster.

"Look, Mike. Just go talk to the professor. Lay off the Tina, and let's try to finish up this term without you gettin' arrested or in another fight."

He paused, then grabbed Mike's arm. "Besides, we gotta get you and Heather together afore we all graduate!"

Mike smiled. "Yeah, she prolly think I'm a mess if she heard me right now."

"Let's just say you don't wanna go runnin' around town tellin' this story when you smellin' like skunk and shakin' like a crackhead."

Mike breathed deeply and finished the last of his beer. "Alright. You right. I'll... I'll ask the professor."

Last person I'd talk to is Mr. Harvard, Buster thought.

"And lay off the fucking drugs," said Jonny.

"That, too. Promise."

"Good, now let's get outta here and find us some tail to chase."

The two pushed back from the table and stood up. Buster sat motionless, rubbing his eyes. *To hell with it,* Buster thought. *I gotta know what the hell he saw.* He reached for Mike.

"You boys leaving us?" Peaches asked, as she stopped at the table across from Buster. She blinked long eyelashes fiercely at Buster while revealing bleached white teeth. Despite wearing a dress and a wig, Peaches loomed large next to Mike and Jonny.

Buster pulled back and threw his hands up. "Something is eatin' this boy up!" he whispered, pointing at Mike, who scratched himself nervously.

Peaches turned from Mike to Jonny. "You boys need another drink?"

"Naw," said Jonny.

Mike shook his head.

"You sure? Have another one and stick around for my show," Peaches said, putting her hand on Jonny's arm.

He shook it off, "No, thanks."

Peaches paused, then turned to walk away, "Thanks for coming, anyway."

"Fuckin' queer," muttered Mike, who seemed incapable of standing still.

Peaches stopped. "Excuse me?" she said, turning with a hand on her hip.

Buster stood up from the table, looking from Mike to Jonny to Peaches.

"I said no, thanks."

Peaches stared at Mike and then popped her lips. "Right. You know, you aren't exactly chickenshit, but you sure got henhouse ways."

Mike stopped trembling, reared back and threw a punch. Instead of landing on Peaches, however, Peaches caught it with her own large hand and squeezed his tiny, bluish-white fist. He winced.

Jonny stepped in. "Let 'em go afore a kick your ass, you fagg—"

SMACK!

Everyone turned to see Oscar with the end of a baseball bat firmly planted against the floor.

"The only ass that will get kicked in this place is yours. If you don't want to know what it's like to have your ass kicked into last week's garbage by a *faggot*, then I suggest you leave."

Jonny, now bright red, cleared his throat.

"Peaches, let go a that boy," said Oscar as he pointed with the bat.

Without taking her eye off Jonny, Peaches opened her hand. Mike mumbled and dropped his fist, shaking it.

Jonny turned and faced Peaches' gaze.

"Tab's on the house. You boys need to leave," said Oscar.

No one moved.

"NOW!" yelled Oscar, as he hit the floor again with the bat.

With that, Mike hit Jonny on the arm. "Let's git, man,

I gotta go."

Jonny backed away, but kept an eye on Peaches.

"Boy, what's got into him?" asked Buster.

"Call me," Jazz's voice floated through the thick air like a parade ribbon, drifting, waiting to be cut.

Mike and Jonny scrambled out the front door into the early night. After a brief pause, bar chatter resumed.

"Just another night at the *old* Magnolia," said Jazz, as she took another drink and propped herself against the bar.

Peaches looked at Jazz Men and then back to Buster.

"You okay, Peaches?"

"I'm fine, Oscar."

"That Mike boy knows something about the professor," said Buster.

Oscar wiped off the baseball bat with his rag and headed back to the bar.

"Looks like that one boy had it out for you," said Jazz.

"Hmmm, well, he wouldn't be the first," said Peaches.

"Won't be the last, neither," said Jazz.

Buster looked at Peaches, "Boy, she's a real—"

"At least the boys are interested in what one of us has to offer," said Peaches.

"*Ladies*," Oscar jumped in, "I will throw both of you out for a month if you don't play nice."

Jazz straightened herself and pursed her lips around a maraschino cherry.

Peaches adjusted her wig and walked toward the back end of the bar. She half-sang, half-spoke, in a pitched nasal voice: "This is a show tune, but the show hasn't been written for it yet."

"I gotta find out what he knows, Jasper," muttered Buster, as he followed Peaches across the barroom, which had come alive in the mere moments that had passed since Mike and Jonny left.

"Hound dogs on my trail... Yes, we gonna have a good singin' night tonight," as she ignored Jazz and continued back to her corner. "Another ginger ale and cherry, please,

Oscar," she said.

Buster realized that Peaches was not entertaining the discussion of the two college students. "You really don't drink?"

Peaches looked at Buster before turning to the bar, "Oscar, you know it's been eight years since I had a shot of demon liquor."

"Don't start now. I like you," Oscar responded.

"You don't have to worry about that—you don't have enough booze in this joint to make me a decent drink," she sipped her drink and winked at Buster.

Buster shook his head.

"It's okay, boo, you can walk around again," she whispered. "No need to stand by me like a lost puppy."

"I know. Just keep thinking about what Mike said."

"Well, he's gone, but you'll find him again, I bet. How about you get a feel for this place? Go check out the people walkin' in." She paused, then added, "Oh. I wouldn't go into the woods around back if I was you."

"Why?"

"Child, you are not old enough yet. Just trust Mama Peaches."

"Who you talkin' to, Peaches Juba Lee?" asked Jazz, as she called down the bar.

"Nothing, Jazz Men, just working through a bit," she sipped her ginger ale before continuing softly, "Tennessee made me lose my rest."

"You know the first thing to go is the mind," said Jazz, as she leaned on the bar.

"The second must be the tits, cause you are sagging all over that poor man's drink," Peaches said loudly.

Jazz looked down. A piece of rubber peeked out from the side of her dress like half a grapefruit, ready to drop into a martini glass. She quickly adjusted her straps and tucked the flesh colored accessory back behind the fabric.

Peaches smiled and turned back to her drink, watching the crowd.

Buster headed back for the pool table. He cautiously navigated the floor, now populated with patrons. A near brush at one table, and another, but he managed to avoid any contact with the living. At the entrance to the bar, by a jukebox, an older woman with a military crew cut checked IDs.

A teenager walked in with two other friends.

"ID?"

"Shh," nudged one as the other giggled. The first one cleared his throat and pushed his chest forward. He wore a tie. The other two squeezed tightly behind him as the door closed.

Well, this oughta be fun to watch. Buster stood near the trio as the bouncer eyed each of them and read the offered licenses.

"This is so cool," whispered the one. Both huddled next to each other, directly behind the first who still quietly faced the bouncer.

"Sign?"

"Excuse me?" he stammered.

"What's your sign?"

"Oh, um, Gemini?"

Gotcha, thought Buster. *Shoulda hit the juke joint at the cross-roads where I... Wait a sec. Maybe I need to start finding these places I remember. Maybe somebody knew me.* Buster felt excited at the idea, then paused. If Buster really had been a loner, would anyone have paid attention to the guy drinking by himself at the bar? He shook off a chill. *Wanting* to be alone and finally *being* alone were entirely different creatures that Buster found should not go together.

"Thanks, kid, but come back when you're twenty-one. With your own ID."

"Aw, man, I told you we couldn't get in," whispered one.

The three turned for the door and Buster followed them out.

Immediately, a damp warmth flushed Buster as he stepped outside.

He relaxed. The door to the bar closed, and the loud chorus of tree frogs filled the night over the sound of idling engines. A firefly blinked, and then another.

"If I could touch again, I'd catch me a lightning bug," said Buster, reaching for a pale yellow-green flick of light that tickled his fingers before flying away.

A couple leaning on the hood of a car wrapped around each other like pretzels. *Ev'rybody needs somebody*, Buster chuckled.

A truck turned into the gravel lot and swept The Blue Magnolia with headlights. It drove past the front of the bar and turned at the corner. Another faded red pickup truck caught his eye, similar to one he'd seen at the station by the university farms. Only half of it faced him. The other half was obscured by the building. Buster followed the crude, partial sidewalk in front of the bar to get a closer look. Someone sat in the passenger side. An orange glow appeared and dimmed as the occupant inhaled on what appeared to be a cigarette.

Buster approached the corner of the building. He still couldn't see clearly inside the truck, which moved slightly. The passenger leaned his head back. The orange moved to the driver's side.

"Hey!" someone shouted.

Someone slapped the hood of a car with the palm of their hand.

"Hey, crackhead!" Something knocked on metal.

The figure sat up and wobbled the truck.

A window crashed. The door opened. The shadow threw the dull orange ember away and jumped in front of the truck. Buster stepped around the corner onto gravel. As soon as he did, a shadow passed right through him, and a wave of nausea rolled from his stomach to his throat as he smelled paint thinner. He leaned against the building, trying to vomit but nothing came up. His skin, or what felt like his skin, burned as if splattered with hot grease. Buster closed his eyes tightly, shaking and dry-heaving, sputtering.

*****

Buster opened his eyes. Although the sun hid behind thin clouds, Buster found himself curled into a ball leaning against a porch column.

"What the f—?" he started, realizing that morning found him at Peaches's house. His stomach fluttered as he looked around. He felt something between a crushing hangover and an extreme consumption of coffee.

He tried to stand, but his legs quivered.

Something buzzed.

No, no. Ple-please. That's too much.

"Peaches? You here?" he called as he rolled over to face the door.

I already done told you... No, it was just me...

The voice definitely was not Peaches. "Hello?" Buster asked as he looked around the porch.

Ple-please, no more... wait. Maybe.

Buster's head hurt as he focused on the voice. Its tenor rang with familiarity.

My har- my heart. Can you pl-pl-please call somebody?

He knew it.

Hell, no, I just wanted t- kn- know.

"Mike!" Buster cried out, and felt a sharp prick on his forearm. If he had been alive, a drop of blood would have fallen onto the porch. Instead, it vanished just before touching the boards. The prick burned as his chest pounded, then fluttered, then pounded harder. A surge of electricity filled his body, and he breathed rapidly.

Oh god, please... stop... my heart...

"Well, look at what the cat drug in!" said Peaches as the screen door opened. "Where'd you run off to?"

Buster strained as he looked at Peaches, whose face went from annoyance to concern. "Buster! What the hell is wrong with you! You shakin' like a leaf." She knelt over him as if to hold him, but stopped and bit her lip. "Boo, I don't know

118

what—"

"I... I don't know... I feel like I'm racing," he sputtered.

Please, more. Make it stop!

"Who's talkin'?" asked Buster.

"Talking? No one's talk...boo. Your arm. That looks like track marks."

Buster palmed his chest and leaned against the porch column.   "My-chest-feels-like-it's-going-to-explode-I'm-hearing-voices," Buster winced rapid-fire. "What's happening?"

"Oh, God, you look like... if I didn't know better, Buster, I'd say you tweaked out of your mind."

Without warning, the tingling ended and Buster retched. He coughed and spit, but nothing appeared. He looked at his arm. The dark line that wrapped his arm like a vine slowly faded. The faint ring in his ear stopped.

The lightness of the world faded into color. Strength slowly returned to Buster's legs. He wiped his forehead and sat up.

"Here, boo, here's you a chair; sit down. Can I get you something?"

Buster looked at Peaches as he steadied himself and pushed off the floor to sit in the rocker.

"Right."

"Thanks, anyway," he coughed.

"Let me see that arm, boo," said Peaches.

Buster turned his arm over.

"Nothing. Not a scratch," she said.

"What's a track mark, Jasper?"

Peaches glanced at Buster. "Just sit there and catch your breath. What the hell happened to you? Where you been?"

"I went outside, and..." Buster rubbed his arm and looked at where he'd felt the prick. The mark had faded as his pulse slowed.

"And what, boo?"

"There was something. Someone. Like the professor."

"You saw him?" asked Peaches.

119

"I don't know. I mean, it was like the time the professor walked through me. I burned all over, it smelled funny, and then I hit the ground."

"You said you heard voices—"

"I think it was Mike," said Buster with a deep breath. "The boy at the bar that I'd seen at the lab. I could hear him just now. Before you came to the door. First, he was telling somebody to stop, then he asking for more. Something about his heart... What?"

Peaches crossed her arms.

"What, Jasper?" Buster smacked his mouth. "Damn, taste something funny. Worse than bad bourbon."

"What else happened?" she asked, still standing firm. "What happened at the bar?"

Buster went backwards. He recounted Mike's story about the professor dumping ants near the reservoir. Jonny's advice. The truck outside the bar. The voice and Buster's ghost-heart racing faster and faster. The voice stopping suddenly.

"And then, you end up here on my porch curled up like a scared little kitten."

"I know. Just came to, right here, Jasper."

"This morning?"

"Yeah, this morning. Must've passed out last night after I went outside. Oh, and he kept talkin' about this Tina girl."

Peaches paused. "Tina ain't a girl, boo."

"A boy?"

Peaches took a deep breath. "Not a person at all, although she is a raging bitch." She walked a few steps toward the end of the porch, scratching her head, then turned back. "Buster, The Blue Magnolia wasn't last night. That was a week ago. You been gone a week.

"A week?"

"Yeah, a week. And I don't think this time it's your weird being-a-ghost thing. Cause that child Mike's a tweaker."

"Tweaker? What are you talkin' about?"

"He shoots up. Meth. Also known as Tina. Sometimes tries to sell it or buy it at The Blue Magnolia, although seems like he doesn't want his buddies to know he goes out there for drugs. Probably turns tricks. Gay for Pay, as they say. High as a kite for days at a time. He's a hot mess, that one."

"Okay, so tell me why I heard him," said Buster.

"I don't know. Somehow, you connected and you feeling him when he's high on meth. And talking to someone. Buster, I don't have a good feeling about this."

"Whadda you mean?" asked Buster.

"That boy saw something, freaked out, told his buddy, and now this," said Peaches. "Did you touch him?"

"I don't know. Somebody outside at the bar, but I—"

"But, nothing! I warned you about messing around with that power. Maybe you walked into him outside the bar." She scratched behind her ear with one finger. "You said it just stopped?" she asked. "Just now?"

"Yeah, so?"

Peaches looked at Jasper and took a deep breath. She picked up a newspaper on the swing and showed Buster the front-page headline: "College Student Missing." Beneath the headline was a photo of a thin blond next to a tractor.

"That's Mike!" said Buster.

"I got a feeling we're not gonna see that boy again."

Buster looked down and rubbed his arms. "Sounded like he was talking to someone just now. Oh, and I heard something about him being the only one. What do you think that means?"

Peaches shook her head. "The paper says they found a small meth lab behind his trailer. Something is not right," she sat in the swing facing Buster.

Buster wiped away sweat.

"You said you saw that Mike boy out at the college, didn't you?"

"Yeah, so?"

"Uh huh," muttered Peaches, as she fanned herself with the newspaper. "You gotta find that boy Jonny. Or that professor."

"What in the hell for? He gives me the willies."

Peaches stopped swinging. "Dammit, Buster, I don't know why you a ghost, why you still here. Or why I can see you. But that boy saw something. Maybe he was just tweaked as high as a kite. But now he's missing. Maybe dead. And you—"

"I what?"

"—you might be the only person who can sort this out."

"And why me?"

"Cause you can. And you heard that little bit about the professor at the reservoir for a reason."

Buster leaned back in the rocker and looked up. "Does everything have a reason, Jasper? Maybe some shit just happens."

Peaches stood up straight. "I don't believe in accidents, boo. If you think *shit just happens*, then sit your ass in that house with Sally and Earl until it finally rots into the ground and I'm long gone, leaving you as a ghost with no house to haunt, no fish to catch, and no one to talk to. Then think about whether *shit just happens*. There's gotta be a reason you connected with that boy."

Buster looked at Peaches and then faced the yard. "I thought you said I was supposed to help Sally."

"I don't know what you supposed to do, okay?! But I know you *can* do something. Maybe it's Sally. Maybe it's Mike. Maybe it's something else. But if you don't do anything 'cept try to catch fish that don't bite, you might as well be dumping them ants or beatin' on Sally yourself. It's like Dr. King said. The worst thing is not what bad people do, but when good folks don't do anything."

Buster stood up and shook his head. "You preach a lot, Jasper. Quote Dr. King when it suits you. I don't know why I keep showin' up here. Just another white man telling a black man what he ought to do to improve himself. Maybe you ought to help me, if you know so damn much."

Peaches's back straightened at the word "man," and

stood facing the yard.

Buster sighed and his shoulders slumped slightly. "But maybe you right. Not like I can fish or do anything else."

Peaches bit her lip.

"But you gonna help."

Peaches looked over at Buster.

"Cause if you right, then it ain't no accident, either, that *you* the only one who can see me. And now *you* know what I know. And you just got a job at the school."

Peaches shook her head and started to talk.

Buster interrupted. "Now, you listen. You get all preachy about God and telling me what I ought to do and how you don't believe in accidents. And you know damn well I can't do much. Maybe *you* supposed to help *me*."

Peaches focused on the yard again.

"You said it yourself. Good folks who don't do anything are worse than the bad folks who causing trouble," said Buster. "And you know what, I do think you right. Somethin' ain't right. I gotta go back. Watching them kids around you reminded me of when I was real little, hangin' out in the schoolyard after Clover, Mississippi had *finally* realized that desegregation was the law. We got to join white kids in schools fifteen years after the Supreme Court said we should. We actually got books. Each of us. Not just the teacher. Working toilets and water fountains."

He continued. "Then, one day in the second grade, three of us were minding our own business by the jungle gym when a pack of white kids chased this scrawny guy over to us. He fell in the dirt and they pushed him down, over and over. Little bastard was crying, trying to get away. One of the rougher ones saw us and made some comment about monkeys on the monkey bars, and all the kids stopped. The little guy stood up. One of the white kids threw a clump of dirt at us, and when the little guy realized some colored kids distracted his bullies, he stepped behind the line. Another kid threw a clump and yelled a word that no child should be called. Instead of running to get a teacher, the small guy said nothing. Not a word. Instead, he picked up a dirt clod, dropped it, then ran away. Don't remember seeing him again, although I'm sure I did. Didn't bother to get help. So, you right. I'm not gonna run away like that kid."

Buster stopped, sweat dripping as if he'd run a race. Each bead vanished before hitting the porch.

"You gonna say something?" he said, finally catching his breath.

Peaches remained silent. Paint chips flaked as she gripped a porch column. She glanced over her shoulder, face unflinching and grey. Buster saw her lip tremble before she put her forefinger over her thumb and pressed against it.

"Jasper?" Buster asked.

"Oh my God," she muttered, then spoke softly, "Strength, no matter the consequence."

"You okay, Jasper?"

Peaches faced Buster squarely, tears mixing with sweat as they ran down her cheeks. "That's why I can see you."

"What? Cause I got picked on?"

"No," she inhaled deep and slow. "I—I am so sorry, Buster Sparkle."

Buster shook his head. "Nah, wasn't your fault."

A bobwhite called from a tree in the yard.

"Yes. It was, Buster," her voice cracked and her lip quivered. "That little kid... was me."

Buster stared blankly.

Peaches continued, "I should have told a teacher. But I didn't." She wiped her eyes, smearing a faint trace of mascara.

Buster started shaking his head. "Hell. No. Uh-uh. Can't be."

Peaches nodded. "It is. Or was. I was getting picked on that day real bad by some older kids. Calling me a sissy. One guy said he was gonna beat me dumb and blind cause his daddy said that was all queers was good for."

"Shhhhhhhit," said Buster, as he faced away and sat in one of the empty rockers. He clasped his hands together and stared.

"I was scared. Doesn't make it right. When they turned to you three, I could catch my breath, cause I knew they'd rather pick on black kids than a seven-year-old fairy."

Buster looked at her, then to his right knee, which vibrated rapidly. "This can't be."

"It was wrong. I was wrong. Now, we know why I can see you." She choked and rubbed tears from her cheeks. "I'm gonna help you and make it right. Cause you right—I can't just tell you what you got to do when you can't do much. You not the only one who has to... That's why I can see you. I'm supposed to help you."

"Don't tell me this is karma or something about God and how you feel guilty—"

Peaches put her hand up as her lips quivered with each word. "No. Don't matter, boo. I got to make that day up to you and clean up my side of the street. Guilt don't matter. Maybe God don't, either. So, I'm gonna help you now, cause I didn't help you back then, and I got homeschooled for the rest of the year until I got bigger. I can't blame it on never seeing you again, cause you aren't the only one who doesn't remember everything. I bet we saw each other in the halls and never noticed. At least, I didn't. Just tell me what you need me to do."

Buster leaned back in the chair and looked up at the porch ceiling. He said nothing as he turned his cheek to the breeze and closed his eyes. "This some twisted world we in, Jasper."

"Maybe. Something upstairs made sure we met again."

Buster grunted. "That was a real dick move, Jasper."

"I know," she answered.

A large grasshopper fluttered through the air and flopped on the porch between them.

"Did you get beat up much at school?" Buster finally asked.

"Mostly names. Got spit on a couple times. A quick anonymous punch in a crowded hallway."

"We couldn't have been in the same grade, because I

don't remember a little white Jasper Cotton getting beat up in the first grade for being a sissy. Then again, my people didn't hang out with your kind. That took awhile. Thrown together, but not shown how to play together," said Buster. "I never got used to the names," he continued. He studied his hands, then looked up at Peaches. "Or the anger I felt for being born into a skin that people hated. You didn't know better. Now, you do. Can't take it back, but can do something different."

"What a small town but big world, that I don't meet Buster Sparkle again until now. So, boo," said Peaches, "what we gonna do?"

"Well, you got that job at the school."

Peaches nodded, "Thank God for being the only person willing to scrub toilets."

"Maybe I'll follow you up there one day and look around while you working."

"That don't sound like much of a plan," continued Peaches. "My cleaning won't take me where you need to go. Maybe you head on over to the farms where the professor is. You bound to see him again."

"If only I could move stuff."

"How would that help?" asked Peaches.

"I could open up files and look for stuff." Buster paused, and looked at Peaches with a smirk.

Peaches stared at Buster. "Why don't I like the sound of this?"

"You can open files and drawers."

Peaches shook her head. "I'm fired before I started."

"No, we can make it quick. I can wait around the lab and when I see something, remember it and tell you what drawer to open."

"You just think all the dirty little secrets is gonna be written down like the answer key for a spelling test?"

Buster didn't answer.

"Boo, it's gonna be a lot harder than that. We don't know what we looking for. You got a dead tweaker and a professor that gives you the willies. If there is something going on up at the school, it is not gonna be written down and put in a filing cabinet in a folder that says EVIL PLAN."

"You right. But my point is, I can go where you can't. And you can do things I can't. So, we gotta work together and find out a few things."

"You gonna be the death of me," said Peaches as she returned to the swing.

Buster smiled. "Being dead ain't all that bad."

"I don't wanna find out."

"It'll be fine."

"Easy for you to say, Busta, you already dead," she said.

"I'll protect you."

"Right. Cause you gonna be the boo police?"

Buster stretched in the chair. "Think we'll ever just sit and laugh?"

"I hope so, Buster, I really do."

CHAPTER ELEVEN

"Have they heard anything?" Heather asked.

Jonny shrugged his shoulders. "Not really. They think it's drug-related, and, unless he was cooking and dealing, nobody cares about one less meth-head."

Finally, we're talking about something, thought Buster. He sat on a short filing cabinet and listened. Two days of waiting at the lab and hoping for something to happen did not prove to be very exciting. At last, the topic of Mike came up.

"Gosh, Jonny, I'm so sorry," said Heather, as she tucked hair behind her ears.

"I knew he used some, but..." he paused. "Part of me really thought he was trying to stay clean."

"After you saw him shakin' like a leaf?" Buster asked.

"But I don't know..." Jonny continued.

"You don't know what?" she asked.

"Something ain't right, Heather."

"You preaching to the choir; now, open up something for me!" said Buster, as he stared at the professor's desk.

Jonny looked around and leaned in. "He was tryin' to tell me something 'bout the professor."

"Is this about the foreign students again?" Heather blew hair from her face as she opened up a compact. "Jonny, you boys has got to learn that just cause somebody don't look like you, don't mean they less than you."

"No, no, not like that." Jonny paused. "This was about the professor, and I told him to ask—"

"Why? Mike cut too many classes?" she asked.

"Naw. He—"

A door opened. Professor Tinsley rustled into the room from the lab toward his desk. "One, two, three..."

Here we go, thought Buster. Interruption or not, Buster found it easier to spy on Tinsley when the professor was actually in the room.

"May I help you with something, Professor?"

"No, Heather, but thank you," he stammered, as he pulled a set of keys from his pocket and unlocked a drawer on his desk.

Buster walked over and looked into the drawer. "What's in there, Mr. Harvard?"

The professor pulled out a small, black notebook, and then locked the drawer again before bolting back into the lab. The door swiftly clicked shut.

Buster pushed on the drawer with his finger. He then tried to pick up papers from the desk. Nothing.

She snapped the compact shut and lowered her voice slightly. "Honestly, he's been weird ever since that man from the physical plant died. And then Mike dying just made him weirder."

Buster stopped moving at the desk and looked up at Heather and Jonny.

"I done forgot about that—that's been awhile, hasn't it? What they say happened?" asked Jonny.

"Heart failure," she said, as she shrugged her shoulders. "Slumped over in his truck right out there in the parking lot in front of the professor. Maybe a year ago? I can't remember exactly, but that's about when Professor Tinsley started mumbling, always rushing around."

Buster returned to Heather's desk.

"That don't make sense," said Jonny. "Not like when the physical plant caught fire a couple years ago and killed that other maintenance guy."

"Well, that's whut everyone else is sayin', although that fire was weird, too. How come the physical plant's sprinklers didn't go off? Those are the guys who monitor everything else; dontcha think they tested them? Anyway, the coroner said the guy must've been sick or something. And with all the grant money Professor Tinsley is bringin' into the school, everyone seems to have forgotten about that plumber, or that he died right outside that door. College said it wasn't related to his job, anyway."

Buster walked closer. *Wait, two guys from the physical plant died? Sally's brother?*

She leaned in. "Something doesn't seem right. I think it's all bullshit. This school is as organized as a bunch of yard chickens." The door opened and the professor walked back in. Heather picked up the telephone and nodded at Jonny.

"No, sir," she said. "No, that's right, not today." Heather hung up the phone.

The professor shuffled through papers on his desk as Buster looked over his shoulder. "Heather, I'm gone to the President's office. See you tomorrow." And in moments, the door to the gravel lot closed behind him.

"What was his name?" asked Heather.

"Who?" Jonny asked.

"The guy from the physical plant."

"Oh, I don't recall. He had a funny last name. Like Tinkle. No, wait. Sparkle. Like that Johnny Cash song, 'A Boy Named Sue.'"

Buster froze.

"Listen, Jonny, I need to get back to work."

"Okay, I gotta get going anyway."

"No!" Buster barked. "Wait! Which guy?!"

"I'm really sorry about Mike. You gonna be okay?" asked Heather.

"Wait! Stop!" shouted Buster. "Go back—"

"Yeah, I'm fine. Thanks, Heather," said Jonny, as he turned for the door.

"You can't just leave like that!" Buster yelled as he ran in front of Jonny. "Which guy was me?! I need to know!"

Jonny turned away from Buster. "I'm sorry if we was kinda rude flirting with you."

Heather laughed. "I can take care a myself, but thank you."

He paused, then turned for the door again.

"Dammit! Wait!" Buster threw his hands up in the air before he dropped to his knees and braced himself right in front of Jonny. *Fuck it, I need to know. Gimme a memory, please, just gimme a damn memory.*

Jonny walked right through Buster. Buster shook and trembled as he remembered crying on the floor, curled up in a ball. He shivered. In his hands was an empty bottle of Jack Daniels. Except Buster knew that it wasn't his hands that clutched the bottle or his head that felt dizzy with booze, but Jonny's, as he cried himself to sleep on the kitchen floor when his best childhood friend still hadn't been found after eight days.

*****

"Well?"

"Well, what, Busta?" responded Peaches.

"What do you think?

Peaches scratched behind her ear. "I think you onto to something. But which guy were you? Either the guy in the fire who died a couple years ago or the guy who died in his truck. And which one was Sally's brother?"

"I can't remember. That Martha woman hadn't been back over yet, neither."

"Start looking at the mail and find an old photo. Surely, you'd recognize yourself. You either Sally's brother, or there's some weird connection between the two of you. You didn't just show up at her house. Just like I see you for a reason."

"Have you found out anything yet?"

"Lordy, child, I just started that job that I got cause I was the only legal applicant willing to start scrubbing toilets. And I didn't know a damn thing to look for until today. So, no. But now, I know what to ask. Besides, can't you let a woman rest?"

Peaches rocked, then tipped Buster's rocker for him. The boards creaked in alternating rhythm as they listened to the cicadas.

"You said woman."

131

Peaches eyed him as if he was a teenager violating curfew. "Yes, Buster. *Woman.* Are we changing subjects already?"

"Why do you do that?"

"Do what, exactly?" asked Peaches.

Buster cleared his throat. "Well, refer to yourself as a woman and stuff. I don't understand."

Peaches licked her lips. "We been over this. Do you need to understand?"

Buster did not answer. "I just wanna know."

"Well, think about it, boo, does it matter? Would you ask a friend to explain why chocolate or vanilla?"

"That's different."

"Really? Do you ask your buddies what they like about being a man when they look at their peckers?"

"Well, no," said Buster, "but how is that the same?"

"Cause most of the time, we don't make our friends justify or explain themselves, except when we have a different opinion. The question *why do you do that* implies that somebody maybe ought to do something different. People don't always have to defend something that maybe can't be explained. Like why some people like chocolate or vanilla. Or strawberry. Do you ever ask someone to explain why they like chocolate better than vanilla?"

Buster shook his head, "No. They just do. But what if I want to get to know you?" he blurted.

"Then THAT, my friend, is the question you should ask. Because that is what makes the question different."

Buster looked at her.

Peaches nodded. "You want to get to know me? Or do you really just think I should act like a man?"

"Yeah, Jasper, I wanna know you better."

"Alright." She paused with a push on her rocker. "It's kinda simple in the end. But getting there wasn't. Mostly cause of what people expect. But sometimes, I feel like a woman. Some things we just feel, other things we know, but can't explain either to somebody else. Sorta how my favorite

132

colors are orange and pink, how I like lightning bugs, like tangerines but hate oranges. When I was little, I had dreams that I was a woman, then I would wake up and cry because something felt... off. I was always effeminate and learned early that it was okay for girls to wear pink and flowers and makeup, but not boys. No one could explain it to me, either. It was always the same: *boys don't do that* or *that's a girl color.*

"After getting chased and teased in elementary school, when puberty hit, I started to work out. All the time. I got big out of self-protection. I even did steroids a couple times and played sports, but, really, I didn't want to be a muscle man, cause I couldn't fit into dresses and didn't feel like a woman. So I quit. All I'd wanted was the ability to throw a punch that would end a fight if somebody came after me, cause I hate fighting and knew that I wouldn't throw a second. I thought, maybe I'm just gay, cause of how I felt around my PE teachers. But that didn't explain what I felt inside."

"So are you gay?" asked Buster.

"The easiest way to answer that for MOST people is yeah, I'm gay. I was born a guy and like guys. But that doesn't tell you my whole story. Who I am is not that simple. It's not about who I like."

Buster's forehead wrinkled. "You still got—"

"Hold it. I'm gonna stop you right there. May seem a logical question to ask, but it's not nice."

"What?"

"You were about to ask me if I still had my pecker, weren't you?"

"Well, yeah," said Buster. *Is that a problem?* he wondered.

"Did you ask your buddies if they had a vasectomy? Or how thick their dicks are? Would you ask a woman if she has fake titties or had a hyster-ectomy? Surgery is personal. And it's not your business for you to know what surgery I have. But mostly, the problem in asking that question is... that it focuses on my dick. It ignores what I'm telling you is in my heart and between my ears. Unless, of course, you have some...vested interest...in what's between my legs."

"No. I guess I don't really want to know about that." Buster leaned back in the rocker.

Peaches tipped both rockers and raised her eyebrow at Buster. "Don't think on it too much, and you'll be fine. Although my bunions might not be." She then lifted a foot to her lap and began massaging her big toe.

A yellow-orange school bus full of arms and backpacks and shouting voices lumbered down Raspberry Lane, away from the town. "Must've already made the pass through campus," said Peaches.

Buster suddenly rose from the rocker and paced the porch.

"You gonna conjure up something if you don't settle down," said Peaches. "Not sure a ghost muttering up a storm across from a cemetery is gonna amount to anything good."

Buster returned to the rocker next to Peaches.

Peaches eyed him as she rubbed her heel and ankle.

Neither spoke for a minute as Buster crossed his arms.

"What's got you all excited now?" Peaches asked.

"I wanna know what happened."

"To who?"

"To me, Jasper!"

"You died, child. That's what happened," said Peaches, as she stretched her foot.

"I know, Jasper, but I mean, how? And which fella am I? Is Sally my sister? If she is, then why aren't there any pictures of me at that house? I wanna know. I don't seem to remember those things. And we aren't the only ones who think something fishy happened."

Peaches put her foot on the porch and tipped back her rocker.

"And then, if I ain't Sally's brother, maybe there's a connection. Aren't you interested?" Buster fidgeted in the rocker as he spoke with his hands.

"Sure, Buster, but I also interested in my bunions. I can't change that you dead, but I can change how tired my feet are."

Buster buzzed his lips as he exhaled.

Peaches turned at looked at Buster. "Want me to push your chair?"

"No, Jasper, I don't want you to push my chair. I want you to help me."

"Help you? I already promised to help you. Why you suddenly all antsy at the moment?"

"I don't know. Wouldn't you be?"

"Sure, but not full-speed every minute. You spent a lifetime isolating yourself—seems like, anyways—so you can wait and just I-don't-know yourself into a stew tonight. My feet is tired from working two jobs, and I got a show tomorrow. Mama needs a new pair of shoes."

Buster paused for a minute. "How's the job at the college?"

"Fine."

"Fine? Since when are you just fine?" asked Buster.

"Since I got these bunions," said Peaches.

"You like the job?"

"Buster, I'm a fift-, forty-plus-year-old queen working in housekeeping services, scrubbing toilets. I have never fit in *so* well—they *so* tolerant," Peaches looked at Buster and continued, "What do you think I like about that job? It pays. And no one notices me, so I can work in peace and come home."

"That's where I worked," said Buster.

"I know, boo, we have been over that a hundre—"

"I mean the physical plant. That's where I worked. You in the same department."

"Yeah, I think we got that covered," said Peaches. She pressed two thumbs deep into the arch of her foot and mouthed her pain into silent words as her eyes squinted.

"I wonder if you work with anybody that knew me," said Buster, as he looked at Peaches' foot.

Peaches eyed Buster. "Just say what you thinking, boo. Can't read minds like you." She turned suddenly, "But don't start messing around with that power. You gotta do this ethical and that has all kinds of wrong written on it. Poking around peoples memories and secrets."

"It's not like I can pick what I learn from somebody. And you gotta find out more too, Jasper; you right where I was."

"Except I just started. I'm a big old queer at a school full of farm boys that, if it weren't for the back of their necks, they'd be lily white. It will take some time. At least wait until I get my first paycheck."

Buster sighed. "At least make a friend."

"Hahaha," scoffed Peaches. "Now *you* telling me how to live? As far as we can tell, you coulda been a hermit. You know how to make friends?"

"Well, I met-" then he stopped.

"Ooo," said Peaches, "you almost said it, didn't ya?"

"What?" grumbled Buster.

"You almost said *Well, I met you.*" She paused. "Watch out—you might end up living a little before too long," Peaches smiled. "Oh, settle your britches, boo, and don't act like you sitting in a dentist chair." Peaches switched feet and began massaging her other toes. "I'll make a friend. And I'll find out about that Buster Sparkle and see what people say."

Buster clapped his hands on the arms of the rocker. A calico cat bolted out from under the porch.

Peaches rolled her eyes. "Don't spook up the damn place. And don't be getting all excited, thinking you gonna hear something you wanna hear." Peaches pointed a finger at Buster. "Sometimes, folks don't need to be digging around the past or regretting on it. We gotta get you movin' forward." Peaches rose from the chair and headed for the front door.

"Yeah, I know you'll be glad when I'm gone," said Buster.

Peaches held the door open for him and motioned for

him to go inside. "I'll be glad when my bunions is gone," she said. "Not sure my life is gonna change much when you finally move on."

"If I move on," said Buster as he walked into the house. "I may be stuck."

"Then get unstuck," said Peaches, as she passed Buster and headed down the hall. "And don't get all mopey on me again, neither," she said, as she turned right into a room with a sewing machine and looked down at the dress that spilled from the table to the floor in a shimmer of glitter.

"You the one who put me up to all this," said Buster.

"Me?" Peaches sat in a stool in front of the table.

"Yes, you. You the one who told me I had to move on. That I had to participate. So, now I am, now we know I died and people aren't sure about it, and you ain't helping me."

Peaches put her palms down on the table. "What else you need? Your missing socks?" Peaches rolled her eyes and returned to the machine. "Lord, you something else."

"How the hell you 'spect me to find out what he up to?"

"Go wait for him. Go follow his ass. Stop pestering me. I promised I'd help, but I am not about to be in a hate crime or get thrown in prison. I'll find something about you. Surely somebody can tell me about you dying — we at least know you were at the college when it happened, either in a truck or a fire."

Buster sat a nearby chair. "I'm trying to do something different."

"So how *is* Sally doin'?" Peaches focused on the soft rattle of the machine as she turned the fabric in a smooth motion.

"Sally?

"Yes, Sally. The woman-whose-house-you-can't-haunt-who-might-be-your-sister? She kick out her low-down husband yet?

"Earl is still around."

"How about you scare him off?" asked Peaches.

"Trying."

137

"Try harder," said Peaches.

"Just how do you expect me to do that?" asked Buster.

"Figure out what makes you go bump in the dark."

"I hadn't quite figured out the details," said Buster. "What are you makin', anyway?"

"Dress," said Peaches, as she smoothed out a bundle of fabric.

"For what?"

"We got a pageant coming up!"

"The Clover Festival?" asked Buster.

Peaches clucked. "The Honey Ball Pageant."

"Honey Ball?"

"No, Honey Ball *Pageant*. Some didn't want to keep it just a pageant. Some didn't want to keep it just a ball. Bees make honey from clover, so there you go."

"Is that part of the Festival?"

Peaches stopped sewing and looked at Buster, containing her giggles. "Really? You think a bunch of drag queens, transgenders, and rest of the LGBTQI-LMNOP rainbow is gonna show up and invade the Clover Festival?"

"Oh. Right."

Peaches eyes widened. "Oh my God."

"What?"

"I'll be damned." Peaches tapped both feet. "Boo, you just gave me the best idea you've had since you showed up at my mailbox!"

Buster's stomach fluttered. "Um, what did I say?"

Peaches smiled. "Just you wait! Won't be the first time a bunch of queens invaded a place they wasn't welcome! This time, it'll be the whole rainbow."

"Jasper, I... I don't like the sound of this."

She started giggling. "Oooo, baby, I think you on to something!"

"WHAT are you cookin' up now?"

Peaches laughed. "You ain't seen nothing till you seen a parade of queens werq!"

"Work?"

"*Werq.* It's got a little bounce when you say it. It's spelled different, too."

Buster's voice wavered and pitched upward, "Jasper, please don't get yourself killed."

"You know, in high school, I was a lineman."

"You don't say?"

"I did say." She looked at him. "What, you think queers can't play a sport?"

"I. I don't know—," said Buster. "A lineman?"

"Just hush," Peaches interrupted as she stood up. "And keep on being impressed. I gotta finish the hem on a gown. Watch me stitch a line straighter than Charlton Heston."

CHAPTER TWELVE

Buster sat in an empty chair. Another visit to the university's lab seemed far more productive than going back to Raspberry Lane. Days in the metal building behind expansive fields of experimental crops ran together like a monotonous assembly line of hours, phone calls, and yawns. Crops grew faster than information. Buster still hadn't learned anything about Tinsley or Mike. Or himself.

Tinsley bent over his desk, reading a spreadsheet of numbers.

"When are you gonna talk to me, Professor?" said Buster. "I've been showing up here a month, and you quieter than a mouse. Somebody needs to talk—maybe you'll actually hear me if I don't go crazy first."

Professor Tinsley scribbled numbers on a chart on his desk, and then stared with an empty glaze at Heather's desk, neat and unattended.

"I don't care what Jasper says—if I'd get anything other than the willies, I'd just walk through you again," said Buster. He stood up and crossed the room toward the professor. "All I know is you smell like the devil and rumble stuff I don't get." Buster stood behind Tinsley and peered over his shoulder. Long columns of numbers were labeled "Batch 45-A" and "Batch 58-B" and "Batch 70." Each rows ambiguously noted "Location," followed by a mix of names, letters, and numbers.

"Counting dead bugs? Or something else?" Buster circled to the front of the desk and leaned closer to the papers and notes. "Damn, this looks boring. How could anything be in that?"

The professor continued without hesitation, marking on the spreadsheet as he went down each row. He then turned to a small, familiar black notebook.

"Well, look at ol' Professor Harvard," said Buster.

"What do you reckon is in that little thing?"

Buster tried to see the page that captured the professor's attention. Still, he wasn't close enough to read the small text and markings that the professor feverishly checked before crossing off entries on the printed spreadsheet.

At that moment, a bell rang, and the professor jolted up, staring Buster square in the eyes, noses touching. Buster immediately sneezed and instinctively wiped his face to rid the smell. Papers went flying and Buster jumped back.

"Sorry about that wind, Professor! Good morning!"

"Good morning, Heather," said Tinsley. "How's that rain?" He scrambled to catch one of the pages.

"Damn, my eyes are burning," Buster rubbed his eyes and stood back from the desk.

"Nothing like a good thunderstorm to cool things down!" said a damp Heather. She leaned forward and let her wet hair dangle in front of her.

"Rain washes away pesticides," muttered Tinsley, as he straightened the pages before putting them in his desk. "Plus, it's mass transit for the colonies."

"Bet you'll get that figured out," said Heather. "My momma says with all that grant money you got coming to the College, you bound to be doing something right."

Tinsley smiled and looked at Heather. "Let's hope so. But it'll be the patent that really makes a difference." Buster watched the professor stand up and put the black notebook into his pocket.

"Doing something right, my ass," said Buster.

"Heather, I'm gonna head into one of the test fields. I'll be back later after lunch." Tinsley pulled a key from his pocket and locked his desk drawer.

"Sure thing."

"You up to no good. I don't know what you got cooking, but something's not right," muttered Buster.

Tinsley lifted a jacket by the collar off the back of his chair and headed toward the lab door. Buster shook himself and followed.

As he opened the door, Tinsley paused as if stuck in thought.

In that pause, Buster bolted through, turning sideways to avoid physical contact. Metal jangled, and the professor continued into the lab, the door clicking shut behind him.

Buster scanned the brightly lit room. People stood scattered at different tables, most wearing white coats, a few in jeans and T-shirts. Near one end of the room, four aquariums full of dirt sat on a long, black table. One student studied something through the glass as if reading the fine print of a newspaper. At another table, a student on a stool peered through a microscope, periodically jotting something in a notebook. Two others stood at a white board and connected lines between numbers and several letters. They seemed to disagree whether one or two lines should be drawn between the letters "S" and "H" on the board in front of them.

Buster saw Tinsley head for another door. Tinsley darted between two rows of tables, almost running into a small female student. Buster followed quickly to catch up.

"Excuse me, Padma, my mind was elsewhere. How are the numbers today?" Tinsley asked.

"The death rate increased to a consistent thirty percent now, Professor," she said, emphasizing each "r."

He smiled. "You remember that last year, we started with ten percent."

"I do," she said.

Buster watched Tinsley.

"We haven't confirmed whether the ants can develop a resistance to this new sample," she continued. "I'm not so sure about this other batch."

Tinsley paused, "Which one is that?"

"This new set of numbers you gave me. Are those from our tests? If so, then these numbers tell me that the ants aren't consuming any of our control toxins. If that's accurate, and this is a new breed on our hands, that could be disastrous."

"Interesting," said Tinsley, as he cupped his hand over

his mouth. "Leave those in my inbox and I'll take a look."

What in the devil are you cookin', Mr. Harvard? thought Buster.

"Still, with the rate for this other set of numbers, in another year, we might be able to wipe out a colony in one generation. But even if we eradicate the Imported Red Fire Ant, we may have a new hybrid showing up in our field test," she said. "Not sure how we can keep up with those."

"There are many, many pests in this country, Padma," said the professor. "Some are worse than the fire ant." He smiled, then turned.

Buster reached for him, then paused and looked at Padma, moving his hand toward her. "*Better watch who you touch, boo,*" Peaches's words echoed in his thoughts. Buster shook his head, realizing that Tinsley remained his focus. He followed the professor out the door and into the brewing summer storm. Overhead, the western half of the sky blurred into the color of charcoal, while the late morning sun still shined in the east.

Tinsley zipped his jacket and scurried toward a Range Rover in the gravel lot. He held his keys out as he looked at the sky.

"Daaaaamn, look at those wheels. Fancy Harvard boy IS bringing in the green," said Buster. "And in a hurry, too. I'm gonna have to get into that truck quick."

Buster caught up with Tinsley as he unlocked the door. Buster took a breath, anticipating his move through the professor. Tinsley pulled the handle, then patted his pockets.

"Dammit," said Tinsley, then ran back toward the lab, with the door of the Rover slightly ajar.

"C'mon, c'mon, open up," Buster gulped, as he glanced back and watched Tinsley disappear through the doorway.

The wind kicked up in a brief gust, and the door quivered open a few inches. Buster reached his hands through the door and pulled. Nothing. Why not now?

Grey clouds swept above. A single drop of rain splashed on the door. Buster heard another land on the hood of the

143

SUV. He shuddered and then tasted water—sweet and cool. Buster looked at the sky and watched a drop of rain falling directly above him. When it hit—or should have—Buster felt a tingle from his forehead to his toes.

So a drop of water goes through me, but I can't go through this here door? Buster rolled his tongue around his mouth, and he tasted rain.

Tinsley came running from the lab, coat zipped tightly.

"Here we go again," said Buster, bracing for the contact.

At that moment, a sudden gust kicked up rain and leaves before pushing Tinsley back two steps. The door blew open. Buster scrambled across the driver's seat into the passenger side. Seconds later, a very damp Tinsley crawled into the SUV and started the engine. He wiped back wet hair from his face.

"Just keep your hands to yourself and we'll be fine," said Buster.

Tinsley unzipped his jacket and put the black notebook in a compartment between the driver's seat and Buster.

Buster reached over and touched the cover. *Too bad I can't read your little book.*

Tinsley faced the rear of the SUV and placed it in reverse. Rain fell in thick, heavy drops, hitting the windshield with the sound of cracking eggs. Crop rows rippled in the fields like tiny waves on a green lake. The vehicle left the gravel lot and turned onto a road that formed an outer perimeter of a group of fields, some empty others in various stages of green.

"Dammit," muttered Tinsley. "This is gonna wash off the test poisons."

"So why did Mike see you at the reservoir?" Buster asked.

The vehicle bounced along under slow swirls of grey and violet-blue overhead. *We gonna end up in Oz if Mr. Harvard don't watch the sky,* Buster thought. *Although, not like it'll hurt me as much as him.*

Tinsley slowed the SUV and leaned forward

briefly. Buster heard several thumps as the Rover drove onto a bridge that crossed a murky gully, and out of the shower. Typical of southern storms, the sky dropped crazy quilt patterns of light showers and downpours, while eerily leaving dry patches.

"Right over here," Tinsley muttered to himself.

What in tarnation is this crazy white man gonna do in the rain? Buster asked himself.

The gully, perfectly uniform and straight, looked like it had been scooped right out of the ground. It stretched into the distant, foggy rain, dividing the farms from another section of land. They crossed the gully and turned left onto another field road that passed by a brown, and still very dry, field.

The wind stopped almost as quickly as it had started. *Ah, shit, that ain't good,* thought Buster. Pink lighting flashed somewhere high above the clouds. *At least I'm already dead.*

Tinsley turned the SUV around at the edge of an open field. He stopped and let down the window and looked at the sky. The rustling applause of rain along a nearby tree line and the hum of the engine waited for the next rumble of thunder.

Buster looked at Tinsley, then back to the thunderhead above. "Mr. Harvard, you better get us back inside afore the sky wakes up," he said.

Tinsley sighed, put the SUV into gear, and headed across another ravine at a quicker pace than when he left. The Rover hit a bump, and both Buster and Tinsley rose out of their seats. The glove box dropped open. A small stack of unopened envelopes fanned out.

"Easy, trigger, I don't hear the sirens yet," said Buster, as he read the return addresses of the letters. Department of Agriculture. Department of Defense. Mississippi Department of Environmental Quality.

"I may be a nobody to you, big guy, but why you keeping letters from the Army and The Man in your car?"

145

Tinsley reached over and crammed the papers back into the compartment and snapped it shut.

Another bounce in the road, and the compartment flopped open again, sending stray letters flying out. Buster reached over to catch one, but it flapped around his grasp.

Tinsley slammed the glove box closed again, ignoring the letters on the floorboard.

Buster then realized they had not turned back for the lab. *Where in the hell are we goin' in this storm?* he wondered.

Tinsley continued down a gravel road that cut through smaller fields of crops. Square, white signs with numbers and letters marked off different plots. Fields gave way to a narrow, unmarked, but paved road that led through a wooded windbreak. The SUV turned east, away from town. Tinsley sped along, passing more fields and an abandoned gas station, before heading under an overpass near a salvage yard full of yawning cars and gaping trucks.

The main road narrowed to two shoulder-less lanes. Another mile, near an abandoned gas station, Tinsley turned right onto an unmarked road. After a hundred yards, he turned between spindly cedar trees onto an old lot. A rusted and yellowed metal shop building about the size of a garage greeted them. The only window Buster could see was a small, dark opening in the door.

"We'd be safer at a trailer park, Professor," said Buster, as he studied the abandoned building.

The SUV rested on a broken cement parking lot. Weeds sprouted through cracks like tufts of hair from a dog's ear. Thick paint peeled from the sides of the building. A vent pipe stuck up from one end.

The driver's door shut.

Dammit, thought Buster, as he realized the professor had left the vehicle. Buster tried to open his door, but to no avail. He watched as the man, hunched over in the steady rain, run to the door and fumbled with a large padlock before vanishing into the shed, leaving Buster in the storm.

You little devil. And of all the places to get stuck. He sat in the car and listened to the rain. Moments became minutes. The wind periodically rocked the Rover like a toy wagon, then stopped. Minutes added up. How long would he be stuck in the truck? Buster remembered a conversation with Peaches.

"*Maybe just think 'bout where you wanna be, boo,*" *She said. "That's what they say for us livin' folks. Maybe it works on dead ones, too."*

"*I don't know, Jasper, I don't think it's that easy.*"

"*Well, if you know how, then do it. But you say sometimes you think about a place you been, and then there you'll be. Is that luck, or something else?*"

Worth a shot. So, Buster closed his eyes and took a breath.

A gust of wind rattled his concentration.

How do I picture inside a building where I never been? He wondered, and opened his eyes. A wet leaf smacked against the windshield. Buster watched water dribble down the glass in uneven rivulets. More leaves flapped in twisting swirls like pages spilled from a notebook.

Wait. I can see the door right outside this truck. Buster closed his eyes again. "Just by the door. I'm just by the door," he whispered aloud. "I'm standin' by the door."

The SUV rocked Buster with the wind as he continued to chant. He pictured himself standing in front of the grey, pock-marked door. He thought about raindrops falling around him, leaves waving past, the smell of rain, the feel of wind on his face. He licked the taste of rain from his lips.

The rocking stopped. *Well, at least I got imagination,* Buster thought as his smacked his mouth and opened his eyes.

"Well, I'll be damned! I did it!" Buster clapped his hands as he stood in front of the metal building. He turned back to see an empty vehicle. He shivered as the rain fell through him.

Buster faced the door of the building. "Well, now

147

what?"

He approached the rusty, padlocked door. There was no gap between the door and the doorjamb. *I'm not even gonna bother*, he thought. Buster leaned and placed his ear against the door. He heard a file cabinet closing and a soft hum.

In front of the building, the worn footpath ended as Buster rounded the wide end of the building. He walked through the grass, silently, but slowly and stepped over the higher, thicker parts. The building was about twenty feet wide, with an air conditioning intake vent the only opening Buster could see. The grass in the rear of the building had been mowed at some indeterminable point, but now grew clustered and overgrown between piles of un-raked clippings. He turned back and headed for the front. With no other entrance or exit to the building, Buster sat, leaned against the door, and exhaled.

CHAPTER THIRTEEN

"But, mama..."

"But, nothing, Carlos. Head up, shoulda back. From the gut," said Peaches.

Buster leaned against the wall of the living room as all eyes steadied on the teenage boy with the clarinet.

Carlos inhaled, put the mouthpiece to his lips, and licked the reed.

No one said a word, nor even scratched a muscle, as warm notes flickered in the afternoon.

Buster did not recognize the tune, but it reminded him of something faint and remote. He watched Peaches nod slightly, eyes closed, tapping her foot. Three others sat in the living room and watched Carlos play his clarinet. Willie poked another boy, who elbowed back. Swiftly, eyes seemingly closed, Peaches popped both on the head with a yellow flyswatter. The two froze, and Peaches resumed nodding as Carlos continued.

Buster chuckled.

"Shh!" said Peaches.

"But Mama Peaches, I didn..."

She opened one eye. "Zip!"

This time, no one protested as Carlos keyed off notes in tempo.

The boy's fingers moved up and down the silver keys and black openings of the clarinet. Buster could not remember hearing one before, but the notes flying out of the instrument sounded like a friendly cousin to jazz on a saxophone. Almost nasally, it hit somewhere between a harmonica and a horn. Carlos' fingers worked swiftly as the tune grew. Buster nodded his head and felt the music from inside and remembered red lights, buckets of beer, and a nightclub on the edge of a Delta slough.

Buster bolted upright. He *felt* the notes: not the way he

felt things from the outside as they made their way through him, but this welled up inside and made its way *out*. Buster placed his hand to his chest.

Buster then put his other hand on his chest.

Peaches opened one eye to look at him.

A faint vibration, not like the hum of Peaches' air conditioner, but like the flow of a warm liquid, a bloodstream of melody, moved inside his chest, across both shoulders, down his biceps and forearms, before spilling into his hands. As the volume increased, the vibration grew stronger. He buzzed.

Peaches opened both eyes.

Buster looked at her, looked at his hands. He pointed to the clarinet.

Peaches smiled. "Carlos, play like baby Jesus is listenin'."

The tune of the clarinet, almost flat, yet full, filled the house and spilled through its tiny cracks into the yard. Buster felt the surge in his chest rise and fall with the volume and tempo. He felt full. He felt different. The hairs pricked on the back of his neck and his arms tingled as if finally waking up from a loss of circulation.

"Boo?"

Buster looked at his hands again and then Peaches. "I... I feel funny."

Peaches glanced over at the boys on the sofa, who steadily watched Carlos play. She shifted in her seat and looked back at Buster. The keys clicked as Carlos ran a sequence and the music reached a crescendo. Peaches jerked her head sharply and briefly to the left. Buster followed her signal and walked into the hallway. The bathroom door stood open.

Buster flipped the light switch. A thousand times before this afternoon, he'd instinctively tried to turn on a light switch and a thousand times before, nothing ever happened. This time, however, the light flickered as if testing Edison's invention. Startled, Buster jumped back, and, between the flickers of light, pulled the shower curtain down as he

150

stumbled into the tub.

The bathroom light shone steady.

Carlos stopped playing abruptly. Buster jumped up and stared into the bright mirror that, only moments before, he could have sworn stared back at him. Now, he saw nothing, and gone was the fuzzy electric sensation in his arms and hands.

Buster heard rapid footsteps coming down the hallway.

"Mama Peaches, don't go in there!"

"S'all right, Willie, nothing but a draft in this old house," Peaches responded.

"Ain't no draft in this heat," said Carlos.

"You know we next to a grave yard," added Willie.

"I heard that! Want my shoe flying at you?" Peaches added as she bounded down the hallway.

Buster reached for the light switch. Try as he might, he couldn't move it. *What the hell*, he thought.

"What are you doing tearing up my house?" whispered Peaches as she turned the corner.

"Who you talkin' to, Mama Peach?" said a voice coming down the hallway.

"Nobody, li'l nugget, I'm just... I'm just," she turned to Buster and whispered, "What the hell am I doing?"

Buster pointed at the mirror and the light. "I flipped it. I saw myself. I.." he stopped talking. Peaches followed his gaze. The audience of boys stood in a huddle behind her.

"Put that away!" she demanded. Carlos clutched his clarinet like a baseball bat.

"You okay, Mama?" asked Willie.

"Yes, Wils, I'm fine. I'm just..." she turned to Buster and the curtain, and spoke louder. "I'm just talking to this here house, asking what in the Lord's name it's doing trying to pull itself apart!"

"Mama Peach, I'm-" started Li'l J.

"You what, little boo?" she turned.

"He's scared, Mama," said Carlos. "We all heard a noise and you talking to yourself."

Peaches stood straight up. "Just a draft."

"Ain't no draft back here, Mama Peaches," said Willie.

"Is someone here?" asked Li'l J.

"Lawd, child, just us. No one is here."

"He ain't back, is he?" asked Carlos.

"What's he talking about?" asked Buster.

Peaches ignored Buster. "Child, do not use *ain't* in my house. And don't look at me like – I know I say it. Sometimes. That man left me for that hussy in Memphis. He is *not* coming back."

"You promised, Mama Peach," said Willie.

"And I am sticking by my word," she said, hands on her hips. "Nobody is here!"

"He wadn't right for you," said Carlos.

"Who the hell is he talking about?" Buster asked Peaches. "And why are we talking about you when I just flipped your light switch?"

"Let's get on back to you playing that clarinet. Jull-i-ard ain't-*is not* gonna come calling when we standing around flapping our mouths!" said Peaches, as she walked through the cluster of kids. "As God is my witness, you are gonna play for that school and show 'em how it's done!"

Buster put his hands up in the air. Shoulders shrugged, and a faint look of confusion crossed more than one face.

"Nuggets!"

Willie and Jerome turned and headed for the living room. Carlos stood still and watched as they turned the corner. He then faced the bathroom, just slightly shorter than Buster. He leaned through the doorframe and reached with his clarinet. Buster stepped back. Carlos quickly looked side to side and used his instrument to open the last bit of curtain that dangled from the shower rod.

"Carlos! We ready!"

"Just a sec, Mama!" he shouted.

"Get on up in here!"

"Washing my hands, Mama Peach," answered Carlos, as he stepped into the bathroom and placed the clarinet on the counter. Buster stepped into the tub to make room as Carlos washed his hands, casting nervous glances over his shoulder. He then left. Buster stepped out and leaned against the doorframe, staring at a mirror that didn't stare back.

Pop! A wave of nausea flooded Buster as Carlos reached back into the bathroom to flip off the light before darting down the hallway. Buster put his head in his hands to rub his eyes. He leaned on the counter to shake his head and found himself in a small dimly lit room with high windows, plain white walls, a bed, and a nightstand.

A young brown-black child played a clarinet behind a closet door, slightly ajar. A toddler with bright eyes watched from the bed, beneath a blanket, holding onto a black and metal case that rested near his pillow. His tiny fingers traced a small sticker on the case of a four-leaf clover. Buster recognized a younger Carlos and Jerome. Buster then heard voices, and followed them in a kitchen where a father slumped onto a table in front of several empty forty-ounce bottles and a Spanish newspaper. A frail, tired woman opened a door and carried in a basket of laundry.

The room rapidly faded, and Buster stood on a wide sidewalk in a wet, bright, loud night. Ahead of him rose a fountain whose water glowed like gold in a stone square as big as a field, surrounded by three buildings of glass and concrete, in turn rising above another expanse of concrete, taxis and more lights. Next to Buster stood an older youth, perhaps college-aged, who wore a tuxedo and carried a black box. On the corner was the faded sticker of a four-leaf clover.

"Carlos?" Buster asked before the sparkles in the wet pavement rolled like a wave, and he grabbed his stomach. Buster heaved and found himself in Peaches's bathroom, leaning on the counter. He wiped his dry mouth and slowly stood up in the dark to face an empty mirror that did not look back.

Buster whispered, but could not finish the sentence. The clarinet resumed, and Buster remained in the dark hallway with his hand over his chest. Flickers of electricity carried through what once were his veins and arteries.

The rest of the afternoon passed quickly. Carlos, Willie, and Jerome, joined by two others, scattered between the living room and kitchen, crossing off math problems in notebooks, feverishly doodling in margins, and reading well-worn paperbacks. Peaches read the paper. Buster, on the other hand, lingered in the bathroom, trying to bring back those moments of tangibility.

"Jasper, this is not gonna work," said Buster, as he finally left and slumped onto the couch.

Peaches looked at Buster, then turned to Carlos and Li'l J sprawled onto the floor, then back to Buster.

"You nuggets want some lemonade?" she asked.

"Oooh, yes, Mama Peaches!" said Li'l J.

"No ice in mine, please," added Carlos.

Peaches looked at Carlos in disbelief. "No ice? Go on and make it yourself. Stuff's in the kitchen," she said as she flapped her fan.

The two removed themselves from the floor, teenage arms and legs like noodles sticking to a hot pot. "Let Wils and Shay have some!" Moments later, Peaches and Buster were alone.

Peaches popped her fan as if hitting Buster on the head. "Boo, what's wrong with you?"

Buster looked up and sighed. "I don't see how this is gonna work."

"Busta, it'll work when you work what you been given. You hadn't got a choice anyhow. No one said it'd be easy."

"Maybe I will go sit in the cemetery or find my way to N'awlins and find some voodoo priest to..."

"Like hell, you will!" Her fan cracked in the air as she flapped it ferociously. "Listen here! Acceptance is your problem."

"Acceptance?"

"Yes, boo. Acceptance. That's the key for all us."

"What the hell, you a psychologist now that you working up at the college?"

Peaches shook her head. "Lord hep me, I'd pop you in the head if it'd make a difference. You sound just like one a my little nuggets." She stood up from her chair. "It's getting warm. Let me turn up the window unit before I set you right."

She crossed the dark room and turned a knob on the window air conditioner. It hummed, then buzzed as it worked to chill the thick air.

"Well, don't wait for the ice to melt! We in here," cried Peaches.

"Okay, Mama!" responded a voice.

"We?" asked Buster.

"Yes, boo, we," she responded. "Maybe you need a little gratitude or a different kind of purpose. Ain't nothing like helping another to get out of a funk. And that is what you is in, Buster: a self-centered funk."

"Self-centered? What have I done to you, Jasper? I don't ask nothing of nobody, nor do nothing to people." Buster sat on Peaches's chair.

Peaches looked at Buster with one raised eyebrow. "And that's not you being at the center of your own universe?" She paused and cleared her throat. "Self-centeredness is the root of all your problems. You tryin' to change the show. You want things to be different. But they are exactly how the good Lor- how they are. You can either accept that you a ghost and keep trying, or you can fuss and fume and rant. But you got a lesson here, and it ain't gonna change until you get it."

Buster looked at her, then said, "You done yet?"

"No, boo. It's time you meet my nuggets."

"Meet? How? Why?"

"Maybe you need another purpose. Something other than being a ghost detective or whining how somebody else—somebody who just might be your family—is living in your house." Peaches crossed the room. "That's my chair—go stand over there till my nuggets get in here."

"Nuggets?!" she belted. "You coming or am I gonna

155

have to call out the National Guard? Oh, and bring mama some lemonade, too, while you're at it," she cried, and cocked her head back toward the door frame. "Lord, boo, can you check that window unit and see if it's blowin' cold air?"

Buster walked over to the air conditioner. He felt a vibration extend from the floor, through his feet and up his legs. Buster waved his hand in front of the air vent. A cool surge passed through him and he shivered. "Yep, it's cranking," he said as he turned around.

Carlos and Jerome skipped into the room with tall, faded plastic cups. Carlos gave one to Peaches.

"Where's Wils and Shay?" she asked.

"They had to leave. Drama club or something."

"And when did they plan on telling me this?" asked Peaches. "I swear it'd be easier to keep free-range chickens in my backyard. Boys, I want to tell you both something."

"What is it, mama?" asked Li'l J.

"Well, child, it's a secret."

He smiled. "Oooo, I like secrets."

"This is a good secret. I have a friend that I want you to meet," said Peaches.

"You ain't—I mean you aren't seeing *him* again, are you?" asked Carlos, as Peaches eyed him.

"No, Carlos, I already told you that I will never see that man again."

"He wasn't right—"

"No, he wasn't, Carlos, thank you," interrupted Peaches, as she straightened herself. "Must you remind Mama of that every time? You just like a little hen. I'm old, not dumb."

"No, ma'am," responded Carlos as he drank from his cup.

"But this friend is different," said Peaches, as she eyed Buster who walked back toward her.

"Is he handsome?" asked Li'l J.

"Well, he's straight, so don't you worry about how handsome he is," smiled Peaches.

Carlos crossed his arms.

"And no, Carlos, it's not like that, either," said Peaches. She paused. "Besides, you can't see him."

The two boys looked at each other before turning back to Peaches.

"Whaddyoumean we can't see him, Mama Peaches?"

"Did I stutter? I mean...you can't...SEE him," she answered and leaned back. She drank from her lemonade and flicked her fan.

"Like an imaginary friend?" asked Jerome.

"Yeah, Jasper, am I imaginary?" Buster asked and leaned against the fireplace.

"Yes. Well," she paused. "No, not really, cause he's more like an invisible...friend."

Carlos laughed, "You feeling okay, Mama Peach?"

Peaches raised one eyebrow at him and clicked her tongue loudly.

"Carlos, sit up for Mama for a second." Peaches then looked at Buster and nodded toward the sofa where the two boys sat.

"You want me to sit, too?" asked Buster.

"Now, nuggets, Mama Peaches has an invisible friend. His name his Buster. He sometimes talks to Peaches. He's actually here today."

Jerome giggled.

Carlos kept his arms crossed.

"Buster, say hello to my nuggets."

"They can't hear me," said Buster.

"I know that! Say it anyway, Buster!"

Buster sighed. "Hello, boys."

Peaches looked at Jerome and Carlos on the couch. "He says hello. He knows you can't hear him like me."

Jerome smiled and waved his hand at Peaches.

Peaches smiled, "He's over there, Jerome, in that chair."

Jerome faced the chair and waved again, "Hi, Mr. Buster," he said.

Carlos shifted in his seat.

"Carlos, what's wrong?" asked Peaches.

"You okay, Mama?" he asked.

"Yes, boo, Mama ain't never been better!"

Carlos looked at his feet.

"Li'l J, pick a number."

"Three," he said.

"Wait, boo, use your fingers. I'm gonna close my eyes," said Peaches. She shuffled her body and cleared her throat.

"Now, Jerome, hold up some fingers." She waited. "Buster, how many has my li'l nugget got?"

"Seven," said Buster.

"Buster says you got seven fingers up," said Peaches.

"Whoa!" said Jerome.

"You peeking, Mama?" asked Carlos.

Peaches squeezed her eyes tighter, "Not a chance, Carlos. Now, both of you hold up some fingers."

"Buster?"

"Jerome has nine up. Carlos ain't playin'."

"Nine and zero," said Peaches. "Carlos, you gonna play?"

"How'd you do that?" Carlos asked.

Peaches cleared her throat. "How about you hold up some fingers first?"

Carlos sighed.

"Buster?"

"Jerome has two fingers. Carlos has one finger," said Buster.

"Buster says Jerome has two and Carlos has one," said Peaches. "That better not be the one I'm thinking of..."

"That's so cool, Mama; is that gonna be in your show?"

Peaches opened her eyes. "I don't think so, nugget. I'm trying to help Buster. You see, he's stuck and don't like it."

"You say I'm stuck. I'm fine as I am," responded Buster.

Peaches ignored him.

Carlos put his hands on his knees.

"You mean, like a real ghost?" asked Jerome.

"A real ghost, boo," she answered.

"Oh," Jerome said, as he shifted slightly toward

158

Carlos. "Is that what made that noise in the bathroom?"

"... but he don't remember bein' alive..."

"Mama," started Carlos.

"... and we not sure how he died. So he's stuck..."

"Mama," Carlos repeated.

"But he ain't accepting what the good Lord—"

"MAMA!" shouted Carlos.

"What, boo?"

"You scaring Li'l J," he said, with his arm around Jerome's shrinking frame.

Peaches looked at the two, then Buster, then back.

"You keep looking over there and talking like he's real," said Carlos.

"But he is, boo," said Peaches.

"Mama," said Li'l J, who looked at the empty chair and back to Peaches.

"I think he's scared, Jasper," said Buster.

Peaches stood up and walked over to the couch. "Now, boo, don't you worry. Buster's not a mean ghost."

Jerome hugged Carlos.

"Mama, this isn't funny," said Carlos.

Peaches sighed. "He's like a guardian."

"You mean, like an angel?" asked Jerome.

Buster laughed.

Peaches scratched her head. "No, boo, he's certainly no angel, but he does keep a watch out when he's here."

"What are you putting me up to, Jasper?" asked Buster.

"Just think of him like he's gonna watch out for you when you's here at Mama Peaches's house. He'll make sure you outta trouble, and that Peaches stays outta trouble too."

Buster laughed, "Like I can keep *you* outta trouble."

Peaches clacked her tongue on the roof of her mouth. "Buster, you can leave now." She looked over in Buster's chair, then scanned the room, as if watching someone leave. "He's not always here and we won't talk about him anymore today. I just wanted you to meet my friend because he's lonely. There aren't any other ghosts or people for him to talk to."

"I'm not lonely!" said Buster.

"He is?" asked Jerome.

"Like you, Mama," said Carlos.

Peaches sat up. "I said that's enough for today. He's gone home for now. Buster don't want to scare you."

"I'm still here, Jasper," said Buster.

Peaches looked around as if she misplaced her keys. "See, like I said, he's already gone. But he'll be back to keep an eye out."

"Can we talk to him?" asked Jerome.

Peaches paused. "Why, child, yes, when he's here, but see, I already sent him home..."

"Jasper, I'm still here," said Buster.

She cleared her throat, "Well, maybe we'll come up with something."

"Hey, Buster!" shouted Jerome.

"Shh!" said Carlos, nudging Jerome as he giggled.

"Hey, kids," said Buster.

Peaches crossed her arms and smacked her tongue.

"Does he have a last name?" asked Jerome.

"Don't ask that!" said Carlos. "Everybody knows you can't use a ghost's full name."

"Why?" asked Jerome.

"Cause it...it—"

"It what, Carlos?" asked Buster.

Peaches wrinkled her forehead, ignoring Buster, and looked back at the nuggets.

"You can't use their full name cause it makes them angry!" said Carlos.

Buster laughed.

"Who told you that, boo?" asked Peaches.

"Everybody knows it!" said Carlos.

"No, child, that's not true with Buster. He was just like you and me once. He has a name and he likes people to use it."

Jerome nodded. "It's res-pect-ful," he added.

Carlos crossed his arms.

Peaches reached over and patted his head. "It's okay, Carlos, you don't have to be scared either. Buster is a friendly ghost."

"Like Casper!" shouted Jerome.

Peaches snorted. "Well, not quite like Casper."

"Is he white?" asked Carlos.

"Why does that matter?"

Carlos shrugged.

"No, he's not," said Peaches.

"So, what's his name?" asked Jerome.

"Buster Sparkle."

Jerome giggled and Carlos snickered.

Buster sat up. "What's wrong with my name?"

"That's a silly name," said Jerome. "Whoever heard of a name like *Sparkle*?"

"Nugget, don't be makin' fun of anyone's name. He's got feelings, too."

"I like it," said Carlos.

Buster smiled. "That's my boy."

"It's like a drag name," Carlos continued. "Almost like Peaches Juba Lee."

"Now, wait a minute," said Buster.

Peaches laughed. "It does have a nice flair, don't it?" She winked.

"Mama, you always said everybody's got some drag in them," said Jerome.

"Well, nugget, Mama Peaches might be wrong on that one. Some folks so vanilla they make a straight line look curved."

"Do you like him?" asked Li'l J.

Peaches paused. "Do I like him? Yes, sugar, why?"

"Then I'll like him, too. Will you let me talk to him when he comes back?" he asked as Carlos elbowed him.

Peaches winked, "Why yes, little boo, you can talk to him when he comes back. Don't need my permission, either."

"He probably needs friends," nodded Li'l J. "Carlos,

will you be his friend too?"

Buster looked at the boys, turned to Peaches, and turned back. "I—"

"He would probably like that, nuggets. We all need friends."

*****

Buster returned to Raspberry Lane the following day to piece together his momentary ability to turn on a light and knock down a shower curtain. Recounting the episode, Peaches quickly shifted.

"Buster, I told you not to touch the kids," Peaches focused on the sewing machine, which rattled several syllables.

The machine stopped as she turned the fabric.

"I didn't, Jasper. Well, I mean, not on purpose! He touched me," said Buster.

Peaches eyed him quickly without losing speed, and continued along the stitch line.

"He reached back into the room to cut off the lights and before I knew it, I was in his house and saw—"

Peaches ceased sewing and put her right hand up, palm facing Buster. "I don't need to hear it."

"But it's goo—"

"Did I stutter? Cause I don't think I did."

"But—"

"But nothing, boo. 'Sides. I already know what goes on at his house. I don't need to hear it from your peepin-Tom, mind-reading ghost tricks."

Buster opened his mouth, but Peaches put her palm up higher.

"You gonna create some bad juju if you don't be careful. Instead of snooping around the head of my little nuggets, why don't you go read that professor's mind and find out why he gives you—and me—the heebie jeebies? Find out what happened to Mike. Find out what he

162

is doing out there in that little metal shack of his."

Buster threw his hands up and walked to the window. "Told you I can't just pick what I learn."

"Okay then. Maybe you ain't supposed to read nobody's mind—especially if they done nothing wrong."

"I didn't do it on purpose, Jasper."

She put her palm down and straightened fabric in the machine to rock again. Buster stood in silence and looked out into the heat of the day.

Peaches coughed. "So. Back to the issue of you learning how to be a ghost. Sounds like all we gotta do is turn off the lights, play a clarinet, and get you reeaal angry. But you still here."

"So?"

Peaches looked at Buster. "You hadn't moved on."

Buster looked at his hands and feet. "Yup. Still here."

"Right. Clearly, you ain't done."

"I hadn't really done anything, Jasper. What if I ain't really dead?"

Peaches frowned slightly and paused sewing.

"I mean, what if ev'rybody got it wrong and I just missin' or hurt or something?"

Peaches stood up and walked around Buster for the door to the hallway.

Buster followed. "I mean, I heard a stories like that in movies. Person isn't really dead, so he lingers until they find him."

Peaches crossed into the kitchen and picked up a newspaper fragment, then turned back. She spread it in front of Buster on a table in the living room. "I'm sorry, Buster. I don't think that's your story."

Buster looked at the strip of paper, torn around the edges. A small paragraph loomed. Buster read aloud: "Local plumber dies at college. Buster Sparkle, 46, died in the parking lot of a lab managed by Prof. Art Tinsley on the South Farms. The coroner's report indicates that Mr. Sparkle died of—"

Buster looked at Peaches.

"I'm sorry, boo, the rest of the page got torn, so I don't know what else it said."

"You knew?" he asked.

"I just saw this yesterday, boo, when I was throwing out papers and saw the headline."

"This is a year old," said Buster, as he looked in the upper corner of the clipping.

"Don't criticize my housekeeping," said Peaches.

"I ain't. I just...dammit. I just hoped maybe I was in a hospital somewhere."

"At least you know you died out at those farms," Peaches paused. "Still. Buster, maybe you got something to do here that doesn't involve that bug doctor. Maybe there's a reason you at that house. That Sally is at that house."

"Maybe so. But why her—even if I am her brother? And why can't I remember anything about dying?" asked Buster.

"Well, did you *live* very much, Buster? Maybe we aren't supposed to remember the dying part. Maybe it's about your life."

He stared at the paper clipping, tracing letters with his finger.

"Lord, half the time I can't remember where I put my keys anyway," said Peaches. "But that don't mean I never had them. Or that they ain't where I last put 'em."

Buster paused. "How's the dress comin', Jasper?"

Peaches looked up from her paper. "Well, boo, if I didn't know better, you was taken an interest in what I do." She paused. "Going well, although I got to have at least two outfit changes for the show. The Clover Festival and the Honey Drag Ball are just 'round the corner."

Buster stood up and walked to the window.

Peaches watched, "You hear somethin', boo?"

Buster shrugged his shoulders. "I think Carlos is on the way."

"How you know that?"

"I feel it," said Buster.

"Why can't you feel me the right lotto numbers?" Peaches asked, as she slapped the paper on the coffee table.

"I'd give 'em to you if I could," said Buster.

Peaches walked to the kitchen. "Don't go nowhere on me, boo, I gonna check on a roast. Tonight's movie night with the nuggets."

Buster stared out the window and lightly pressed his fingers on the glass. A faint smudge lingered momentarily before it faded. Was it real? Moments later, Buster watched as Carlos skipped up the walk from the street. Jerome and Willie and another kid followed.

"Mama Peach! Mama Peach!" cried Carlos as he bounded in the door.

"Hey, nugget! Back here," she cried, as she left the sewing machine and headed into the hall.

Buster watched as the children tumbled into the house like calves running through a farm chute. Bags and band instruments piled themselves in a corner. Six feet followed Carlos into the back.

Buster heard footsteps run back. Li'l J stood at the front door and looked at the ceiling. He arched his back and shouted, "Buster! I'm home, hope you had a good day!" Then he ran, almost stumbling, back to the kitchen.

The sound of excited voices and laughter filled the back of the house. Buster cross the hallway for the kitchen.

"Mama! Mama!"

"Guess what!"

"Carlos has somethin' to tell you!"

The voices crossed like ballgame chatter.

"Well, nuggets, Mama Peaches can only hear one of you at a time!" she said, as she closed the oven door.

Buster stood in the kitchen doorway and watched Carlos and the others swarm around Peaches like bees.

Li'l J wiggled as Willie sat at the table and picked up a cracker. The other boy, Buster realized, was Shayla when she removed her baseball cap. Carlos halfway smiled.

"Well?" Peaches asked.

Carlos silently handed a piece of paper to Peaches.

She looked at him, then the paper. "What? Detention? Did you pass biology? Cause repeating that would be worse than detention," she said as she read.

Li'l J wiggled.

"Shhh," whispered Shayla.

"Wait," Peaches looked up at Carlos, then the paper, then back to Carlos. The paper began shaking in her hand. Li'l J started jumping.

"I got the audition, Mama Peaches!" cried Carlos.

"Well, boo, I can read!" cried Peaches, as she towered over Carlos and squeezed him as the rest of the kitchen cheered.

"Ju-lee-ard! Ju-lee-ard!" chanted the other kids, while Carlos quieted.

"What's all the fuss about?" asked Buster.

"It's just the audition, Mama Peaches," said Carlos.

"Yeah, an audition that no one in Clover, Mississippi ever got before!" cried Shayla, as she gave a fist bump to Carlos.

"He still gotta get in," said Willie.

"I outta smack you, Willie," said Peaches, as she squeezed Carlos.

"It's okay, Mama, Willie's right. Plus, I got to go there to audition," sputtered Carlos.

Peaches released him. "Go where?"

"New York City!" shouted Li'l J.

"New York City! New York City!" chanted the kitchen.

"How am I gonna get there, Mama? My momma and dad can't take me or pay," said Carlos. "The school won't pay for me to go, neither."

"What's Jull-ard, Jasper?" asked Buster, who stood against the wall.

"It's a music school, Bu—" she interrupted herself.

The entire kitchen froze in silence. The kids looked at Carlos and to Peaches.

"Is Buster here?" asked Jerome.

166

Peaches shook her head, "No nugget, he not—"

"Then who you talking to, Mama?" asked Shayla.

"No one, Shayla—"

Willie interrupted, "You was, too, Mama Peaches. You was—"

Shayla elbowed Willie.

"—*were* about to say a name."

"Hey, Buster!" giggled Li'l J.

"Who's Buster?" asked Shayla.

Carlos chimed in, "Peaches's house is haunted by a dead straight man!"

"No, it's not haunted, nugget! Now, shush!" said Peaches.

"Buster is our *friend*!" said Li'l J. "And I'm *his*!"

Shayla looked at Peaches. "Is this for real?"

Peaches sighed, "Yes." She turned to Buster. "Julliard is a music school."

"It's the best," nodded Li'l J, as he put his fist into the air. "And my big brother is gonna go!"

Shayla's eyes widened as she followed Peaches' gaze to an empty space in the doorway.

Willie matched Jerome's hand with a fist bump.

Peaches continued while reading the letter, "Carlos applied and sent an audition tape. Now they want to meet him in person. No one from Clover, Miss'ippi has ever been. But he has to go to New York to play."

Li'l J glanced back and forth between Peaches and the empty doorway. "So, is Buster really here?"

"So, who is this Buster cat?" said Willie, as he caught a pretzel in his mouth.

Carlos stood with his arms crossed.

"That's a fancy school, ain't it?" asked Buster.

"Yes, it's a great school," said Peaches, as she straightened her hair and turned back to Carlos. "Carlos, Peaches is so proud of you! We are gonna have to celebrate this!"

"How am I gonna get there?" asked Carlos.

"Well, he's got to go," said Buster.

Peaches looked at Buster then to Carlos. Shayla remained frozen while Li'l J skipped around the table. Willie continued eating pretzels.

"Mama Peaches, don't play games right now; I got to figure how I'm gonna go," insisted Carlos.

"He's got to, Jasper! I see it! He gets—" started Buster.

"No!" shouted Peaches, as she spun and faced Buster. "You a good man, Buster, but nothing good is gonna come of fortune telling—"

"Whad he say, Mama?" asked Li'l J.

"Huh? Nothing, nugget, he just spoutin' off."

"Is- Is- there a ghost here?" Shayla stuttered.

Li'l J hugged Shayla around her waist. "It's okay, I was scared, too, at first."

"No. He told you something," said Carlos.

Buster started to speak.

Peaches looked at Buster. "I said no. I don't wanna hear about it."

Carlos uncrossed his arms. "What is it, Mama Peaches?"

"Settle down, brother," said Willie. "You know you'll get in. Cool act, by the way, Mama."

Peaches looked at Carlos. "We gonna get you to New York. Somehow, someway. I don't know if you gonna get in, but we gotta try. Buster thinks you gotta try, too."

Carlos looked at the empty doorway Peaches had previously addressed. Unknown to Carlos, he made direct eye contact with Buster.

Jerome started skipping again. "Carlos, I have ten dollars in my piggy bank I'll loan you."

"Why won't anybody answer me?" shouted Shayla. "Who is this Buster dude, and why are we talking about him like he's here? What the hell is wrong with you people?"

Li'l returned to hug Shayla. "Mama Peaches has an invisible straight friend who watches out for us. Now, let's have pizza cause Carlos is going to Ju-lee-ard! Ju-lee-ard!" He pumped his fist in the air.

"It's an audition," said Carlos. "That I can't afford to get to." He sat at the table and picked up a pretzel with Willie.

Shayla sighed and shook her head, slumping into a chair next to Willie. "You people are crazy."

CHAPTER FOURTEEN

Buster's awareness of time was as reliable as a gospel preacher stopping early for Sunday dinner. According to Peaches, Buster would disappear for days or hours, yet, for Buster, he existed in a rolling blackout that ran together. A season had passed, this he knew, because school had started, grass was brown, and early October still carried the weight of summer's drought.

"C'mon, Jasper, see if they will send you over to clean at the lab," he'd pleaded. "Tinsley's got a notebook he keeps real close, and its usually there."

"Boo, it ain't that easy. From what I hear, he got some kinda federal grant and the government is all up in his business. I can't just ask to show up, after asking about the maintenance guy who died out there, without looking like I'm up to something. They do background checks on people."

"Don't they do that anyway?"

"Maybe," said Peaches.

"But he IS up to something and nobody seem to know."

"Buster, you just keep trying that secret shack of his out past the salvage yard and you'll find something."

"You find something out about me? The plumber who died?"

Peaches wrinkled her mouth. "Not much. You worked hard, alone, and fished. People knew you, but didn't. You were like the neighbor that you wave at and say hello to, but still don't know a damn thing about."

So Buster left Peaches that morning, or perhaps the day before, with the intent of finding the secret shed where Tinsley had, unknowingly, taken him many weeks prior.

First, Buster had thought of the farms. If he focused on where he'd been and where he wanted to go, he could get there, and he'd been to the farms. *Maybe I'll find the professor's car and ride out there with him again,* he'd thought.

But days, perhaps weeks, of watching the professor in the lab really hadn't gotten him any closer to the strange little black notebook the professor kept, or the secret lab. If it was, indeed, a lab.

Instead, Buster decided to head for campus. Perhaps it would stir up memories that might be helpful. He found himself standing outside of the small building where Jasper had applied for the job. Not exactly useful, but someplace new, nonetheless, so he turned and kept walking.

"Try putting one foot in front of the other. You'll end up right where you need to be. Trust your feet," Peaches had *told him.*

The main campus stretched without any apparent direction or organization.

How did I find my way around this place when I was alive? thought Buster. He passed in the shadow of a large football stadium that rose from of a tangled, knotted intersection of roads. Not a parking lot in sight. *Where in the hell do the cars go?*

A coed ran past him with a dog.

"Hey, buddy," said Buster, as the dog jumped and barked.

"C'mon Petey," said the student, as she gave the leash a quick jerk.

The puppy looked back and yelped before running to catch up with its owner.

"Good idea, Petey," said Buster. "Stick with folks who can feed ya. Not like I got a treat."

He continued along a sidewalk that meandered around old and new buildings. Nothing looked or felt familiar. *Why is this not ringin' any bells?*

Twenty minutes later, Buster passed between two buildings and found himself in the middle of a giant, open, rectangular brown lawn, marked by a crisscross of sidewalks. A flag pole rose from the center. Still, he recognized nothing.

Students in brown and white ran and somersaulted in lines. "Go, Ox, Go!"

Buster took a long detour toward a grove of cypress trees near the southern end. Buster looked up at the sun, *At least I coulda been helped out with the heat.*

He reached the end of the lawn and stepped under the trees. Slightly cooler and drier, Buster smelled dirt and decaying leaves. He stood between two roots of the old cypress and leaned back. Most of the lawn and its cheerleaders were obscured from view.

Buster rested his head back against the bark. *So. If Sally is my sister, why don't I remember?* he wondered. The darkness of the shade cooled him in the still air, and he inhaled deeply. *Am I stuck cause I don't know? And how do I help her if I can't kick Earl out?*

He tapped the back of his head against the bark, looking into the pattern of blue and black above. Too dry and dark to resemble snowflakes, too thick for cobwebs, the thin leaves of the cypress formed a fractured quilt against the backdrop of the open sky.

Buster closed his eyes and continued to tap his head against the bark, which hardened as he repeated. He could picture the shed easily. He couldn't remember the maze of back roads that the professor drove to reach the hidden building, but he recalled passing the salvage yard. Another memory sparked. He'd known about the salvage yard outside of town: that's where he remembered taking sacks of beer cans. But would that help him find the shed?

If he couldn't force Tinsley to take him, Buster had to find a way. What did it take to conjure himself to a place he'd only seen once?

Buster thought of the leaves parting above him and a hot blue sky changing and filling with cool clouds: Indian summer. Buster smelled barbecue and heard cheers of a football game as he fingered the rough bark at his sides. Small strips pulled easily as Buster remembered sitting in the end zones, cheering and watching players dance across the field.

So fishing wasn't the only thing he enjoyed, but college football and clean throws and Hail Mary touchdowns. The flood of memories felt dizzy and uncertain, disconnected, yet familiar. He smiled remembering a final seconds kick for a field goal win, and a quiet grandfather holding him up to cheer with the crowd. Buster remembered his grandmother and her familiar absence, which stung like the hot burn when Jonny possessed him after Mike's disappearance. A grandmother and a best friend, unknown to each other, but both missed, both connected only through memories given to a ghost. A ghost with vague history, uncertain purpose, loosely tying worlds together.

The rough bark had worn smooth to his touch. Buster opened his eyes to find that he stood not on campus, but leaning against a forgotten metal shed. Parked ahead of him was a green Range Rover, backed a few feet away from the door.

"Daaaamn!"

Buster approached the door of the building. It was closed. But, it was a start. An enormous start.

Hope I didn't just sleep for three weeks.

He waited.

Buster walked to the corner. *Maybe there's a window I missed.* Buster headed for the other end of the building and tried to kick a rock. Nothing.

He walked around the parked Rover and looked at the building. Any possible gap in the building might let him look inside or find a way to get through. Its roofline sloped upward. Near one end, a vent hood and two pipes rose from the top.

That's it, he thought. *Maybe I can see down in there.*

Buster headed for the front of the SUV and climbed onto its hood, then its top. He stood up and looked at the building. The eave started barely four feet above and in front of the top of the car. With a hefty stride, Buster might jump from the car to the building.

Buster took the only step back he could and, with all his

173

might, lunged. For a brief moment, he grabbed the overhang. His feet swung rapidly for the door of the building, and he lost his grip. At that moment, the door opened, and Buster's feet plunged right through the chest of the professor. Nausea rushed through Buster as he crumpled at the professor's feet.

"Ow!" he yelled, hitting the cement floor.

As Tinsley peeked outside, Buster crawled away and curled up. *Damn, you sonofabitch.*

The latch clicked.

Inside, Buster climbed upright and wiped his mouth. The hard landing hurt briefly, then faded, as intangible as Buster himself. The shed was slightly warm and smelled of stale bread. Bulletin boards, covered in papers and notes, lined a wall at the end under a very tiny glass window block. A dry erase board, smudged with greenish-black ink, leaned against the wall behind a desk with an old computer wired to several other pieces of equipment. In the center, under a giant kitchen vent, was a table with an odd assortment of glass tubes, jars, and containers. Several small aquariums rested on a table that seemed unlikely to support their weight. A dim light hung above the glass boxes half-full of dirt, each covered with a clear hood.

Buster stood and walked over to the aquariums. He touched the glass, and his print faded quickly as he removed his finger. Was the print real? He touched another. As his eyes adjusted, he saw ants. Hundreds, if not thousands, circling inside each aquarium, as if to greet his fading ghost prints. Some tiny, some large. Each looked different from the next. Inside one aquarium, pellets scattered like birdseed seemed to annoy the ants. Another contained a pile of pellets that the ants swarmed like tiny vultures, as if trying to devour them even before carrying them away.

Damn! thought Buster, looking at a small mouse, barely alive, attacked by a horde of fast moving ants. He shivered and walked to the next aquarium. Ants made lines along a greyish white shape, perhaps four inches long. *What in the hell?*

Buster looked closer. The shape was bent in two places. "Hell, that looks almost like...Oh my God...," he sputtered.

Buster gripped the table and turned away as the image of a human finger imprinted itself in his mind. His hands outstretched, Buster steadied himself, searching for a sturdy grip. His left hand felt something.

Beneath his fingers rested a familiar metal golf tee. "Mike," Buster whispered.

At that moment, a metal latch clicked. Buster's heart pounded in the fleeting instant. Although he was invisible and dead, Buster still felt that his discovery by the professor would not be welcome.

He turned and looked up. The professor's back was to the room as he bolted the door.

"Yes," said Tinsley.

Buster rose. Tinsley turned into the room, talking on a phone with a cord that stretched back to his desk.

Damn fool's gonna knock off shit like that, thought Buster.

"I know," he said as he returned to the metal desk.

Buster watched.

"I'm working on that, I told you." Tinsley scratched his head. "No, I need more time."

Tinsley sat at the desk and opened a drawer. Tinsley leaned back in his chair as he turned on the computer and waited. Buster walked over.

"Look, you wanna cause more damage, stop wasting your time on —"

Tinsley put his head in his hands. Buster leaned in, but still couldn't hear the other caller.

"The boy is dead. He was a meth head anyway."

Tinsley clicked a few keys and drummed his fingers on the table. "NO!" He sat up. "There's no need for that. I promise to deliver."

Buster stepped behind Tinsley to look at the computer screen.

"The other was just a random—it's fine."

The monitor screen flickered. On the desk were two photos, one of an island and the other of a young girl.

"Yes, sir."

Buster peered around Tinsley, the other caller barely audible. A brilliant blue sky almost pulsated in the background of the overgrown island. Tinsley traced his finger along a rocky shoreline of the photograph.

"Plannin' a trip, Mr. Harvard?" asked Buster.

"No! Please, you won't have to do that!" shouted Tinsley as he stood up, brushing Buster's face. "I promise I'll finish the work."

Buster jumped back. His nose burned. Instead of nausea, Buster felt a wave of panic as he saw a teenage daughter waving from cheerleader practice on the drill field. He rubbed his eyes and looked at the professor, who now sweat steadily from his forehead like a glass of water on a hot day.

"I still don't like you, Mr. Harvard," said Buster.

CHAPTER FIFTEEN

Three drag queens and a ghost squeezed themselves into the makeshift storage / dressing / bathroom, where Peaches revealed the grand idea. Buster recognized Lucy and Stella from Peaches' house.

"What do you mean an 'invasion'?" asked Lucy Furr.

"An invasion. Like taking over," said Peaches.

"Are you crazy?" asked Buster and Stella simultaneously.

Peaches looked at Stella. "Probably. But that hadn't stopped me before."

"Didn't that happen with some drag queens somewhere up north?"

"Fire Island. 1976."

"Oh, that's why I don't remember, I was still in diapers," said Lucy.

Stella snorted as Peaches clacked her tongue.

"What?" asked Lucy.

Stella rolled her eyes and threw an imaginary sash over her shoulder. "It'll be a fabulous form of civil dis-o-bedience."

"Jasper, is this what you dragged me in here for? Cause I don't like the sound a this," said Buster.

"Peaches, where in tarnation did you come up with such a hair-brained scheme?" asked Stella.

"Lord, it's probably them brain cells fried from all those years of poppers," said Lucy.

Peaches flashed a big smile. "It was a little friendly neighborhood ghos—"

"What?" stammered Buster.

Lucy put her hand down on the table. "Ah, hell no. Your pretend friend is now—"

"I ain't pretend—" said Buster.

"—givin you ideas?"

"What pretend friend?" Peaches asked.

"Knock it off, doll. The nuggets told Stella about your lonely ghost. That's sweet and all, but seriously. Have you lost your damn mind?" asked Lucy.

Peaches looked from Stella to Lucy and back. "Why does it matter where I got the idea? Nothing wrong with telling them about Buster!"

Stella and Lucy glanced at each other, then silently stared at Peaches.

"Don't look at me," admonished Buster.

"Whatever. My point is that I think it's time we showed Clover we are just as much part of this community as the rest of 'em."

"Now hold on a minute, Jasper," Buster tried to interrupt. "I didn't tell you to parade around town in a dress. You gonna get yourself in trouble."

Stella clapped. "I love it. Since when are we gonna not participate? The nuggets need our support. And we got every right to be there as anybody else."

"My nuggets need to see their elders—"

"Watch it," said Lucy.

"Oh, get off it," said Stella. "We older. Bout time we stepped up to the plate and showed them kids that it's okay to be who God made us."

"Jasper," pleaded Buster.

"That's more like it, girls. Asides, half them boys won't even know the difference. Maybe we can even get some of the queens from Tupelo to come down," said Peaches.

"Tupelo?" asked Lucy.

"Well, don't curl your nose up. My mama's people was from Tupelo," said Stella.

"Course they were—"

"Ladies!" shouted Peaches. "Let's be civil about this. I bet we can even get Oscar and the boys from The Blue Magnolia to help us out."

"How?"

"Publicity! He'll get the word out! We'll have a whole rainbow at the Clover Festival!" exclaimed Peaches.

178

Buster shook his head. *I don't like this.*

"What's wrong, boo—"

"Who you talkin to, Peaches?"

"Wait—is that Casper?"

"Uh," Peaches looked from Lucy to Stella and back. "No, you, Stella, what's wrong?"

"Pssssh, ain't nothing wrong with me! I should be asking you the same thing!" answered Stella.

Peaches rolled her eyes. "Uh, so you like the idea?" she asked.

"Fab-so-lutely!" Stella said.

"Wonder if sweet old Jazz Men will show up?" asked Peaches.

"Of course she will. If there's a pot to stir, she'll be there with a giant spoon!"

"And a knife," added Lucy.

Peaches smiled. "This could be the best Clover Festival yet!" She winked at Buster out of the corner of her eye.

Stella leaned in and touched Peaches' knee. "Babe..."

"Got a bit of mascara in my eye," Peaches muttered as she looked into the mirror and wiped her eye. "Let's get to work on those dresses. I'll convince Oscar to join our parade."

"The nuggets are gonna be so proud," said Stella.

"Let's get out of this tiny sweatbox bathroom and get to singing. Miss Jazz Men will be all aflutter if we don't get out there shortly," said Lucy.

The three, followed by Buster, shuffled out of the storage-bathroom-dressing room. Buster sneezed as the plume of hairspray and perfume trailed behind.

They split in the cool bar and watched Jazz Men on stage. Her sequin dress made Jazz look like a swizzle stick missing its glass of booze. She turned and spoke to the far side of the bar. "I got that man home and it was about as useful to me as a cup of de-caffeinated coffee. I mean, what's the point of a big, black muscle bottom if he's just gonna stick his heels to Hea-van?" She threw her head back as she sang the last word. The small bar crowd laughed.

"Hmmph," grunted Peaches. "Bet she wears a hood at home."

"What's that mean?" whispered Buster.

"Child, you don't even need to know," she whispered back.

"I see my sista Peaches is talkin' to that imaginary friend of hers again," Jazz called out.

Peaches squirmed on the barstool.

That's why you single, guurl, you gotta...talk...to a few men once in awhile." She winked at a broad man in a black cowboy hat. Someone whistled.

"You prolly right, Jazz Men," shouted Peaches. "I mean, at least you try. But then again, men only rent what flies, floats, or fucks, and I'm not looking for a tenant." She sipped her ginger ale.

"Whooo, girl!" shouted someone from the back.

"Easy, now," said Oscar, stifling a laugh.

Jazz paused, mouth turned slightly, then she cocked her head and smiled, "That's right girl, I ain't selling out for just any ol' country boy that walks into this bar."

Another whistle.

Peaches murmured, "Hmm-kay."

Buster stepped back as a thin cowboy walked past. "Hey Peaches, baby," he kissed her cheek.

"Well, look at who the cat drug in," she said as she kissed back. "You lookin' sharp in those sting-ray boots. Should I call you Elvis now?"

"Haha, well, don't try to get me onstage to sing like him, sweetie," answered the man, as he tipped his cowboy hat.

Buster returned to Peaches's side at the end of the bar. "So not only is he a crooked ass, that professor, but I think he murdered that boy Mike."

"Boo, you right. But we gonna *have* to discuss this later. I'm working tonight and I'm about to cut this bitch off," said Peaches, as she eyed Jazz Men on the stage.

"Cut?

"Not for real, sugar. Just put an end to this. She woke up on the wrong side of someone's truck this morning. We play nice on stage here, unlike them queens up in Mem-phis."

Peaches stood and picked up her microphone. "Thank you, Jazz, for that insightful performance."

Jazz Men smiled and stepped back.

"Don't forget your tips, guys, gals, and go-betweens, cause, all girls, 'moes, and hoes gotta eat up here tonight." Peaches sparkled under a spotlight, throwing light around the room. The swizzle stick walked away.

Buster faced down the bar. "Damn, I wish I could have me a real drink," he said.

The music began. "Speaking of men," she began.

"Oh, lordy," groaned a voice in the crowd.

"You feel me, too?" Peaches asked, ignoring the comment. "I loved a man once. Once was enough."

Someone laughed. "Amen!"

"I thought it was love, anyway. Turns out, it wasn't real."

Buster noticed a half-full glass, unattended on the bar.

"Come to think of it," Peaches continued, "I think Miss Cheryl Lynn said it best." The music grew louder.

Peaches immediately turned, and her body froze in position as she belted out, "*What you find-ah...*

Wait a sec. If I can taste rain, thought Buster, staring at the mug, *I wonder...* Buster stuck his finger straight down into the beer.

"*Whatcha feeel now...*

It felt barely cool as he swirled his ghost finger in the glass. The liquid didn't move as the bubbles tickled him. Buster pulled his finger out and licked it. He smiled, realizing he'd tasted the drink before even his hand reached his mouth. *Fuck, that is one good beer.* He turned and faced the stage where Peaches pointed to the audience.

"*Whatcha knoooowa ... to be real!*"

Buster looked back at the bar. No one had come by to claim it. He hadn't tasted the fuzzy tingle in months, and the warmth flushed through him quickly.

"*Whatcha fiiind now,*" Jazz Men joined Peaches onstage.

He puckered. "Kinda bitter. Not quite like I remember." Buster shrugged his shoulders and proceeded to stick his finger into the mug again.

"*Whatcha feeel now...*" Lucy joined Peaches, reflecting a murky green sparkle of tiny lights on her dress.

Without moving his finger, the heady buzz ran from his hand, along his arm, to chest, then spread to his mouth and head, as if with the flow of blood. He smacked his lips.

The level of beer did not change in the glass, but Buster tasted it on his tongue as if he'd really taken a drink.

He put his finger in again. He felt a slight hum.

"*Whatcha knooooowa... to be real!*" Buster looked up right as Peaches pointed in his direction with a singer on either side.

Buster looked down the length of the bar. An unattended glass of dark liquid stood next to a patron, singing along with the music, who leaned on the shoulder of the tall cowboy. The familiar taste of bourbon filled Buster's mouth. Another glass sparkled of gin. He peered over another shoulder and was greeted by a bright red drink with a cherry on top. He shuddered and proceeded to the next as bar patrons clapped in sync with the music as Peaches belted lyrics.

Drink after drink, Buster stuck his finger into each open glass, tasting the sweet, the tart, the sour, the bitter, the grape, and the barley of every type of alcohol being served that night at The Blue Magnolia.

"*It's got to be real.*"

He stumbled as he walked away to find an empty chair. "Ah hell, no," he laughed.

"*It's got to be real.*"

The music stopped, and the bar stood in applause. Buster saw Peaches, center stage pointing directly upward, surrounded by Lucy and Jazz Men. "Whew!" Peaches exhaled.

"Thank you, thank you, baby doll," said Peaches, as she nodded and picked up a few dollar bills. "Now, welcome to our show tonight! Not like them Mem-phis Queens," said Peaches. "We left lip syncing back in junior high, didn't we, Jazz?"

"That's right, Peaches Juba Lee. We here to sing, to be real, and to entertain."

Buster chuckled.

"On tonight's roster, we have Miss Jazz Men, Miss Lucy Furr, followed by our special guest, Miss Stella Ruby," added Peaches.

Buster peered close, "Why them ain't wom—Ooh, right," he said.

"Miss Lee," said Stella, as she stepped forward.

"Yes, Miss Stella?"

"Thank you kindly for the invitation to your little soiree this evening."

"Child, you can speak plain here...this ain't a high cotton establishment."

"Hey, now!" shouted Oscar.

"Hay? Oscar, I think you got plenty of hay for them boys out back to...sit on," said Jazz.

Stella stood straight. "Boys? Sit on? Miss Lee, I think you brought me out here to tempt me. My momma warned me about these kinda places."

Buster snickered and slid off the stool. Peaches held a hand up to block out a spot light and look in his direction.

"Stella, bless your momma's heart, but she was more social than that."

Stella's mouth dropped open in mild disbelief. "Why, you think so?"

"I do. I think she was right generous and friendly. In fact, I saw her name and telephone number on a bathroom stall," said Jazz, as she winked very long and noticeable eyelashes at the crowd.

Stella frowned and put her hands on her hips.

Lucy turned. "Now Jazz Men, don't lie. You've never been in a church bathroom your whole life."

The crowd laughed.

Buster laughed and slapped his knee. "Damn, I'm drunk." Peaches eyed his direction.

"Jazzy, you might need to get on your knees and beg for the Lord's forgiveness," said Stella, as she smiled at the crowd.

Lucy smiled before stepping into the light, "Oh, she gets on her knees and begs alright."

"That's enough, Miss Lucy," said Peaches. "We got a show to kick off tonight. Shall we, ladies?" Peaches turned and flashed an emphatic smile at her stage companions and hastily threw another look in Buster's direction. "We might actually have us a live audience tonight, so let's get on with the show, shall we?" Peaches walked down two steps from the small stage, leaving Lucy to sing the next number as Jazz retreated to the side out of the light.

Peaches made her way over to Buster's stool, pausing to smile and check on patrons as if looking over produce in the store. Buster drummed on the counter as he swayed and watched, then hummed a few notes while mouthing words to a song that was not playing at that moment.

At the bar, Peaches motioned to Oscar. "Ginger ale, please." She glanced over her shoulders and learned in to Buster. "What's gotten into you?"

Buster stopped swaying and smiled. "Youshore can beltout themtunes," he hiccupped.

Peaches' smile turned to a gaping mouth. "Are you drunk? How in the hell did that happen?"

Buster chuckled. He took his finger and stuck it into Peaches' drink that Oscar just placed in front of her.

"Well, I'll be damned."

Buster shrugged his shoulders and stuck his finger in a forgotten beer mug nearby.

Peaches curled her nose. "That just looks nasty, boo."

"Sure doesn't taste like it," he said.

"Just don't get drunk and start possessing folks."

"Peaches, doll, why you down at that end of the bar?" cried a voice.

Peaches eyed Buster. "Don't get all Exorcist on me and ruin my show!" Buster sneezed into a fit of snickers, and Peaches turned and left him struggling to stay on the stool.

CHAPTER SIXTEEN

Buster opened his eyes. He looked at his hands and feet and the room around him as the blackout faded. He sat on the floor in the living room of his house. Or Sally's.

Earl sat in his recliner, drinking beer and eating from a heated television dinner. From where he sat, Buster saw Sally eating her dinner alone at the kitchen table. Earl hovered over his food, as if protecting it from an unseen scavenger, while mechanically shoveling it into his mouth. Sally sat straight up, napkin folded in her lap, quietly chewing and glancing intermittently at Earl.

Why'd she let your sorry ass back? thought Buster.

"That's liberal horseshit!" shouted Earl at the barely audible television.

Buster moved closer and Earl turned up the volume.

"Earl, could you please keep that down?" Sally called from the kitchen.

Earl grumbled and turned the volume up.

"This new breed of ants is a lot like the Argentine ants, which makes them harder to kill," said a recognizable voice on the television. Onscreen, Professor Tinsley stood with the research station and the farms behind him.

"Art Tinsley is professor of Entomology and Toxicology at Mississippi Agricultural College here in Clover, researching new toxins to kill ant colonies, and believes he has made a major breakthrough into a multi-billion dollar industry for pest control."

Buster stared at the screen. *Well, look at Mr. Harvard.*

Tinsley spoke, "We've managed to increase the death rate for predominate ant species, but this new hybrid has been a bit more challenging. Still, we managed to develop a breakthrough, and hope to have a product available for farmers and gardeners soon."

A reporter continued, "Professor Tinsley's research has

brought the university more than ten million dollars in grant funding, and his study of neurotoxins on ants has won critical recognition, resulting in additional co-funded grants from major agri-corporations. This additional funding has helped the university build key partnerships with the private sector."

Earl laughed after drinking his beer. "Wish that sonofabitch would give me some a that money. I'd tell him all he's got to do is pour diesel fuel on them buggers and light a match. Boom!" he simulated a mushroom cloud with the motion of his hands.

"Earl, I wish you would eat with me at the table," said Sally.

Earl didn't respond.

"How toxic are these new poisons, Professor Tinsley?" asked the onscreen reporter. "Is it safe for the environment?"

"Won't hurt any of your daylilies if that's what you're worried about," he smirked. "But, just don't go drinking any of it, just to be safe."

Earl mocked with a simulated laugh.

Buster flinched and felt a tingle along his spine.

A plate rattled in the kitchen. Buster looked at the empty table and heard pots and pans banging in the sink.

Earl groaned and turned up the volume, as he extended his arm toward the kitchen and stuck up his middle finger.

"I'd be careful if I was you, buddy. Might make good ant feed one of these days," said Buster, as he headed for the kitchen.

Sally turned the faucet on steady. Water splashed in the sink as she less-than-gingerly put dishes and pots aside. The volume of the television increased.

"We've never seen a growth in the ant population like this," said the newscast. "The new hybrid is appearing all over the county in no discernible pattern of migration. Almost like they are dropping out of the sky."

Earl turned off the television.

Should be asking Mr. Harvard a few more questions,

Buster thought, and turned back to Sally.

Cabinet doors smacked loudly as Sally put away spices.

"Goddammit!" shouted Earl.

"Why is he still here?" Buster asked.

Sally began humming.

"Too bad Carlos ain't here to play his music to calm you both down," Buster said.

Sally turned on the small kitchen radio and adjusted the dial to a classical station.

Pop! Buster broke with intense fever and nausea. *Fucking African cunt. I need a fucking beer. Maybe I'll go over an see Sharon after her shift ends.*

"Earl, please don't drink more beer tonight," said Sally.

Buster steadied himself on the counter with one hand, as Earl walked through him for the refrigerator. Buster felt intensely hot from the inside out, and all he could picture was the redhead at the liquor store. Except Buster knew those were Earl's feelings and thoughts.

"Fuck you," said Earl.

"Excuse me? Who let you back into this house? Was that begging and apologizing all horseshit?" asked Sally.

The next moment was only a moment, but to Buster, it blurred into frozen memory. Earl grabbed a beer and in one motion, slammed the refrigerator door shut, sending magnets of crocheted flowers across the kitchen. With his free hand, Earl then smacked Sally across the cheek, sending her sideways into the wall at the end of the counter.

She stifled a cry.

Buster flushed and said, "You son-of-a-bitch."

Earl turned to walk away.

Sally blurted, "Is that how you treat your whores, too?"

Earl stopped, facing Buster. In a flicker, he paused. Buster watched the pupils of Earl's eyes contract, then dilate into a bloom of wide emptiness. Rejecting Peaches's admonition that some thoughts should remain secret, Buster inhaled and immediately thrust his hand into Earl's chest.

188

"No, Earl. Don't," said Buster.

Earl turned. Buster saw Sally's face before Earl backhanded her into the wall. He dropped the beer.

Instinctively, Buster tried to grab Earl's free arm before it flew forward to plant a fist on Sally's opposite cheek. Unable to stop Earl from hitting Sally, Buster lost his balance, and only caught fragments of Earl's hate and spite. Sally tried to catch herself, knocking over the radio in the process. The volume shot up. A symphony blared loudly, first ringing in Buster's ears, and then, in a brief pause in the music, a clarinet solo matched Earl's other fist as it hurled toward Sally.

Buster's heartbeat drummed in his ears as his entire body vibrated. The clarinet played louder.

"No!" screamed Sally.

Again, another hand, this time pinning Sally against the wall, where she wailed. A firm kick landed in Earl's crotch. He grabbed her throat and squeezed. Buster tried to pull Earl's arm free, but flares of anger and bile surged each time he touched Earl. The inhuman rage that consumed Earl spread to Buster like a flame.

"You're a cunt, Sally. Nigger cunt. Always have been and always will be," spit Earl, as he rolled up the sleeve to the arm that pinned Sally to the wall. "Now, give me what's mine."

Sally wilted like a soap bubble dying in the sun.

"Don't give up, Sally," said Buster.

Sally wailed, limp. "Please," she cried.

Earl forced her to the ground and spit.

Buster quivered with anger, angst, and fire. A familiar tingle ran through his hands, and a cold electric clarity that tasted like metal and felt like ice water shot through Buster. In that split moment, he looked at Earl, then Sally, then Earl again. Behind both, Buster noticed the previously barren kitchen wall displayed photographs that he'd never seen. Until now. Photographs of Sally. Of Buster. His Nanna and grandfather. Their house. The house that Earl now dared to set foot inside. Buster stepped for a nearby photo and stared at a photograph of himself standing next to Sally on the porch of the house.

Yes, Sally was his sister. Absence in life, and death, did not change the thing he could not remember until now.

Buster trembled. His heart thundered and his ears rang as the clarinet hit a crescendo. Without even touching Earl, he saw what Earl intended to do with Sally before. And after. Buster's arms and hands flickered.

Earl reached for the light switch and cut it off. "You don't like it when I fuck with the lights on, so this is for you," as he unzipped his pants.

The rancid darkness heated Buster; he howled. A sound he'd never made and never heard before, but a sound that flushed from every piece and memory of his existence and every emotion that he ever felt. A sound that defied his between-ness.

Even the boards of the old family home did not budge as the world fell silent for two complete seconds.

Then, the clarinet broke the silence, as Earl remained utterly motionless and Sally's sobs stopped. Three heartbeats, two human breaths, and a very angry ghost.

This was it. Buster reached for the small skillet on the stove.

"Sally!" he shouted, as he passed her the iron pan.

Sally and Earl made eye contact with Buster. Neither spoke.

"Now, Sally!" said Buster.

As Earl blinked with recognition at his dead brother-in-law, Sally gripped and swung the pan, smacking Earl in the nose.

"Fuck!" he said and covered his face.

She swung again, this time hitting the side of his head, knocking him off her. Sally scrambled back and took another swing at Earl, hunched on the floor, and squarely connected with his right knee.

"Holy fuck, you crazy bitch!" screamed Earl, as blood

dripped through his fingers from his nose.

Sally stood firm.

Flick.

Lights on. The course of energy that previously flooded Buster drained rapidly as the clarinet softened. He looked at Earl. In a brief moment, he saw a glimmer of recognition staring back with bewilderment. Buster turned to see Sally, at the end of the kitchen by the telephone with the skillet in her hand standing over Earl, ready to swing again. "Get out, you worthless asshole!" she screamed.

Earl glanced at Sally, then the spot where he knew he'd seen her brother, and scrambled to his feet. "Witch!" he spit before stumbling through the kitchen, limping and bleeding.

She gasped while clutching the pan. "Bu-bu-buster?"

The moment of familiarity lingered.

Buster turned to Sally, "Can you still see me?"

She ran through Buster for the front door. Instead of nausea, Buster felt an ocean of relief, protection and safety. In that brief moment, he saw himself through her eyes, something between hallucination and reality, but visible nonetheless. An absent brother showing up.

Skillet still in hand, Sally said nothing, as Earl grabbed his keys and limped out the door. Buster stood next to his sister as she exhaled and finally released something held tightly within.

She turned and looked back toward the empty kitchen. "Thank you," she whispered.

"I'm sorry it took so long," answered Buster, knowing the words weren't heard.

CHAPTER SEVENTEEN

"Buster, I can't show up unannounced at that man's shed," said Peaches.

"Jasper, it's the only way to find out what he's up to." Buster stood on the porch outside her screen door. "I'm telling you, there's somethin' out there in that shed of his."

"Boo. I'm sure there is. But *I* am telling *you* that I am not about to go snooping around a shed in the sticks. In Mississippi."

"It ain't in the woods."

"Buster. I don't care if it's in the center a town in a strip mall under a neon light. I am not gonna just walk up to a professor's secret shed or barn where I got no business. Especially one that is up to no good. This may not be 1960, but it is still Mississippi. I am not about to test equality and tolerance because a dead black man tells a queer like me that a crazy white professor is hiding something in a rusty metal building. Do you want me on the 6 o'clock news?"

Buster sighed and put his hands on the back of his head. "But—"

Peaches walked to the door and whispered loudly. "But nothing. You just don't know what it's like to be me. Maybe you never will. No matter how many times I tell you. I can't go snooping around outside a crazy white man's shed any more than you could if you was alive."

"But, Jasper! I found Mike's metal golf tee there. He was feeding those ants a finger! Maybe Mike's! I think he killed that poor boy. He's working on something real awful."

"Go to the pol..." she stopped, then sighed. "Right. You can't do that." She paused. "You know that's not a school building?"

Buster lowered his eyelids. "Of course. But he's doing something there."

Peaches breathed deep.

"You know I got to have your help. All we got to do is open the lock, get in there, see what he's got, then go."

"You got a key?"

"Padlocks. I saw the combination. And most of the stuff in there ain't even locked up. He's got some small, black notebook that he keeps near him everywhere."

"You tellin' me that a professor is working on some top-secret evil project but doesn't even lock up his desk?" Peaches tilted her head down and looked at Buster.

"Strange, I know. It's not like the movies. Anyway, it's not like anyone else is around that building."

Buster paused. "Please, you got to help me. Can I come inside? I can feel you keeping me out of your house, or I'd be in there now."

"You fine right where you at—I'm not gonna cast you away any further than my porch. How's Sally?"

"What? What's she got to do with this?"

Peaches shrugged. "You so worried 'bout what you want, I wanna know how she is. Ever since you scared the bejesus and spooked Earl, I hadn't heard a peep outta you bout your sister."

Buster sighed. "Dunno."

"What do you mean you *dunno*?"

"I don't know. When I wake up or come to, I'm never there. I try to go back, but then it always gets foggy, and I find myself somewhere else or waking up here."

Peaches did not respond.

"Maybe I'm done there and can't go back," said Buster.

"Humph," Peaches clacked her tongue. "Say that again?"

"I can't go back."

"Naw, boo. The part about you being *done* there. Sound like you still gotta reason to be here that you still need to finish."

Buster chuckled, "Why do you think I'm buggin' you then? Clearly, I ain't done with you, cause you still see me.

193

You gotta help me." He smiled with his argument.

Peaches put her hand on the doorframe and pursed her lips to the side. "Alright, Buster. Say I go out there with you. What's your plan? Break down the door? Steal the computer? Tear up the man's chemistry set? What if he ain't doing nothing wrong out there but just working on a little science project? Then, I'm committin' a felony. And Parchman ain't exactly my idea of a fancy resort, and I doubt that Chris Maloney is there waiting for me."

"Who?"

"Never mind," said Peaches.

Buster shook his head. "I'll figure it out when—"

"No, boo. You got to know exactly what I'm gonna do, or we are not going. We aren't going to the Piggly Wiggly and figuring out what we're gonna have with the chicken."

"Okay," Buster put his hands to his mouth and exhaled. He turned and paced. "I got it. We'll go. I'll give you the combination. Have you got a camera? You can take pictures of his equipment and the ants, and we'll find his black notebook."

"You know it's bad when ants get involved. We might need the green berets."

"I'm not joking, Jasper! He's feeding the ants a human finger!"

Neither spoke for a minute as Buster's comment settled between them.

"Right."

"Plus, there's his files, and he's got a desk. Plus maps. Even if we don't know what to find on his computer, we can look at them."

Peaches put a hand on her hip. "Still sounds like we not sure what's for dinner. And that's not a plan."

Buster stopped pacing and looked at Peaches.

"Don't give me them ghost puppy eyes, boo. If we are gonna pull a 007 and trespass, then we are gonna trespass *right*. Maybe you should stay out there long enough to see where he's hiding everything. Find out what we need from his computer. What he's hiding in his desk. Why he's growing ants out there. Why you think them maps is so important. If we are out there, then we need to make it quick."

Buster's shoulders drooped.

"What?" asked Peaches.

"Too bad we can't copy stuff from the computer."

Peaches looked down.

"Now what?" asked Buster.

"Willie can."

"What?" asked Buster.

"Willie knows computers."

"Hot damn, Jasper! Why didn't you say so?"

Peaches shuffled. "I don't know about this, Buster; it's one thing to get me out there, but I can't drag one of my nuggets into this."

"Can he teach you?"

Peaches put her hand on the door. "Maybe so. That might work. I can go to the library and maybe he can show me on one of their computers."

"Okay, then. You find out from Willie, and I'll see if I can find anything else out," he said.

"Buster..."

A telephone rang.

"Yeah, Jasper?"

Peaches shook her head, "Aw, nothing, boo, I got to get ready for another show. That's probably Stella calling me now."

Three days later, Buster had convinced Peaches. She worked up the nerve, and they rumbled down the road for the salvage yard, where Buster hoped his memory would spark. He knew better than to share this one hurdle. As the car headed past the scrap yard, they hit a hard pothole.

A memory flickered, and Buster recognized the narrowed road ahead.

"Lordy, don't break my transmission," said Peaches.

"Jasper, see that abandoned gas station up there? Turn

in and park there."

"Buster, you sure this gonna work?"

"Yeah, Jasper. I promise it'll be quick. Get a couple things out of his computer. Find that little black notebook. Then go. Wish you had a camera," said Buster.

"Me, too. He better not have this notebook on him," Peaches said.

I hope you right. Buster kept to himself.

The two sat in Peaches's brown, faded car under an awning next to the abandoned gas station.

"This isn't much cover."

"How come?"

"We're in front of an abandoned gas station. Not exactly inconspicuous."

"Look around, Jasper. You see anybody out here?" asked Buster.

"That's my point. When you the only one, everybody notices." Peaches looked around.

"Yeah, true. But you parked. Could be waiting on somebody."

"At an abandoned gas station in the middle of the sticks. Cause that don't sound suspicious neither." Peaches wrung her hands together and peered through the windshield. "Thank God I didn't put on my heels." Her view crossed twenty yards of a recently mowed patch of brown grass to spot the back of the metal shed. Surrounded by what might be considered a field under larger circumstances, the shed showed no signs of life. Buster peered at the gas station, which faced away from the metal shed.

"You right about there being nothing out here but abandoned buildings, scraggly trees, and a stray dog," Peaches said, as she surveyed beyond the perimeter of the old gas station. "Just the right spot for a six o'clock news alert."

"You didn't wear a dress, so you should be fine," said Buster.

Peaches rolled her eyes and stared sideways at Buster. "You really think that's what being queer is about."

"Just sayin'."

"So what we waitin' for? A signal? Cause someone like me sitting alone in her car—"

"Dammit, Jasper, knock it off!"

Peaches folded her arms and looked away.

Buster looked around once more. "Okay, you ready?"

Peaches pursed her lips and tilted her head back toward him. "Remember that you came to me. You will respect what I have to do to protect myself. Without my help, you may end up lingering until the sun don't rise in the east and there is no one around you to pester."

Buster shook his head, "Jasper, I don't get where you coming from and don't know what I said that's wrong. But you don't have to lecture me on being different. Right now, you simply look like a dude in a car in an empty lot in the country. Nothing looks outta place this second. I didn't mean to snap. Let's just hurry and get this done and get outta here."

Peaches did not respond.

"Aw c'mon, Jasper, I'm sorry. Was I wrong? Let's go," he said.

"Say that one more time—"

"Let's go—"

"No, the other part about you being wrong," said Peaches.

Hell no. "Really? You are gonna make me apologize?" Buster asked.

Peaches stared back at Buster with neither smile nor frown.

"I don't know what it's like to be you any more than you don't know what it's like to be me. Can we stop fightin' over being different, get out a this damn car, and be done with this?"

Peaches nodded and opened the door. The zzz-zuu chorus of tree frogs welcomed them. Peaches motioned for Buster to crawl from the driver's side, and they stood in the glow of the October sunset dipping behind the tree line. Not a human in sight. The abandoned service station marked the fringe of a tiny community that looked like it had died during an era when everything closed at five and nothing opened on Sundays. A couple of trailers and small frame houses were questionably inhabited. A stray dog under a nearby oak looked up from his rest.

"Well, come on," said Peaches. "I'm not gonna hang out here after dark."

Buster turned and saw that Peaches was already a third of the way across the field. The short, brown vegetation rasped and crunched beneath Peaches' footsteps.

Buster looked back. The car was now halfway hidden by the gas station. He looked ahead, and Peaches remained absolutely still.

"What is it?" Buster asked.

Peaches motioned.

Buster followed her direction. "A snake?"

Peaches nodded.

Buster stepped closer and leaned over. "Looks dead," he said. Buster then squatted above it. He looked at Peaches. "You afraid of dead snakes?"

Peaches nodded.

"Then just walk around over there," pointed Buster. The snake suddenly rattled and weaved through the dry grass and Buster jumped back.

Peaches yelped and ran ten yards far to the right as the snake continued in the opposite direction directly past Buster. *Well, must be a good thing if a snake can't see me*, he thought.

Buster met Peaches by the corner of the building, where she hopped from one foot to the other and rubbed her arms as if cold.

"You okay, Jasper?"

"Yeah, I'm fine. If you gonna tell me you can talk to snakes, then I'm outta here."

"No, Jasper. Don't think it even knew I was there. Not like your butterflies."

"Humph. Maybe you ain't so bad after all," said Peaches, as she glanced over his shoulder, as if watching for the snake to come back.

"Jasper, that snake is more scared of you," chuckled Buster.

"Easy for a ghost to say," said Peaches before turning around. "Let's get in heah and be done with this place. I got the heebie-jeebies."

They proceeded along the building's side when the crunching sound of car tires on gravel interrupted their walk. Peaches leaned stiff against the building as Buster continued.

"Just kids," he muttered as he watched the car disappear behind a thicket of trees. "C'mon."

The front of the building was partially shielded from the gravel road by a row of cedar trees. The faint dust cloud left in the car's wake rolled across the grassy lot.

Peaches coughed. Buster smelled the dry dirt mixed with a faint odor of oil. "Smells like my grandpa's old barn," he said.

"What'd you say?" Peaches asked.

"I said it smelled like my grand—" he paused and turned to Peaches. "I'll be damned. I remembered something else."

"Seems like doing something besides trying to fish is helping you, Buster," Peaches peered around the corner looking for more cars.

"Bound to be right once in awhile."

"Don't sass me—you still need my help," said Peaches as she headed for the front door.

Both looked up and down the road before facing the lock on the door.

Peaches paused.

"This is it," said Buster. He pointed at the lock and looked up at Peaches. "What?" he asked.

"For somethin' top secret, I expected a bit more," she said.

"Maybe he ain't that smart."

Peaches laughed. "Right. Raising ants and researching poisons and getting grant money. Even you call him 'Mr. Harvard'? More like a Dr. Frankenstein or something."

Buster shrugged. "Maybe too many locks who make it look like something important's in here?"

"Yeah, not like a rusted shed with a single padlock is really gonna stir up suspicion that someone stole the Mona Lisa or is hiding Jimmy Hoffa's body." Peaches took a breath and pulled out a white glove.

"Oh, yeah, good idea," said Buster.

Peaches mimicked Buster and said, "Oh, now you think you the only one with a plan." She turned the dial as Buster muttered the numbers he saw Tinsley use.

"Stuck," said Peaches.

"Well, give it a tug, Jasper. It's a rusty shed."

The lock popped open. Peaches grasped the doorknob. "Ready?"

"Yep."

The latch clicked and within moments, the two stood inside the professor's dark lab.

"Hit the light, boo," said Peaches.

"I can't," said Buster.

"It's dark as molasses; can you move in the dark?"

"Sometimes," said Buster.

"Then sometimes do it now," said Peaches.

"Nothing. It's gotta be something else," he said. "You scared, Jasper?"

"NOW," she said.

"You try. The switch. Just move your hand over. There."

Peaches bumped into a table. "Ow!"

"Easy, Jasper," warned Buster. "We can't tear up the place."

"Dammit, I tore my favorite jeans." Peaches looked at a small rip of fabric snagged on a corner that winked open like a part in window blinds.

200

"Watchit!" shouted Buster, as he pointed at a tall glass beaker that wobbled on a wire stand. Forgetting about the hole in her jeans, Peaches leaned forward and grabbed the beaker just before it made a final dive off the stand for the hard tabletop.

Peaches looked wide-eyed at Buster, who shrugged his shoulders. She turned for the wall where Buster pointed, and saw the switch. Moments later, a dim light flickered on overhead.

"Well, this just looks like a messy office," said Peaches, as she rubbed her eyes to adjust.

Buster walked to the row of small aquariums. "I don't know what kinda office keeps bugs." The lights brightened with a double flicker.

"Well, maybe an office for a crazy professor who cuts up frogs and puppies," she said, as she glanced around the room of aquariums, maps, geometric-looking drawings, and an old computer on a paper-covered desk.

Peaches joined Buster. "Guess you right about this being some kinda lab."

"These the ants?" asked Peaches.

"Take a look for yourself," said Buster as he walked over to a desk across the room. "Think somethin's in these papers?"

"I got no idea—your guess is good as mine," said Peaches as she eyed the walls of the lab: maps, charts, small aquariums, large ones. "I wish I had a camera."

Buster pointed at a drawer. "See what's in here."

"I thought you knew where stuff was," Peaches said as she joined Buster at the desk.

"Well, sorta. I know there's got be somethin' in here," he said.

"Boo, I ought to whip you!" She covered her mouth. "Oh. God. Wait, no. That was the wrong thing to say."

Peaches started again, "Dragging me out here with a plan only to get me out here and tell me your only plan was to get me out here and figure it out once we got here!" Her hand was on her hip.

Buster ignored Peaches and scanned the papers on the desk and the adjacent cabinet. "Lookit this—Department of Agriculture," he muttered as he pointed at the top of the letter sticking out from a pile. He looked at Peaches. "Turn on the computer for us."

Peaches pursed her lips and clacked her tongue.

"Please, Jasper," he said.

Peaches cocked her head to the side and pressed a button on the computer. "Do you even know what we looking for in this?" she said.

"You got that disk Willie gave you?" he asked.

Peaches turned on one foot. As Buster stared at the monitor, the light flickered overhead.

"Child, you gonna be the death of me," muttered Peaches, as she stared at the tanks and grow lights. "What in the hell am I trying to find?" she asked.

Buster watched the computer screen, "Dammit, this is takin' forever. You'd think a fancy professor would have a new, shiny one." He walked his fingers across the top of the desk and pages, pausing to flick in the event that something different would happen and he'd move a few pages. His fingers stopped. Buster looked down. The page was blank, but he felt something. Buster looked again. The imprint of notes covered the page as if waiting for a reader.

"Jasper," he said. "Come 'ere."

Peaches said, while remaining slightly bent, studying the contents of a wastebasket, "Whatyoufind, boo?"

"Somethin', I reckon. Don't quite know, but I think Mr. Harvard left a note. Can't really read it," he muttered, looking at Peaches, who'd turned back and walked to a large aquarium. Buster fingered a small, black notebook. "Hey, this looks like it!" he shouted with relief.

"What they eatin'?" Peaches asked, as she hunched over and peered into one of the glass tanks.

Buster answered, "You didn't believe me? Did you hear me? I found his notebook."

"Uhhuh," mumbled Peaches before asking, "Believe what, boo?" She moved to the next aquarium. "These here look kinda re—oh my God! No! These ants is eatin a...Whoo, lawd baby Jesus!" Peaches stepped back and fanned herself.

"Mike's?" added Buster. He looked at files on the metal desk.

"This boy ain't right in the head," she muttered. "We got to get outta here!"

"Not till we take something with us," said Buster. "The computer ain't even on yet!"

She looked at Buster. "We need to go. Now. Maybe he got some secret fancy silent alarm or something."

"Now? But the computer just turned on, and we got nothing!"

"*Now*," she said, as she straightened herself and stood at the door. "C'mon cause I'm cuttin off the lights."

"We can't just leave without getting somethin' on Mr. Harvard!" shouted Buster.

"We can't take all this! We got to go afore he shows up!" Peaches backed further away from the glass tanks for the professor's desk. Buster didn't budge as he stared at Peaches.

"Fine. I'll take this," she said, as she grabbed the small, black notebook at Buster's fingers and crammed it into her pocket.

"We all the way out here and he's up to no good. We don't exactly know what's in that!" Buster pointed to the notebook.

"Buster. You're right. He is up to no good. But we gonna be in a mess of hot water that is beyond either one of us if he catches us, and I got a feeling," she said as she stormed for the door.

Buster followed, pleading, as Peaches cut the lights and motioned him out. She turned and pulled the door until it latched, "We gonna make do with what we got, boo." Outside, she fumbled with the padlock.

Her back to Buster and the road, Peaches steadied her hands with the hook of the lock. A moment of calm penetrated the thick air as she heard the snug, metallic click of the lock at it latched. "Lord, have mercy for whatever's going on in there," she muttered quickly, as she put the palm of her right hand on the door.

"Shit. Jasper, act like you knocking! And don't turn around!"

Her shoulders tightened. Peaches slowly released the lock with her left hand and rapidly knocked with her right.

"Sugar honey iced tea, sugar honey iced tea," murmured Peaches. "What is it?"

"Just act normal-like," said Buster.

"Normal-like? What's *normal-like* gonna mean here?" Gravel crunched behind them under the wheels of a car. "Oh, baby," said Peaches. Her voice quivered.

"Stay cool, Jasper."

She nodded.

Buster added, "And don't cry."

Peaches wiped her face and took a breath.

"Don't start singing no gospel either."

"Hush! Don't talk to me like I'm a child," she whispered hoarsely and shot Buster a schoolmarm glare. A car door shut. "Showtime!" said Peaches as she turned and smiled.

"Hi, mister! Is this your business? I'm sure glad to see you. I'm going door to door to tell folks about a gospel revival my choir is having."

Art Tinsley said nothing as he looked at Peaches, then at the door behind her.

"I knocked on all the houses, but came back by here one last time. Thought I heard an air conditioner, so I thought maybe somebody was working inside."

Tinsley said nothing as he glanced at the closed padlock.

"Cat got your tongue?" she asked, then followed with, "Anyway, it's Wednesday night from seven to ten after family night services. We'll have food and singing...Bring your family, cause all is welcome! Oh, I already said family,

204

didn't I? Of course I did, cause it's family night..." she forced a nervous laugh at her own joke.

Buster watched Tinsley turn his keys over and over in his hand. "He ain't buying it."

Peaches reached out her hand. "Lordy, it's hot. Nice to meet you. Please be sure to come." She turned and walked.

Tinsley said nothing as he spun his key ring around his finger. Buster stayed behind and watched the Professor, as Peaches turned the corner.

Tinsley looked at the door and the closed padlock, then the corner where Peaches had turned, then back to the door. *He ain't buying her story.* "Keep walkin', Jasper," Buster shouted. He could hear Peaches breathing in the distance. *C'mon, just be calm. Just be calm.*

Tinsley fingered the combination padlock, then turned and walked to the edge of the building.

"Where you goin', Harvard?" asked Buster, as Tinsley peered around the corner at Peaches.

"Hey!" he shouted, as Tinsley watched Peaches walk to her car.

She didn't answer.

"Hey!" He repeated. She turned slowly.

"You didn't say where this revival is. My daughter loves to sing—maybe I'll bring her. Did you say you got any flyers with you?" asked Tinsley, as Buster stood next to him.

In the distance, Buster heard Peaches mutter, "Oh, hell."

"I ran out," Peaches turned and faced them both, "but might have one more in my car. Lemme check."

She turned and continued. Tinsley took one step forward.

We in trouble now, thought Buster.

Tinsley took another smaller step as Peaches reached the pavement.

Buster began to jog toward Peaches and looked back at Tinsley, who started crossing the grass, his brown shoes glistening in the setting sun.

Buster shouted, "Hope you have that flyer, Jasper, cause

you got a friend coming."

Tinsley kept a steady pace across the small field as Peaches reached her car and open the rear door.

"Where is that damn thing?" she muttered, forcing a steady, deep breath as she shuffled through a pile of mail, newspapers, a boa, some shoes, and several dresses.

"Find it?"

"Oh, thank God," said Peaches, as she stood from her car. "Here you go," she called out. "Missionary Lutheran Church, Wednesday 6 p.m."

Tinsley approached and took the flyer. "You like to sing?" he asked.

Buster waited nervously.

"Do I like to sing?" as if right back onstage, Peaches smiled and turned to face an invisible audience. "He asked if I like to sing. He's asking. Sing." She turned back to Tinsley. "Mister, does Dorothy want her little red shoes?"

"Dorothy?" Tinsley asked.

Peaches shivered, then looked at Tinsley with a wrinkled brow. "Dorothy. As in Oz."

Tinsley said nothing.

"Well, Mister. I got to get on to choir practice." She smiled. "Them notes ain't gonna sing themselves."

Tinsley looked over her shoulder at the pile of dresses in the back as Buster crawled through.

She turned from Tinsley, closed the back door, opened the driver's door, and sat down, fumbling with her car keys. "Oh, hell, Buster, where you at?" she whispered.

"I'm here."

Peaches jerked briefly. "Oh! Don't scare me like that, boo," she glanced back as she started the engine. "What, now I'm your chauffeur? Hell no. Get your ass up here."

"Nobody can see—"

"Don't fuck with me, Buster. I got a crazy professor burning a hate crime in my head whilst I back outta this parking lot."

Buster looked past Peaches as the car turned in the lot.

"He's just standing and staring."

Peaches stopped and put the gear in drive. She turned, flashed a smile, and waved before driving off.

Buster watched as Professor Tinsley looked at the flyer in his hand, then reached onto the ground to pick up a piece of paper.

Peaches breathed in and fanned herself. "Think he knew we was in his secret lab?"

"Oh, dammit, Jasper, I think you dropped something when you opened the back door," he said from the passenger side.

"Dammit, boo! Don't just jump in the front without warning!"

Buster turned around one last time. "Well, I don't think he tryin' to follow you, but he's reading something that I think fell outta your car."

Peaches leaned back as she gripped the wheel, "Oh, lord, I hope I didn't drop any mail, cause that sonofabitch is gonna know where I live."

"Well, you ain't takin your time now," said Buster.

She glanced in the rearview mirror, then looked at Buster. "Well, you better come up with a plan quick, cause no doubt your professor will be lookin' for me if he thinks we was in his lab. And if my electric bill ain't in the back seat, he got my address."

*****

Tinsley stood at the door of the metal building and fingered the padlock. Still locked. He breathed and turned a dial, then opened door into the dark lab. He flipped two switches. Tinsley blinked at the quick flicker of lights as the hum of a fan greeted him. He leaned back against the now closed door and scanned the room, before staring at the aquariums.

Satisfied, Tinsley turned. "Ow!" he groaned, as he walked into the corner of a table covered with beakers that trembled and rattled like the crystals of a chandelier. He rubbed between his leg and the table and realized his khakis were caught on a splinter. His fingers felt something stuck to the table that pried easily with a slight tug. Between his fingers, Tinsley held a small fray of dark fabric.

He cursed, then bumped another table, knocking over a beaker as he bounded for his desk. He stumbled into his chair, where he threw open a drawer, spilling papers onto the floor. He sighed heavily and reminded himself to fix the desk and add a second lock to the front door. Tinsley leaned back in his desk chair and looked at the flyer that the strange, effeminate man gave him, and a recent utility bill addressed to #3 Raspberry Lane.

The sound of a beaker rolling across the table caught his attention, but he made no movement to stop it, nor did he flinch when it stopped rolling because it had fallen from the table. Not even the shattering glass on the cement floor phased Tinsley, because his computer screen blinked, and he knew that it had recently been turned on by someone else.

CHAPTER EIGHTEEN

"We ready, ladies?" asked Peaches as she walked into her living room. Buster followed behind.

"As ready as a virgin behind the bleachers," said Lucy as she studied a copy of *Vanity Fair*. Stella leaned over Lucy's lap to read along.

"Easy, girls. We got company coming up the walk," Peaches peered out the window.

"She better not be talkin' about Casper!" muttered Lucy to Stella.

"If you are gonna talk behind my back, at least make an effort to do it *behind my back*," said Peaches before she opened the door to backpacks and arms and laughter. "Hey, little nuggets!"

"Hey, mamma!" Li'l J shouted.

"There's my little man," said Stella.

"Sup, Mama Peach?"

"C'mon in, Shayla. Willie, don't you look fine and dandy. Carlos, don't brood today. We are gonna invade and need our shiny happy faces."

"Hope y'all got your permission slips," muttered Lucy, as she flipped through a copy of *Essence*. "Oh, honey, look at this week's crush."

"Don't tempt me, now! That is one fine black man," said Stella. She pushed the magazine away and straightened Jerome's collar. "Don't you look like a grown man," said Stella.

"I'm going for Executive Realness!" he shouted, nodding his head.

"Lord, help us all," said Lucy.

"Is she always that mouthy?" asked Buster.

Stella snapped her fingers. "Well, you got it baby! You as real as it gets!"

"Kool-Aid anyone?" Peaches called from the

kitchen. "Fruit punch!"

Willie, Li'l J, and Carlos, and a couple more of their friends piled toward the kitchen like a litter of puppies fumbling for a biscuit. Buster stood at the window and pressed a finger into the glass, looking for prints.

Shayla remained on the couch and studied a spot on the floor. Stella cleared her throat and made eye contact with Lucy, nodding at Shayla as she headed for the kitchen.

"What?" Lucy asked Stella before glancing at Shayla. Lucy rolled her eyes and folded the magazine. "What's got you all cross today?"

Shayla shrugged, and then tugged on her baseball cap and sunk further into the couch. Lucy curled her mouth to one side returned to her magazine. Shayla began to bounce a knee as she tilted her head back and stared at the ceiling.

"Well, if you don't talk, I won't ask," said Lucy as she stood up. "Keep that sugar pouring, Peaches! Stella, got a live one in here for you!"

Stella and Lucy passed each other in the doorframe, Lucy ignoring Stella's stares.

"Shay, something mighty intense going on in that beautiful head of yours," Stella said, handing her a glass. "Wanna talk about it?"

Shayla turned the baseball cap backward as her knee wobbled. "Aunty Stella," she stopped.

"It's alright, sugar, spit it on out. Ain't nothing so awful as when it stays inside our heads."

"Miss Stella, I don't get it. I always liked girls."

Stella chuckled. "Shay, you won't be the first lesbian in this town, let me tell you that. Coach Bende..." Stella interrupted herself. "That isn't it, is it babe?"

"No, Miss Stella. I'm confused. I think. I think I have a crush on Willie," Shayla blurted.

Stella sat up. "Well, that's okay."

"But he's gay and I'm a girl who likes girls. I don't understand. Why do I like somebody that won't like me?" she whispered, looking at the hallway.

"Well, hold on, Shay, you jumping like a frog to all kinda conclusions and making all kind of assumptions about what he like and don't like. You just finding yourself, too."

"But that's the thing. I can't figure out what I like."

"Who says you got to figure that out right now?" Stella asked.

Shayla shrugged. "Seems like y'all know who you are."

Stella laughed. "Sugar, you got a long way to go before you even *start* to find out who you are. Some of us never find out. Go ahead. Like Willie. Or don't. Maybe even let him know. Maybe you find out you're both into each other and that labels don't matter. You like who you like. No one else can control that. Now, don't pout too long or you'll trip on it. Here, let's go get ready to invade."

Stella and Shayla headed for the kitchen, followed by Buster, as the door opened and more feet and ponytails and baseball caps scrambled into Peaches's little house. The morning carried on as kids made signs. Peaches and Lucy adjusted taped cleavage into dresses tailored for their frames.

"Big bones make big broads," muttered Peaches.

"Honey, don't try to make it sound like anything other than a couple of queens, squeezing themselves into sequins, who are strong enough to kick a redneck into next week if threatened," responded Stella, as she took a safety pin and adjusted a strap on Peaches's brightly colored dress.

Buster stared, then looked away. It didn't seem right, but then again, he saw two grown men putting on dresses and taping their chests into a different form. Even after months of spending time with Peaches, this new world remained foreign and obscure to him, and he couldn't help but stare in a matter that would otherwise be called rude and insulting. Or perhaps, he realized, that it was still rude and insulting, and not okay. It didn't appeal to his sensibilities as a straight man to gawk at the feminine-like breasts of two whom he still considered men, but who clearly presented and thought of themselves differently.

"Ready?" Peaches asked Stella, glancing at Buster.

"Yes, ma'am," smiled Stella, as she puckered and checked her lipstick. "Ruby red like me," said Stella.

"Hope my mascara don't run in this here heat," said Peaches as she looked once more in the mirror. She pulled an eyelash.

"You sure about this?" asked Buster.

"Let's invade Clover!" said Peaches, as she checked her chest once more.

The trio left Peaches's back bedroom and walked down the narrow hall for the front living room. Peaches stopped in the doorframe and smiled as she surveyed a room of glitter and sneakers. Her nuggets had brought friends, all shades and all neighborhoods getting ready for the Clover Festival. Stella spotted Li'l J and stepped over teenage legs and limbs and plastic cups of lemonade.

"What are they makin', Jasper?" Buster asked.

Groups of two and three huddled around white, pink, blue, and yellow poster boards, markers scattered between stickers and smiles and laughter.

Buster read each one softly. "Be You. Be True." "Be Fabulous." "God Loves Me, Why Can't You?" "Love Your Neighbor. Even if She's Straight."

Buster watched Peaches carefully, yet quickly, wipe a tear beneath her eye.

"You okay, Jasper?"

"Huh? Yeah, Buster, just a eyelash," she whispered, then turned and clapped her hands three times. "Why, look at all of you! You are just amazing!" She swallowed hard. "Honey, that one might be a bit much for this little town," she said as she looked at a young teenager with a French braid.

Buster read her poster: "Gay Couples Don't Have Abortions."

Stella gasped. "Where'd you get an idea for that one?" she asked.

Lucy cackled. "Some old biddy is gonna have a stroke over that one. I love it!"

"My cousin Mary Sue saw it in Et-lanna when she was

there this summer and there was a Pride Parade with rainbows and flags and shirtless guys everywhere, and she saw this poster and wrote it down even though she had to pee before her mamma and daddy decided to—"

Peaches interrupted her with a hug. "Thank you, sugar. I love the lime gree—"

"It's CHARTREUSE!" cried the young girl.

"Yes, of course!" added Peaches.

"Jasper, you sure about this?" asked Buster.

Peaches raised a hand to address the room. "Nuggets— I think I picked up a few new ones today, I guess—this gonna be one festival that we'll never forget. Y'all remember that God made all of us, and you deserve to go places and be welcome and loved just like anybody. You gonna tell your grandkids and your friends all about how this sleepy town woke up when we, you, invaded the Clover Festival."

"You tell 'em, Mama Peach!" shouted Willie as he gave Shayla a high-five.

She bit her lip and looked at Stella, who winked.

Li'l J gave Willie a fist bump, and then walked over to hug another kid hunched over a poster.

"Now, you just smile and walk and be brave, and keep an eye out for each other," continued Peaches. "Don't say names and don't fight anybody. If people hate on you, it says more about them than it does you. Stick together."

"Are we gonna be safe? There some crazy people in this town," asked one boy Buster didn't recognize.

Stella stood up, "Yes, you'll be safe, just go about your business and smile. Good people live in this—"

Lucy cleared her throat.

"Good people live in this town," Stella repeated.

"'cept Professor Harvard," grumbled Buster.

"Is Buster gonna come, too?" Li'l J shot to his feet and bounced twice.

"I'm here, little buddy," Buster said.

Carlos groaned.

Someone giggled.

213

"Who's Buster?" asked a new face, who'd tagged along for the excitement of the First Invasion of Clover.

"Just what we need: queens, queers, and Casper to scare the daylights outta the folks in Clover. They'll truly have an exorcism," groaned Lucy.

Stella snapped her fingers. "Must you always be so persnickety? Seriously, Lucy. These kids are having fun. Who cares if they wanna believe in Peaches's imaginary ghost?"

"Ghost? Is this house haunted?" whispered one of the new kids.

"He's—" Peaches stopped. "Listen, let's not fight. Not today. Our power is our people," she added.

Lucy rolled her eyes. "*Our* people? How many times have I got to hear some gay boy tell me he's into *masculine muscle straight-acting jock-types* only? Or make some snide remark about drag queens and trannies and clowns? Don't even get me started on pronouns or whether bi-sex-u-a-lity is a *phase*," she emphasized. "*Our* people only want to be like everybody else: free to love and not get beat up or spit on. But being like everybody else also means this church thinks that church is going to hell," she pointed from one side of the living room to the other. "That neighborhood is better than this one," pointed behind her and to the floor. "How successful you are is based on what car you drive *or* whether your summer is spent at the public pool, a bug-infested cabin in the woods, or a big house at the beach." Lucy wiped sweat from her brow.

"No, you talk about *our people*, Peaches, and you forget that *our people* can be just as judgmental and ornery as the rest of them. No. Kids," she turned to the wide, green faces staring at her, "This parade we gonna throw is not about being gay or straight or blue or green or rich or poor. It's about being free. Being true. Accepting ALL people the way the God made 'em, and not hurting each other. And if you don't believe in God, then that's up to you, because you still part of this universe and you in it for a reason, so own your

214

heart and listen to what's there and love EVERYBODY. So, no, Peaches, this is more than *Here and Queer.*"

Lucy paused. "I need some diabee-tees. Here, baby doll, pass me my cup. This bitch is on a roll," she paused to drink. One of the younger kids giggled. Two teens snickered and another elbowed one of them. "Whew, now I'm ready. Are y'all?"

Murmurs and nods.

"Well, are ya? Cause I'm not invading unless you damn sure you ready to strut your stuff!"

Cheers went up.

Peaches tucked her smile into a corner.

"Be you, be true, and go show Clover what you got," Stella cheered, now on her feet.

"Be You! Be True!" a kid shouted.

"Be You! Be True!" said another.

Willie joined.

Stella nudged Shayla, who joined in the growing chant "Be You! Be True!"

"You okay, Jasper?" Buster leaned over and whispered to Peaches.

"I," her voice cracked. She nodded faintly and whispered, "I didn't have this when I was a kid."

"But they do," said Buster as he watched Carlos, Willie, Shayla, and Li'l J giving fist bumps to their friends, who compared posters and signs they made to post at the Clover Festival.

Lucy called across the jubilant room. "I think they ready, girl," she smiled.

"Thank you," mouthed Peaches. "You ready, Buster?" she whispered to the side.

He took a deep breath. "Na, but I guess you gotta, don't you?"

"Yep," Peaches nodded and hugged Carlos as he walked past her.

"Let's go!"

With that, the house emptied as bodies jostled onto the

porch, across the front lawn, and onto Raspberry Lane. A mini-parade in itself, the group of drag queens, gender benders, gays, straights, in-betweens, and outcasts turned by the cemetery, under the empty gaze of the broken confederate monument, and headed toward Clover's main section of town. Joining athletes, students, and townspeople walking in the closed road, Peaches's parade merged into the small, college-town fair with bright colors and flags and tenacious smiles of excitement.

"Lord, Jasper, I hope you know what you doin'," said Buster, as he caught the eye of one college boy who looked a bit longer than what made Buster feel comfortable.

Peaches looked back at the trail of kids who clustered and mingled. "Say a prayer, Buster. It won't hurt you," she whispered.

"I like your t-shirt, Li'l J," said a young girl they met at the intersection of Main and Cochran Street.

Peaches added softly, "I think they'll be just fine."

Ahead, people flocked like bees around the drink and food tents that lined the street. The Clover Festival buzzed. In a lot by the Presbyterian church, tractors that hadn't seen a field in four decades had been cleaned, greased, and brought in on flatbeds for men in overalls to argue over which model Grandpa used on the back forty after coming home from The Pacific. Corn dog, fritter, and watermelon stands were parked next to a water truck. A line formed at the beer truck.

"Why, it's not even noon," said Stella.

"Peaches, what's the difference between a gay man and a straight man?" asked Stella.

"Here we go," said Peaches.

"A six-pack!" Lucy snorted. Stella elbowed her in laughter.

"Girl better get some new material if she wants to keep workin' The Blue Magnolia," retorted Peaches.

"Speaking of, where's Oscar? I thought he was gonna come help us out?" asked Stella.

"Mama Peach, me and, I mean, Willie and I are gonna

216

get some water; do you want something?" asked Shayla.

"No, but thank you."

"What is with that girl and Willie," asked Lucy. "Is she his puppy dog?"

Buster caught a glance between Stella and Peaches.

A drumhead snapped. A few heads looked around and then went back to chatter.

Four or five more snaps in rapid succession.

"What in the hell is that?" asked Lucy.

Several people now looked around.

A drum roll caught everyone's attention, followed by a loud whistle.

"Oh my god, no," Stella turned and stared down a side street where the crowds had focused attention on someone, or something, coming toward The Festival. "I think we found Oscar."

By the time Buster saw the motorcycle, the entire crowd had parted to make room for drummers snapping the heads and rims of their snares. But what followed the drum corps was unlike anything Buster had ever seen, even in months of spending time with Peaches and her house of nuggets.

A group of dancers, whom Buster guessed had to be in their twenties, followed a lead dancer in two single file rows. They wore high boots and short shorts and tight t-shirts, and walked with determination. And face stubble.

"You go, girl!" shouted one of the drag queens over the rat-a-tat of drumsticks on metal rims.

"Mama Peach! They're J Setters!" shouted Carlos.

"Honey, I don't think that's the Jackson State dance squad," said Stella.

The motorcycle rumbled up to Peaches. Shirtless and sparkling, Oscar smiled at Peaches.

"Lord, Oscar, were you hit by a unicorn?"

He reached out with both arms, welcoming.

"Don't you dare touch me with that glitter," said Lucy, pointing her finger at him.

"I told you I'd help my girls out," he winked at Stella.

"I just brought a few friends to help me."

"Friends? What'd you do—round up all your exes for a family reunion?" asked Lucy.

Oscar turned around. "Damn. You're right. I forgot a couple," he said, as he turned back to Peaches and Stella. "You ladies ready for this?"

"Have we got a choice?" asked Lucy.

Oscar smiled and shook his head while his motorcycle growled. "I won't be able to stay on hog this long in this crowd, so better make our entrance quick."

"Just how you like 'em," said Lucy.

"Love you, too, baby cakes," as he blew her a kiss.

Lucy tilted her face so her cheek faced Oscar. She put her hand over her heart and exaggerated a curtsy.

Peaches rolled her eyes. "Are we just gonna stand and watch the two of you flirt, or we gonna get on with this parade?"

"Yes, ma'am," said Oscar, as he turned and nodded at the lead dancer, who blew a whistle and immediately executed sharp, rapid dance moves in the middle of the street. After a few seconds, the lead abruptly stopped, head turned toward Peaches, and blew a kiss in her direction. The row of dancers behind and to the left of the lead initiated the same sequence of moves, and five counts later, the row to the right kicked off. The entourage hypnotized the crowd with angled arms, body paint, heels and sequins, and testosterone. One woman placed her hand under her husband's jaw to close his mouth.

Another whistle, and this time, four sharp strikes on a snare followed by a drum cadence turned into high steps as the dance squad marched forward.

"Salt an' peppa, baby!" called out a teenager.

Peaches smiled wide as she and her own parade screamed with cheers and claps.

Li'l J ran up to Peaches, "Mama Peach! Mama Peach! Oscar brought people!"

"Yes, sugar, he sure did," she said, then noticed Buster.

"Close your mouth, boo, you might catch it."

He looked at her, then back at the dancers. "Are those boys?"

Peaches laughed loud. "Some might be. Does it matter?"

Guess it really don't, Buster thought, and slowly shook his head.

"Where y'all from?" asked Stella.

"Mem-phis," shouted the leader, waving as they passed ahead. Eight counts later, the entire dance troupe turned and waved at the crowd.

"Lord, bless that bartender," said Stella.

Peaches turned her palms up and glanced at the sky, "She do indeed, She do indeed."

The drumming and whistles dulled slightly as Oscar and his gang turned a corner. Buster watched the rest of the crowd return to its water bottles, barbecue, and chattering, voices louder and livelier, as if a big pot of coffee had been passed around.

Willie, Shayla, and Carlos walked by Buster and waited.

"Man this party is ragin'!"

"When you gonna stop quotin' white girl shows?" asked Willie.

"Whatever!"

"*Clueless*," said Willie.

"*Breakfast Club*," said Shayla.

"*Steel Magnolias*," added Lucy, overhearing the trio.

"Next thing you know, it'll be *Laverne & Shirley*," added Peaches.

The three teenagers looked at Peaches with furrowed brows and stares.

She sighed. "Never mind."

The Festival resumed, the street cleared by dancers, and Buster had to shuffle quickly to avoid people. A brush with a hand here, an arm there, would tingle uncomfortably, but not nearly the same threat of possession for Buster as Tinsley. Still, each touch left him queasy and uncomfortable, feeling the hurt, love, or sadness of strangers and learning that at least two dads wore their wife's underwear in secret. One secretly tried on his daughter's cheerleading outfit, and another woman didn't want to wake up. He felt the nerves of a young man fumbling an engagement ring in a pocket while he chatted with a young woman.

Damn, I didn't think about how to avoid getting possessed, he thought, as he barely avoided a silent couple frowning and looking in opposite directions. Fortunately, they dropped hands and stepped apart briefly, allowing Buster to slip between them sideways. He didn't need to know the unspoken words of their argument.

"Jasper?" he called out. "Damn, where'd he go?" Buster scanned the crowd as it briefly parted. A few sequins later, Buster headed for Clover's main street, toward big hair that floated above caps and pompoms. He turned onto a sidewalk behind a row of vendors. Mostly empty, other than some kegs, cardboard boxes, and strollers, Buster caught up to a wig teased into the shape of a ball.

"Jasper, thought I'd lost yo—" he exhaled, dodging a five-year-old on a scooter. "Jasper," he repeated and stepped in front, only to realize that he'd lost Peaches in the crowd. "Dammit," he muttered, as he felt a pop along his spine, smelled cotton candy, and thought *I hope papa lets me have a funnel cake.* Buster rubbed his face, only to open his eyes and see a young girl with pigtails racing through him, on tiny legs, to hold her father's hands.

Buster stood quickly and stepped aside to avoid another possession. He headed for the water truck where a few people had gathered.

"Where the hell is that quee—" he stopped himself. Buster scanned the faces of Clover. Was that a drum strike in the distance? The Invasion had dissipated in the crowd, but not without leaving rainbow stickers on parking meters, tents, even on the back of an older woman's wheelchair. A sign that read "Aloud and Proud" in rainbow letters was taped to the side of a moving truck parked near one of the concession stands. Beneath, someone had scribbled "Fairies

220

eat poo."

That ain't gonna be good for the kids, Buster thought. He exhaled. *All that work just to be safe*. He started to walk away when he noticed three teens in cheerleader outfits walk past.

One pointed at the sign. He recognized her from before.

"My daddy says being gay is wrong," said one with a slight curl to her lip.

"I bet he does," grumbled Buster. "Wonder if he's the one trying to wear your cheerleading skirt in the closet?"

"He says love the sinner, hate the sin," she finished.

"He must hate not being able to wear a dress," said Buster.

"Seriously, Mary Jane Tinsley? This *isn't* the 1990's," said one in the middle.

Buster froze at her name.

"What makes it a sin?" asked the third.

"It's in the Bible, Karen," said Mary Jane. "Leviticus or something."

"Have you actually *read* the Bible?" said the second cheerleader.

Mary Jane started to nod, then stopped.

"Okay, great! So you know that Leviticus was a book of laws for a bunch of nomads? And it says a lot of things are wrong. Like eating fat. Tearing your clothes." She paused, "Having sex during your period."

"Why are you looking at me like that, Karen?" Mary Jane asked.

"So what you and Steve did is fine, but being gay isn't?" Karen asked.

"Picking up grapes that fall off the vine—"

"No way!" said Karen.

"Totally. Look it up. There's some messed up stuff in there," the unnamed cheerleader continued. "Like mixing fabrics, trimming your beard, cross-breeding animals, cutting your hair at the sides, and, wait for it," as she turned and pulled her waistband down, "getting a tattoo!"

The girls squealed. "Suzie! When did you get that?"

"Last week," Suzie smiled, "But, hold on, I'm not done." Suzie pulled out a poster marker from a pocket in her pleated skirt and walked to the sign.

"Mary Jane Tinsley, being gay is no more a sin than you wearing that cotton-lycra top of mine or eating bacon. So, shut your face. Which I say because I love you, even if your dad is wrong. Let's go get snow cones!" and just as they'd arrived, the three cheerleaders left in a whirl.

Stunned, Buster watched the girls disappear into the crowd. He turned and read "Don't H8 What U Luv" written in large, red letters, followed by an arrow that pointed toward the slur. A surge rushed through him as he remembered another era when college students came south to stand up for strangers.

Moments later, Buster felt sick from the smell of rotten eggs. He looked up quickly and recognized professor Tinsley from the side. Tinsley stared straight ahead with penetrating hatred, locked onto a target. Buster followed Tinsley's gaze through heads and shoulders and polite gaps in the crowd, directly to a head of hair teased high and tight above a dress that looked ablaze in the midday sun.

"Shit, Jasper, he's found you," muttered Buster, standing up and looking for the fastest way to get through the crowd.

Tinsley didn't move as bodies swirled and sweated between himself and Peaches, who stopped to get snow cones with two of the nuggets.

"How the hell does he recognize Jasper?" said Buster, as he looked from Tinsley to Peaches, then back.

Tinsley put his hand in his pocket and proceeded to walk into the crowd.

"Hey, Professor!" Jonny sauntered up with an outstretched hand. "Hot out here, idinit?" he said.

"Hi, Professor Tinsley," said a soft voice.

"You two?" Buster asked, as Heather held one knee and hold Jonny's other hand.

Tinsley accepted and shook the outstretched hand,

mumbling acknowledgment, then continued past toward the snow cone truck.

"Well, that's kinda rude." Jonny muttered.

"Shhh, he's been really moody lately, anyway," whispered Heather.

Buster looked for a part in The Festival crowd to reach Peaches first, but had no luck.

"Jasper!" he shouted.

"Jasper!!" he shouted louder.

A dog barked.

"Not now, dammit," as Buster stepped back from an elderly couple.

"Jasper! It's me! Buster! Professor Harvard's comin' your way!"

The dress stopped winking under the bright sun as Peaches stood still.

Two of the nuggets kissed her cheek and headed off into the crowd toward a dunking booth.

Peaches did not move as Tinsley stepped cautiously through the crowd.

"Jasper, don't just stand there," Buster called, as he ran around a couple arguing over a corn dog and crossed the street. He stepped up on an abandoned cooler by a crafts vendor. He waved his arms. "Here, Jasper! I'm here!"

Peaches slowly turned, snow cone already melting into sugar water and dribbling down her hand.

"Just be yourself. Maybe he don't know it's you!"

Peaches's chest rose, then fell as she licked the ice in her hand and turned, only to come face to face with Art Tinsley.

"Oh, ex-cuse me, sir," stumbling over syllables.

"Don't I know you?" he asked.

Buster strained to hear.

"Why, I don't think we've ever met," said Peaches, tilting her eyes slightly down past his gaze.

"Didn't you give me a flyer about a revival?" he asked.

Peaches paused. "Re-vi-val?" She flashed a bright smile. "Sugar, I don't think you'd be interested in any of the singing

223

venues that I go to."

"You seem familiar," said Tinsley, as he eyed her boa.

"Unless you been to The Blue Magnolia, I don't think we've ever met," Peaches tugged at a part of her dress that stuck to her skin.

"Lord, don't tell that man where you work!" said Buster.

Tinsley continued to stare.

"Well, toodleloo," said Peaches, as she turned into the sweating crowd.

"Don't look back, Jasper," said Buster, as Tinsley watched the six-foot-three pillar of sequins and hairspray weave and sparkle on heels through The Festival.

Buster hopped down from the cooler and managed to join Peaches in a break among the crowd.

"Boo, don't try to talk with me here, cause I'll look certifiable," she whispered.

"Don't worry, Jasper, I just lost you. Looks like our friend found you, though."

"What's he doin'?" she whispered, and pulled on a loose curl.

"Just watching at the moment."

"I can feel the holes he's putting in the back a my head," she whispered.

"I wish you wouldna told him where you work," said Buster, and he looked back at Peaches.

"I panicked, boo! I was just makin' conversation," Peaches paused. "Hi, how are you?" she smiled at a couple as they walked by. "Why am I still talking to you?" she whispered coarsely. "People already staring at me."

"Fine. Just wanted you to be okay."

Peaches smirked.

"What?"

"Why, if I didn't know better, you thinking about me," she whispered.

"You make it sound like I don't care 'bout nobody."

Peaches licked her teeth and clacked her tongue.

"What?"

"Nothing, Buster, you just keep watching that man behind me and make sure he don't put a real hole in the back of my head." Peaches fluffed the back of her hair with her right hand.

Buster glanced back. "Don't see him."

"Let's hope we don't for awhile. I don't need him up in my business."

I really hope that wasn't mail you dropped at the shed, Buster thought, but he was too afraid to say aloud. Buster scanned the street, wondering why the nape of his neck tickled.

CHAPTER NINETEEN

The progression of the day crept across the cracks of the porch boards like a sundial. Buster sat in one of Peaches's rocking chairs and waited. He couldn't remember how long he had been there, but warm days had a tendency to extend themselves into forgetfulness. Peaches wasn't home, so Buster decided to wait on her porch and pass the time.

A monarch butterfly fluttered above drooping spider lilies near the advancing shadow. A faint fall breeze directed the insect from its task and carried it under the porch shelter.

Buster held his hand palm facing up. The butterfly flapped and blinked its wings as it approached. Hovering slightly, it attempted to alight and dropped onto Buster's hand, missing, then trying again, each time passing through his illusory fingers.

Buster smiled. "Kinda tickles." The butterfly lost interest and clumsily flapped toward a table.

Moments later, Buster heard footsteps on the dry walk and looked up to see Li'l J crossing the lawn.

"Hey, buddy," said Buster, as he stood. The butterfly flapped a path back to the flowers. Li'l J jumped onto each step with two feet before reaching the porch. He dropped his book bag and knocked on the door.

"Mama Peach!" he shouted.

"Jasper ain't here, little man," said Buster. "Where's your brother?"

Li'l J forced an exhale and crooked his nose to the side. He knocked again, the screen door rasping in the dry heat. "Mama P!"

"Too bad you can't see or hear me, Li'l J," said Buster. "I don't know where Jasper is." Buster stretched and yawned. "Actually, don't really know how long I've been sitting here waiting, neither. Guess your brother has band practice."

Li'l J gave one last rap on the door with his other fist

shoved into his pocket. He looked around before sitting on the top step of the porch. He bent over to tie his shoe, then reached under a cracked barren board and retrieved a key.

"You rascal," laughed Buster, as Li'l J hopped up and darted back to the front door. The screen squawked as he swung it open quick and wide with anticipation. Li'l J turned the key and opened the front door, and disappeared into the empty house like a mouse down a hole.

"Hi, Buster!" cried Jerome from inside the house.

"Out here, little man," answered Buster.

Before the screen door had time to smack shut, it flew wildly open as Li'l J returned to the porch. He held the screen door open with his foot as he picked up his book bag. With both doors wide open, Buster hustled through. *Watch him sometime, boo*, Peaches had said. *You may learn something*.

The muffled, dark inside of the house smelled heavy, like a quilt. Li'l J headed down the center hall to the back left for the kitchen. Buster followed.

"How is school?" Buster asked.

Li'l J dropped his bag by a chair in the kitchen, rattling it on its shiny four legs. Li'l J opened the refrigerator and pulled out a pitcher of pink liquid. Buster watched Jerome retrieve a glass from the cupboard and pour himself some of the drink.

"Pour me a glass, little man," teased Buster.

"Want some, Buster?" shouted Li'l J.

"I'm right here."

"It tastes okay, but Mama Peach don't—doesn't add enough sugar," he called out.

"I'll just dip my finger," said Buster. "Don't think it'll hurt," as he reached over the table and put his finger into the pitcher as Li'l J finished pouring.

Buster licked his finger. "Not bad, but shore not sweet enough."

Li'l J pulled a notebook from his bag and it flapped on the kitchen table with a loud SMACK. He began writing in the notepad.

"What kinda homework you got, Li'l J?" asked Buster, as he looked down at the scrawl in the lined paper.

Numbers and signs marched across the page in formation as Jerome began to solve math problems.

Buster shook his head. "Not that I could help you even if you asked."

Li'l J looked up and faced Buster.

Buster tilted his head, then asked, "Did you hear me? I know it's dark, but I need music to—"

Jerome stood up from the table. He looked through, then past Buster, and continued for the door. Buster turned and looked at Jerome, who peered out of the kitchen into the hallway.

"You okay, little buddy?" asked Buster.

He looked back into the kitchen, then down the hallway toward the front of the house.

A board creaked.

"Hello?" cried Li'l J. "Buster?"

Buster stood from his chair. "I heard that too, buddy," he said, as Buster stepped around Jerome and into the hallway.

"Who's there?" cried Li'l J.

"C'mon, cut the radio on, Li'l J. Gimme some music," whispered Buster as he stepped into the hallway, digging a toe into each step. Another creak. "That definitely ain't me," he said.

"Who's there?" they both called.

"I'm gonna call 9-1-1!" shouted Li'l J, as Buster heard him lift the telephone from the receiver.

Buster turned to face Li'l J, "Do it!" Footsteps broke the silence. Buster again smelled burning matches and rotten eggs, and bent over to catch his breath as he broke into full body sweat. Sounds warbled like a siren in his ears as Buster strained to look into the kitchen.

"Hey! You're Mary Jane's da—" shouted Jerome.

"Shit!" came Tinsley's voice, as a chair turned over on the floor.

"What're you doin' in Mama Peaches's house?" asked Jerome.

Tinsley stumbled backwards into the hallway, passing through Buster again. Buster grabbed his knees, spitting out nothing while his entire chest burned like fire. Tinsley's voice argued with someone in his head.

"Where you going?" Li'l J asked before whispering, "Hey, Buster, are you really here?"

Buster couldn't focus as he heard Tinsley. *That faggot stole my notebook with those numbers.*

Li'l J asked, "What's wrong, Mary Jane's dad?"

"Wrong house, I gotta go," stuttered Tinsley, as he bumped into a table and knocked over a lamp, crashing in front of Buster.

"Mama will be here soon—"

"Fuck!" Tinsley tripped and grabbed onto the narrow bookcase, knocking books off. As he pulled himself up, the bookcase tipped. Tinsley limped to his feet in the kitchen.

Buster watched through blurry eyes as the bookshelf tipped over, spilling books like dominoes. One book hit Jerome in the face as he threw his arms up. The unbalanced bookcase, now emptied, knocked Jerome in the head as both fell to the floor. Li'l J, unconscious, faced Buster, who shivered in a fetal position as a rolodex of images and numbers from three years of Tinsley's work flipped through his head. *Tinsley bred ants that he had released throughout the county after perfecting a poison that would target the new invasive hybrid. A malignant hero of gardeners everywhere. Both could be sold, the poison legitimately and the hybrid species on a growing black market that would overpower and turn on an obscure greedy man like Art Tinsley.*

The kitchen door banged on its wooden jamb. Buster shivered on the floor as strange voices in his head shouted, and he saw a photograph of Mary Jane from the parade, clutched in Tinsley's hands.

Seconds turned to minutes. "Hey Li'l J," whispered

Buster. The young boy looked asleep, pinned under a stack of books under the bookcase. Minutes grew as Buster shook off the nausea. He rose to his feet and tried to lift the bookcase. A dark pool collected under Li'l J.

Buster paced the dark hall. *Jasper,* he thought. "Jasper!" he repeated, as a feeling of dread and panic consumed him as Li'l J grew pale.

"JASPER!" he finally shouted with every emotion he could stir. The air shifted as fine particles of dust from the books, the back of the shelves, the hall table, and between the very floor boards—if not every board of the house—rose into the air and flew away from Buster in every direction as the house inhaled and sneezed.

Three miles away, Peaches fervently wondered if Carlos could make his audition. What had Buster seen about Carlos's future? Tempted, she refused to allow herself to ask. She shivered—what had Buster learned about HER future when she stepped into him? Had she given him that memory of being bullied? What was going to happen? She shuddered again, this time dropping the toilet brush.

As intense and bright as the Mississippi sun, Peaches heard Buster calling for her.

CHAPTER TWENTY

Buster leaned against the wall near the foot of the hospital bed.

"Lil J, how you feeling, my man?" asked Willie.

The monitor beeped.

"He still out, nugget, so don't wake him," said Peaches.

"It's been two days," said Willie. "When's he gonna wake up?"

Peaches shook her head.

Shayla crossed to the opposite side of the bed. She put her hand on the bed rail, then moved her hand to the blanket near Li'l J's uncovered hand. "When do you think his parents will come back? You really don't need to be here when they get back, Mama Peaches."

Peaches nodded, "Okay, boo."

Shayla slid two fingers into his hand, then all of her fingers lightly wrapped Li'l J's, as if holding the paw of a newborn kitten, still asleep.

"Where's Carlos?" Buster finally asked.

Peaches looked at Buster, then around the room. "Willie, where's Carlos?"

Willie shrugged.

Shayla silently pointed toward the door.

Buster turned and walked into the hallway. Carlos slumped in a chair and drew his hoodie tight around him. His knees bounced up and down as his shuffled in his seat.

Buster sat next to Carlos.

Carlos sniffed and sat up.

"I knows you can't hear me," said Buster. "But, you doing okay?"

Carlos sighed and slumped back.

Buster rubbed the back of his neck as he looked at Carlos.

"Shoulda skipped practice and gone with him,"

231

muttered Carlos.

"He out here, mama," said Willie.

Buster looked up and saw Willie standing in the doorframe.

"Boo, come in here and say hi. I think your brother is wakin' up."

Carlos bristled and rose from the worn chair that wobbled when he moved. He walked head down past Peaches and stood at the foot of the bed. Willie waited next to Peaches.

"Well. Go on."

Carlos glanced at Peaches, then walked to the side of the bed opposite her.

"Well, I know you are not throwing shade in my direction," said Peaches. "Say hi to Li'l J. Maybe he'll wake up."

Carlos blurted out, without looking away from Jerome, "He wouldn't be hurt if he didn't listen to all your stories, Mama Peaches!"

Peaches stepped back. Willie and Shayla stared at each other across the hospital bed, then to Carlos, then to Peaches. Buster looked at Jerome as the monitor flickered.

"If he hadn't listened to you, he would've run! He wouldn't have thought a ghost was there protecting him!" Sweat dripped from Carlos. "That crazy story about a stupid ghost!" Carlos spit in the room.

Buster watched as Li'l J moved his arm. "Jasper..." whispered Buster.

"Not now," whispered Peaches.

"See?? Who you talking to, Mama? Ain't nobody there. It was just a story! But Jerome thought it was real! He actually thought he had a ghost protecting him, so he didn't have to run! Buster does not exist!" shouted Carlos.

A sharp pang stung Buster as Carlos shouted.

"Now, boo," started Peaches.

"Don't call me that!" Carlos trembled as tears poured down his face. "He didn't have no one around him! It's your fault that I wasn't there, cause you told me I had to stay at school and practice for an audition I can't even pay to get to!" Carlos screamed.

"Carlos," said Shayla.

"Carlos, baby, did you think you were supposed to be there?" asked Peaches.

Buster looked again as the monitor flickered. Li'l J turned slightly.

Peaches looked toward Buster and Jerome.

"Stop it!" Carlos choked back his tears. "No one is there!"

"Mama," said Willie.

Carlos sobbed and gripped the bed railing. Shayla still held Li'l J's hand as Peaches walked around the bed to Carlos. She wrapped around him with her arms and he choked on his own tears.

Buster turned and leaned over Li'l J, whose eyes slowly opened. The heart monitor flickered again.

"Mama, what's wrong with that machine?" asked Shayla, as she pointed at the green screen.

"Does that look funny to you?" asked Willie.

"Hey," said Jerome.

Buster looked down. Li'l J's eyes were half open.

"I think Li'l J's talking," said Shayla.

Not to me, thought Buster.

Jerome smiled. "I knew you was there," he whispered.

"Li'l J, Mama can't hear you," said Peaches, as she loosened her grip on Carlos.

Buster looked at Peaches, who kissed Carlos on the forehead.

"Hey, Buster," Jerome giggled softly.

Buster abruptly turned to Li'l J. "You—

Jerome pulled his lips into his mouth and muffled a giggle.

"Lil J, who you talkin' to?" asked Shayla.

"Hey, my man, feelin' better?" asked Willie.

Jerome slowly propped himself on his arms and smiled

at Buster.

"Can you—" Buster started, then stopped his question.

Jerome put a finger close to his mouth and shook his head, giggling. Buster stepped back as Peaches and Willie and Shayla and Carlos surrounded the bed. Jerome slid between their bodies as a nurse walked into the room.

Jerome giggled and ran on bare feet to the door, grabbing Buster's hand, then letting it go.

Buster looked at his hand and realized nothing happened. A nothing which actually meant something that Buster didn't want to be true.

"Wait, I don't," said Buster, as he stepped into the hallway. Jerome stood facing him in a hospital gown, giggling. Buster stared back into the hospital room, where four figures remained huddled and focused around the bed while a heart monitor beat slower and a red light flickered above the door. Somewhere down a hallway, a buzzer sounded. He slowly turned back to Jerome, who now held his hand up to Buster.

"Buster, come play with me?"

Buster stepped toward Jerome as another nurse ran for the room, brushing through him. Buster's skin tingled and the hairs raised on his arms. *Another one today. Been here 16 hours already and I need to see my kid. This one's parents better get here.* Buster held Jerome's hand and looked over his shoulder. The red light was steady and an even steadier beep sounded.

"It's okay," said Jerome. "We'll go this way," and he tugged on Buster's hand.

"Li'l J, where are we going? Wait, no. You...you need to get back in there," Buster whispered hoarsely as he looked back to see the nurses standing over the bed, as Peaches and the nuggets clustered against the wall.

Jerome shook his head. "I can't. But it's O.K." He emphasized the "O" and "K" with a thumb in the air.

Buster followed Jerome down the hall as a doctor ran past. Buster felt a warm surge in his face. "Li'l J, I don't wanna take you anywhere. Please go back in there."

Jerome stopped and stared at Buster, placing his arms on his hips. "Whatever you want to be, you be." He smiled. "I'm not gonna be shady. I'm just gonna be FIERCE!" He laughed and proceeded to skip. "Now, come play!"

Jerome turned another corner, and Buster ran three steps after him to find Jerome at the far end of a brightly-lit corridor facing another hall. Jerome spun around and smiled, waving.

"Li'l J!" Buster whispered loudly as he started for Jerome.

Jerome giggled and ran out of sight down another hospital wing. "Bye, Buster!" he shouted as he ran. "Tell Mama—"

"NO!" shouted Buster as he ran faster. "Jerome! Get back here!"

Buster ran as hard as he could, dodging another nurse pushing a patient in a wheelchair. Buster reached the next corner of the hallway with no sight of Jerome, as a long wail echoed along the hospital floor.

CHAPTER TWENTY-ONE

"Busta! BUUUUSTA!"

He jerked. Somewhere in a blend of sleep, memory, and awareness, Buster walked along a fence in front of a house.

"Busta Sparkle, get your ass out heah NOW!"

Buster stopped and closed his eyes and focused on the image of a white, hand-painted mailbox. Moments later, he stood in the sunny square patch of Peaches's front yard.

"Dammit, what good is being able to see a ghost if you can't call him when you need him?"

"Out here, Jasper," answered Buster, just as he saw Stella slowly walk past, long legs in spiked heels like appendages to a giant brown grasshopper.

"Lord, she talkin' to that imaginary friend again?" muttered Stella, as each step plunked with the sound of deliberation. The final step creaked as she pushed off into the shade of the porch.

"Bout time you got here," Peaches said, sticking her head out of the door. "Uh, hey Stella."

Stella looked at Peaches, slowly turned to look behind her, then back to Peaches. "Are you talking to me? Cause I swear you looked right past me as if someone was in the yard."

"Pshhh, girl, c'mon in. Almost done puttin' my face on."

Stella propped open the screen door and leaned against the wood frame. "You think this a good idea, Peaches?"

"Why wouldn't it be?" asked Peaches.

Stella licked her teeth with her tongue, then made a clacking sound. "Oh, I don't know—the fact that Li'l J and Carlos's family never liked you? The fact that Li'l J got attacked by a burglar at your house when they thought he was at school? The fact that I am a transwoman and about to go to a holy rollin' church service? The fact that Carlos's papa blames you for Carlos being *funny*? I know it ain't much to worry about EXCEPT THAT WE LIVE IN CLOVER, MISSISSIPPI!"

"Wasn't just any burglar," mumbled Peaches.

"Do what?" Stella asked.

Peaches cleared her throat and straightened her dress. "I don't care. Be You. Be True. That's what we tell the nuggets."

Buster stepped onto the porch behind Stella. Peaches looked at both of them. "We are *going* to Li'l J's funeral. He'd want it that way."

"In a dress?" Buster asked.

Stella shrugged. "Suit yourself. But I got my mace in case someone gets religion and tries to cast a demon outta me." Stella tucked hair behind her ear. "Unless of course it's Brother Earl. He could cast anything out of me he wanted."

"Hush! You sound more like Lucy right now. You better remember why we there!" said Peaches. "We are going as we are, cause that's what Li'l J would want!"

Stella turned her hands up into the cool November air and stepped away from the door, and Peaches went back inside. Buster watched her sit on the rocking chair and light up a cigarette. "Imma just suck on my cancer stick a bit before we get on the road."

Buster sat in the rocker next to Stella. The two of them listened to Peaches's singing, muffled by the house. Buster looked at Stella, who chewed on the back of a finger. He watched her pick up a compact and look at herself.

"Lord, get me through this day," she muttered. Buster noticed her fingers shaking slightly.

"You look pretty," he said, before looking ahead. "Guess I never thought I'd think that about a—well—don't matter, you look nice. Even if you can't hear me."

Stella doubled over, shaking.

Buster turned back at her.

"Dammit!" she sobbed, then coughed hard. "We shoulda planned for someone to be here every day," she said.

Buster looked at the door to the house, then back to

Stella. "I'm really sorry," he said, reaching out, almost patting her back, then stopping. "Damn, I wish someone else could hear me. Li'l J didn't do nothing wrong. It ain't right, but it happened. I know who did it. That crook won't get away."

She inhaled deeply and straightened her spine. "Peaches is right. Li'l J wouldn't want us to change. We going for him, as we are." She inhaled again, and then extinguished the cigarette on her heel.

"Peaches! Let's get a move on!" she shouted to the light blue ceiling of the porch.

"Stella! I almost ready!"

"Jasper, I'm going, too!" said Buster.

"Damn right, you are," Buster heard Peaches mutter between notes. *"I need you, boo."*

"Need me?" he whispered. "What in Sam Hill am I gonna do?"

Stella turned and looked in the door. "Well? Shall I send out for the carriage, or we gonna take the train? They not gonna wait on a bunch a queens, especially one as white as you."

"Well, don't get your panties in a knot, Stella, cause I am on. My. Way." Peaches charged through the door and almost bumped into Stella, who eyed her from head to toe.

"What?" said Peaches.

"No dress?" Buster said.

"Classy, like Jackie-O," said Peaches.

"Right," said Stella. "Cause Jackie-O wore a size..." she stopped herself. "Although, I'm sure she'd be flattered that you wearing that flashback jacket. But did she ever wear a pantsuit?"

"There's a compliment in there somewhere, so, thank you," said Peaches.

"What thrift store sold you that furniture cover, anyway?"

"Go on, then. Keep it up. See if I don't try to convert you myself while you stewing in that church for Brother Jones."

"Brother Earl."

"Whichever. They all the same. One down-low brother to another, not being honest with themselves or their wives. Bless their hearts." Peaches walked off the porch and headed for her car.

Buster followed. "You sure 'bout this?"

"Yes, boo, now just settle down. We going to church," she whispered.

"Peaches, doll, what did you say?" asked Stella.

"Nothing, you little hussy, now get your ass in my car. Not the back seat, like you accustomed too."

"Whoa, now, you outta save that sass for Lucy. We are picking her up today, aren't we?" asked Stella, as she walked around to the passenger side. "And are you planning to drive from the back seat?"

"Oh," said Peaches, as she nodded while she held open a back door of the car for Buster.

"You sure you okay, Peaches?" asked Stella.

"Yes, babe, I'll be alright," she said, opening the driver's door. "We'll pick up Lucy on the way. Let's just get to the church before they lock out the rainbows and unicorns."

After picking up their final passenger, the brown car turned onto the black tar road past a bramble of bois d'arc trees. It curved behind a heavily-bricked, towering complex of buildings set off by a six-foot iron fence. On the other side of the fence, a playground manicured itself under outstretched oak trees.

"Well, there's the church that ate Clover," pointed Stella.

A large group of white children chased each other up and down a long slide. Two college coeds in lipstick, skirts, and cotton sweaters stood under the limber arch of an old crepe myrtle, talking and casting glances toward the mangle of kids.

"Yep," said Buster. "Looks like—"

"Isn't that where you went, Peaches?" asked Lucy.

Peaches didn't respond.

Buster leaned forward, "Yeah, Peaches, is this where you grew up?"

"If you call it that," said Peaches. "My grandparents thought nothin' beat a good Christian education, until some choir boys thought it fun to play smear-the-queer. With a real queer. Little Tommy Snickers pulled me behind the holly bushes to show me something. Then, he pulled out his tiny doodle and screamed 'Don't touch me faggot!' His buddies then used me like a punching bag."

"Wait. Tommy Snickers? That isn't the bastard who got arrested for raping that junior high cheerleader a couple years ago?" asked Stella.

"The one and the same," said Peaches. "Although he tried to claim consent. Now he's at Parchman."

"Tell me how a fourteen-year-old consents to a forty-eight year-old bald, fat man. Well, karma sure is a bitch," said Lucy, "Cause that's exactly what his nasty white ass is now."

Buster watched the swing sets disappear as the road dropped into a hollow. At a drainage creek, the car made a sharp turn.

"That don't right anything," said Peaches, as she reached for the radio. "I need to sing and get my mind offa this."

"Well, we here, doll, you'll get your singing soon enough."

Buster saw a short brick and wooden structure behind two cedar trees at the back of a gravel lot full of cars. The doors stood propped open, and several members of the congregation stood outside. A broad youth wearing a football jersey stood by the door.

"Mmmmhm, that boy is fine. Black like the depths of my Africa," said Lucy.

"You did not just bring Langston Hughes into your gay cougar fantasies."

Lucy sighed, "Fine, Peaches, but I am only tryin' to lighten your day. You about as glum as my Aunt Ethel without her happy pills, Cheetos, and *Oprah.*"

Peaches pulled the car into a second gravel lot across the street.

"I'll be damned," said Buster, as he tingled from the inside out.

Peaches glanced back at the rearview mirror.

"This was my church," he said.

"Aw, hell," Peaches muttered.

"What now?" asked Stella.

"Lord, girl, you just keep talking to yourself like we ain't here, and you are gonna get locked up," said Lucy.

Peaches checked the side mirror and stepped out of the car. She opened the rear door to get her purse, allowing Buster enough room to get out. Stella and Lucy got out of the other side of the car.

"You had to put me in the ditch with these new heels, didn't you?" said Lucy, as she looked down at the ground and pulled gently on her dress.

"Lord, she is on a mission today," Stella said to Lucy as she nodded towards Peaches, who was now halfway across the unpainted road. "You think she's okay?"

Buster crossed the street and stared at the lettering on the church and the small steeple.

He stopped at the sidewalk, looking back at the gravel lot, then his feet, then the church. "Ain't had a reason to go to a church yet. Here goes nothing," said Buster, as hesitated and then took a firm step onto the church lot. Nothing. "Well that's gotta be a good sign," he exhaled.

Peaches looked over her shoulder with a raised eyebrow.

"Well, at least I ain't cursed," said Buster, with hands outstretched.

"At least one of us isn't," Peaches said under her breath as she shook her head.

Buster and Peaches waited for Lucy and Stella to approach. Lucy nodded at a man smoking a cigarette.

"Don't stir up trouble," said Stella as she leaned over to Lucy.

"Sugar, they don't even have a clue about me," said Lucy.

"Maybe they won't even notice. I don't quite stick out like you and Peaches."

"And just what in the hell does that mean?" interrupted Peaches.

Lucy stared at Peaches like she'd stolen a boyfriend. "Aside from your linebacker days, you and Stella are two of three white people here," she swept her hand across the church lawn.

Peaches remained silent.

"Nothing spells segregation like cemeteries and Sundays," added Stella. "So far, looks like it's me, Peaches, and that old man over yonder that diversify this flock."

The foursome approached the front doors of the small church. The chatter of a congregation inside spilled into the faintly cool morning. Two gentlemen in suits stopped talking. Both looked at Peaches. A third walked inside.

"Good morning," said Lucy as she nodded her head.

"Morning, sister, how are you today?"

"Fine now, brothe—" she smiled before Stella elbowed her.

"—well, no, not really. It's an awful day. I can't walk into God's House lying, can I?"

"That's right, sister, but come on in, He'll forgive you."

"Yes, She will," muttered Peaches.

Although Peaches towered over them, the two men ignored her and smiled at Stella and Lucy, who looked like beanpoles in comparison in the fall sun. The three stepped inside the church, warm with bodies. Chatter nearest the door "How awful" and "Poor Carlos" followed by "The mother" stopped like the chorus of crickets at an intruder. A hundred pairs of eyes followed Peaches. A few sniffles escorted an "I never" as they walked to a pew. A low whispered "queer" was followed by a "shush," and Buster turned to watch Peaches keep her head up, as Stella and Lucy nodded at people in the crowd as if they knew everyone.

Buster watched as some faces bent toward each other, others which stared straight ahead, and still others which emphasized disapproval of the white gender-bender who just walked into their midst.

Once they sat dawn, the chorus of crickets slowly resumed a broken pattern of rasped chirping while waiting for the service. Buster stood in the aisle. Ahead, he saw a small casket. In the corner, members of the high school football team wore jerseys and sat obediently, shoulder pad to shoulder pad.

Buster looked around the tiny sanctuary full of fans and sweat. The warm bodies had returned to their pre-funeral murmur of nodding heads, opinions, and assessments. Near the front, he saw an empty pew where a placard noted "Family." He didn't see Carlos. A large woman in a pink suit sitting against the wall fanned herself between whispers to the woman by her side and glared at Peaches, who was easy to spot, being a full head above everyone else.

Buster looked around the rest of the church. Although most of the congregation managed a placid pretext of ignoring Peaches in the fifth pew from the front on the left side, noticeable heads broke the surface of the lake, bobbing and leaning and whispering. No one seemed bothered by Stella and Lucy as they sat and fanned themselves, safe in the churchgoers' perception of them as women. Even if they accompanied the weird white man in a dress.

Buster remained at the end of the pew and looked at Peaches, who raised an eyebrow to ask "*Where you going?*"

"Just gonna walk around. It's too warm," followed by, "I don't know why I'm whispering."

Peaches smirked slightly, then also fanned herself and sat quietly, as Lucy and Stella leaned into each other like aunts reuniting over Thanksgiving dinner. Buster looked around the compact church.

I think I been here, he thought. He looked for Carlos, before remembering to look in the section reserved for family. He recognized Willie and Shayla sitting in the second pew from the front near the football players, so he walked over to them after an usher passed.

"How's Carlos?" Shayla asked Willie.

He shrugged. "He's not talking."

"They know anything yet?"

"Nah, not like they'll investigate when they think it's a random burglary," said Willie.

Buster fumed. "It wasn't a goddamn-random-burglar!"

"Think he still blames Mama Peaches?" she asked.

"Nah, but his momma sure does. But she was at work, so she's just upset that Li'l J and Carlos were going over there behind her back. You know she thinks Peaches is why Carlos is gay," he whispered.

Shayla shook her head. "I'm nervous that Mama Peaches is here," she said.

"But she's got Lucy and Stella with her."

"Whatever. Cause those three will never stir up trouble in a Mississippi church." Shayla bit her lip and looked over her shoulder. She waved her fingers in response to Stella.

"It'll be fine," said Willie.

"Sure—cause no one's noticed yet," said Shayla, as she nodded toward the lady in pink whose frosty glares could have otherwise grown icicles from the collective sweat of the congregation.

"Why is she so bent out of shape?" asked Buster and Willie together.

"Cause she in a church where gays and queers and other outcasts aren't welcome. Specially if one's white and wearing a dress," muttered Shayla. "Guess Miss Stella and Miss Lucy's got them fooled."

Buster looked back at the trio, Stella's long neck and limbs more slender than the squat woman behind her.

"I can't wait to leave this town," said Willie, as he shook his head.

"Where you gonna go?"

"Atlanta. I wanna get into Morehouse."

Buster swelled and smiled.

"Morehouse? As a gay black man?" asked Shayla.

"Shhh!" whispered Willie. "Yeah, why?"

Buster stepped out of the way of a couple walking past. Shayla dropped her voice. "Hear of Adodi or Keiron Williams?"

"What's that?"

"Who. Willie, if you wanna get out of hell, don't go running toward purgatory."

He scrunched up his nose. "Say what?"

"At least do your homework. If you wanna leave Mississippi so you can be who you are, better make sure that you go someplace where you can *be*. Or at least know what you're getting yourself into."

"Shhh," said Willie. "No place is perfect, but right now, any big city is better than this. Look at the way that woman curling her nose up at Mama Peaches. And they wanna talk about love and baby Jesus and being *Christian* when they being anything BUT."

Buster looked back at the woman in pink, who leaned into another next to her.

"They can't all be hateful where it's bigger," he muttered.

"Not everybody, Wils, just the loud ones," Shayla nodded toward the back of the church. Both Willie and Buster turned to see an elderly couple stop next to Peaches. They watched her turn and put her hands up and jump up, standing almost twice as tall as the two. She hugged the woman, who kissed Peaches's cheek. Peaches looked like she would snap the man's spine like a pretzel as she gave him a bear hug. He shuffled, smiled, then winced in pain as Peaches quickly put him down and covered her mouth in apology.

A nearby churchgoer softened as the elderly woman introduced Peaches to her. Stella and Lucy simply stared in amazement, as Shayla added, "See, not everybody hates."

Exactly what I told Jasper, thought Buster.

Willie grunted. "Still, I wanna get outta here. Maybe me an, I mean, Carlos and I should go to New York City together."

"Think his mama gonna let him go audition?" asked

Shayla.

Buster felt cold.

"As if. They haven't got any money, especially not after a funeral," said Willie.

"But he's got to go!" Buster blurted, louder than he expected, then turned before remembering no one could hear him. He looked back at Peaches, who'd cast a glance his way, but continued chatting with the elderly black couple. "Carlos has to go! He has to!" he pleaded, despite knowing they couldn't hear.

Shayla nodded, "Too bad he isn't eighteen yet, or he could just go."

Willie smiled and nodded. "Ah, but see, that's not far off now, is it?"

"Wait—you right! But without money?"

"I don't have that kinda money," said Willie.

"We gotta think of something," Shayla and Buster said together.

"Maybe Mama Peaches already has something cookin'."

At that moment, a door hinge squawked and quieted the congregation into a murmur, as a line of faces dressed in deep purple robes filed in from a side door and stood in a small area to the left of the pulpit. The door closed behind a shuffle of feet and one beat later, a tambourine snapped. As the metal zils rolled rapidly, the choir hummed softly. Some of the congregation joined.

Buster watched the lady in the pink suit tap her foot. Buster heard a drum stick count off four beats before the choir clapped and stepped, purple robes rippled in rhythm. The hum grew louder and the tambourine rolled lightly. A woman wearing a gold collar that bloomed out of her robe like an oversized flower stepped to the front.

Her eyes closed as she held up her hand. A guitar struck a chord that vibrated every loose board in the wooden church. Buster turned to watch a man in a suit with a long jacket walk to a pulpit and clap in unison with the choir.

"My fellow brothers and my lovely sisters, born of this

friend we have in,"

"JESUS," sang the choir, as the preacher pointed upward.

"Blessed be his name."

And with that, the giant flower of a woman belted out an Amen that took at least ten syllables to finish. Buster felt the boards vibrate under his feet as he scouted a place to sit. The family pews still remained empty, and Buster wasn't sure whether he wanted to be sitting there when the family joined the service.

The zils continued to rattle, and the choir hummed as the preacher covered his heart with his hand.

"Isn't it wonderful to know we have a friend in,"

"JESUS," chimed the choir.

This reminds me of something, Buster thought. The choir turned faces and palms toward the ceiling.

"All your sins and grief to bear," continued the preacher, as he spoke in rhythm to the music. "What a privilege to carry."

"EVERYTHING IN HIM TO PRAYER!" the choir flashed a wave of hands like sunflowers. More hands lifted from the congregation, and a small woman near the front rose and held her palm to the sky.

"Sally!" exclaimed Buster. "Good to see Earl isn't with you."

By now, all attention was on the choir and the preacher, and everyone seemed to have forgotten the white gender-bender in a dress.

A tiny saxophone buzzed brightly and warmed Buster. He spotted a place to the side opposite the choir where he could stand. The voices in purple robes hummed as the Reverend walked toward the congregation, where he met a young woman in a black dress walking down the aisle, clutching the arm of a disheveled man in a work shirt and jeans.

"Is she drunk?" muttered Buster, as he leaned against the wall. The broad reverend almost engulfed the woman as he hugged her.

"Carlos!" Buster bolted back to his feet as he watched the reverend shake the hand of Carlos' father—the disheveled man—who then grabbed the boy's shoulder and brought him forward. A large, squat woman clung to Carlos like static. A small entourage followed.

The Reverend escorted them to the pew marked, "Family" and headed back to the choir as he continued, "Oh, what peace we forfeit, what pain we bear, all because we do NOT,

"CARRY EVERYTHING TO HIM IN PRAYER!"

The saxophone riffed a chord into a solo, and Buster wiped his forehead as he began to sweat heavily.

Damn stuffy in here, he said and rubbed his chest. Hand- held fans flapped against the heat like lazy butterflies. Buster watched an elderly man in sunglasses, facing him from across the church, rock from side to side in tune with the music. A long white cane, grasped tightly between his fingers, laid back on his shoulder.

The preacher and choir faced each other in reverie, and a few congregants rose from their seats to join the choir. The bright saxophone shrilled and Buster massaged his ears. Tears formed in his eyes. He winced. His ghost sweat dripped into nothing as he stood near a woman fanning widely.

Buster looked back at the congregation. The man with the shades, still facing Buster from across the room, stopped swaying. The man with the cane struggled to his feet.

Don't heat up, old man, thought Buster.

"TAKE IT TO THE LORD IN PRAYER!" the choir shouted, and the saxophone buzz continued.

"Whew, I'm woozy," said Buster as he tilted his head back.

The old man raised his hand, but couldn't put his arm above his head.

Is he pointing at me? thought Buster.

A woman near the blind man rose up and placed her

hand on his shoulder. He murmured something. The woman nodded and patted him.

Buster flushed. He now sweat profusely as the choir and saxophone competed with each other for Amens from the pews. He itched tremendously and began scratching under his shirt.

"TAKE IT TO THE LORD IN PRAYER!"

The old man took a step and shouted, "I see!"

The woman next to him smiled and faced the ceiling.

"That's right, my brother, you see the way in Jesus!" smiled the preacher.

"No, you fool! I can see a man over there," and he pointed his white cane directly at Buster, who immediately stopped scratching.

"See?" shouted the old man.

Buster looked at his hands, which flickered twice, then back at the old man. Some of the choir stopped singing and the Reverend looked in Buster's direction, then back to the old man. The band continued softly, and half the choir continued singing while others hummed and looked at each other and the preacher in confusion.

"Ain't nobody there, Brother," said the Reverend. "Are your eyes playing tricks again?"

"Like hell. He's scratching himself."

Buster looked at his hands, which flickered again, then at Peaches, who didn't move. The saxophone riffed into a crescendo and Buster felt dizzy.

I gotta leave, he thought, as he remembered Carlos and the clarinet. Buster stepped away from the wall and headed across the church in the direction of the blind man.

The man turned to follow Buster he passed and paused next to Peaches, who looked more confused than the choir that couldn't decide whether to sing, hum, or stop altogether. People in the congregation seemed distracted and began looking at the choir, then the congregation, then the preacher, then the ushers. Several followed the gaze of the old blind man.

"Noooooooo!" wailed Carlos's mother, Mary, and the music abruptly ended with a muffled cymbal crash.

Buster's wave of nausea quickly passed as he reached the door of the church.

"YOU!" yelled Mary, as she rose from her seat and pointed at Peaches. Buster looked from Mary to Peaches and back.

"Well, hell, now I can't see a damn thing," grumbled the old man as he sat down with the help of the woman next to him, who nodded and patted his shoulder.

Peaches looked around, then pointed at herself. "Me?" she mouthed silently.

Half of the entire church stood in the interrupting pause of the service. Floorboards creaked.

Carlos tried to grab his mother's hand. She flung it away.

"YOU!" Mary yelled again, as she swaggered across the church, still pointing at Peaches. "It's your fault that my Little J is gone!"

Peaches didn't move. Buster watched Carlos's mother stand at the end of the aisle.

"Sister," attempted an usher.

"Don't *sister* me!" she scowled at the man. "You let IT in here!"

Buster heard a gasp and looked back at Peaches, who sat rigid, the color completely drained from her face. Stella reached over and held Peaches's hand.

"No. She didn't," stammered Lucy, as she left her mouth open.

"If my baby hadn't been around the likes of you, then he'd be here today," her voice creaked high as she doubled over and grabbed a pew, trying to approach Peaches.

Buster turned back to Peaches who sat frozen and pale, as if made of wax.

"Jasper?"

Peaches did not respond.

"Well, I never," muttered Stella.

"Sister, ain't nobody's fault here," continued the

Reverend.

"I'M NOT TALKING ABOUT A BURGLAR!" she cried. "*It* already trying to turn my baby Carlos gay," gasped Mary, clutching her chest as she stepped another pew closer. Carlos, bright red, looked at his feet. Shayla and Willie stared in disbelief.

Two men in suits rose and stepped beside Carlos' mother. "Sister Mary, don't make this harder on yourself," said one of the men.

She choked and continued sobbing as she stumbled. The men caught her before she hit the ground.

"I don't want *it* here!" she screamed. "YOU AREN'T WELCOME. Not today!" Her face wretched, and her mouth gaped wide like a scream; yet only soft stifled, staccato cries came forth. "Not today," she whimpered.

Buster looked back at Peaches, who slowly rose from the pew. "Jasper," he said.

"Peaches, baby," said Stella.

Peaches turned quietly and stepped into the aisle. Silently, steady, she walked away from the pulpit toward the doors. She wobbled slightly on one heel as she stepped passed Buster. She paused, then continued quietly into the bright open door. The older couple stood up to follow Peaches.

Stella turned back to Lucy. "Let's go."

Lucy stood up and waved her finger in the air, "Some house of *God* this is!"

Stella grabbed her hand and pulled her into the aisle. "Hush."

Lucy jerked away "You let me be," she stammered, before turning to the congregation and shouting, "All y'all better check your own damn closets afore you cast any stones. Especially you, broth—"

"Come on!" interrupted Stella, pulling Lucy down the aisle.

"And stop staring at me like you want—hey there, sugar!" she flashed a smile before Stella gave her a final yank

251

out the front door, calling for Peaches.

Buster turned and watched the two men with the Reverend help Carlos's mother return to her seat, where Carlos sank his face into his hands. One row over, Shayla and Willie stared at the floor, Willie holding Shayla's hand.

Buster twitched. "Well, I'm not done here, Jasper," he said and walked over to Mary. Buster opened his mouth, then stopped. Buster looked at Carlos, who shook and inched away from his mother. Mary leaned back against the pew with her hand over her heart, legs slightly splayed. Buster leaned over, careful to avoid touching her, and said softly, "I hope one day that someone loves you as much as Peaches loves your kids."

Buster stepped back from Mary, whose eyes opened wide. A beat broke the silence. The Reverend motioned and said, "Go Down, Moses!"

Buster then turned toward the open church doors and ran. He stepped into a brightly lit haze. As he crossed the church lawn for Peaches's car, the glare grew until he found himself lost in a thick, bright fog.

*****

The house folded into its own shadow under a midday sun. Even for Mississippi, the fall day was hot. The earth sank like an overcooked casserole, brown and deflated. The metal skin of the car in the drive popped lightly from the heat.

Buster stood on the porch of #3 Raspberry Lane that seemed less asleep and more closed off from the world.

"Jasper?" he called.

Not even a cricket chirped.

The window unit groaned and rattled as it woke.

Buster knocked on the door. It rapped back with an echo, but the house didn't move.

He closed his eyes and pictured the empty living room, dark and cool. He inhaled deeply and tasted Aqua Net on

252

his tongue. Buster opened his eyes and saw himself standing in more shadows inside Peaches's quiet hallway, his existence less and less bound by challenging rules. The window unit hummed in the living room.

"Jasper? Is that you?" Buster heard a sniffle. A faint heartbeat beckoned him to the kitchen. "I know you'se here." There was no response. "I stopped by to check on you."

Go away, he heard. Not a whisper, but a thought. Clear and direct and, if thoughts had tones, unwavering in self-defeat.

Buster followed the echo of the thought to the end of the hallway, and turned into Peaches's kitchen. In the dark, at her table, Peaches faced a bottle of whiskey and a full glass of bourbon in the middle of the table.

"Thought you didn't drink," said Buster.

Peaches looked up from the glass to Buster, then back. "I haven't in eight years and four months and five days. I thought I would sit here awhile first."

"Why?"

Peaches shrugged.

Buster approached the table. "Did you bring the funeral here? Cause you hadn't been this gloomy since I met you."

"Are you even real?" asked Peaches.

"What in the hell kinda question is that?" Buster responded.

"For all I know, I've been talking to myself all these weeks and months," said Peaches, as she stared at the bourbon.

"You gonna let me sit, or am I gonna have to stand here?"

Peaches pushed a chair away from the table with a foot.

Buster sat. "I don't know what *real* means to you, Jasper. But you ain't been this way since I met you. This ain't you."

"Do you know me, Buster?" Peaches looked at him.

Buster sat back.

She continued. "You show up in my life,

253

unannounced. I don't know why, really. My guilt? But you weren't there when Li'l J needed you."

"I was here, Jasper. You seem to forget that I have a few challenges, being a ghost and all."

Peaches said nothing.

Buster shook his head. "So, it's my fault?"

"No."

"Then what are you talking about?"

She sighed. "Never mind," she answered, moving her left hand from her lap to the table. Buster saw her fingers tremble. A heartbeat quickened in the dark kitchen.

"You thinking about drinking?" asked Buster.

"*What the hell does it look like?*" Peaches both thought and said in two distinct voices, one angry and another afraid.

Buster shrugged his shoulders. "Dunno. Thought you said there wasn't enough to make you happy."

Peaches didn't move. "When did I say that?"

"At that bar you took me to. Where you work." Buster could hear Peaches breathe in, then exhale.

The air conditioner wheezed and grumbled from the living room as it turned on.

Buster heard the drip, drop, and drip from a faucet. He turned to look at the sink, full of dishes.

"So, how long you gonna stare at the whiskey?"

"Not long enough." Peaches then picked up her left hand and pulled the glass closer to the edge of the table. A ring of sweat outlined where her hand had been.

"You talk like it's gonna be bad," said Buster. "So, why you doin' it?"

"You wouldn't understand," said Peaches, caressing the glass as if handling fine crystal.

"Why? Cause I ain't gay? Cause I ain't lost a friend? Cause I ain't been called a bad name before?"

Peaches looked at Buster. "No. You wouldn't understand cause I hadn't stopped thinkin' about this bottle since I walked out of that hospital, wondering how the hell I could be so careless."

"So this ain't just about the church."

"It's about everything, Buster. The hospital. Li'l J. Li'l J getting hurt HERE in MY HOUSE. The church. That rich school that won't help Carlos get to New York City so he can audition. About Clover. About that crooked professor who murdered Mike, and now Li'l J, and I can't prove it without sounding like a complete nutcase. About me seeing you and not knowing why the fuck I gotta ghost running around me like I'm some kinda voodoo woman, and whether or not I've really just lost my mind because I didn't stand up for a black kid on the playground when I was gettin' bullied for being queer."

"So, how that bottle gonna fix it? Seem like to me you going to the problem and not the solution."

"Oh my god. You are not gonna quote me and think that proves anything. You. Don't. Exist. You just a bad acid trip that manifested my guilt for something I did a long, long time ago."

"If I don't exist, then why am I here?"

"I don't know, so why don't you *git*?"

Buster tensed in anticipation. Nothing happened.

He lifted his hands, which had instinctively gripped the edge of the table, and turned them over to look at them. He looked at Peaches, who stared back.

"You must not really want me to go," he muttered.

"Why?" said Peaches, trying to look unsurprised.

"Cause I'm still here. You didn't cast me out of your house."

"Go find someone else to spook," said Peaches. She looked at the glass and reached for it.

Without pausing, Buster stood from the chair, shoving it back and over. The metal frame smacked the linoleum floor as Buster's arm swept across the table, knocking the glass from Peaches's hand and sending it—and the bottle— from the table through the air and firmly into the cabinets by the kitchen door. The sharp clink of glass was followed by the smell of rotten apples and maple syrup. Buster looked

255

from the bottle, cracked in half on the floor, to Peaches, who looked from the empty table to Buster while massaging her hand.

Neither spoke as they turned from a locked gaze to the table to the now booze-soaked cabinets.

"You. You just—"

"Yeah, I did," said Buster, as he looked at the puddle of bourbon on the floor.

"Maybe you are..."

Neither spoke as the kitchen clock ticked off eighteen seconds.

"I gotta make a call," blurted Peaches.

Buster looked at her. "To who?"

"My spon...doesn't matter. Don't go nowhere," and she shuffled quickly out of the room.

Buster looked at the brown puddle as it collected in grooves in the tile, drawing a grid across the floor. Buster reached for a dishrag on the counter, but couldn't pick it up.

"Great. Back to square one," he said, as he heard a voice in another room.

Buster followed the voice to the sewing room. Peaches sat at the machine with her back to the door, telephone perched between her shoulder and her ear, tissue in another hand. "Show me how to live," she muttered.

Buster wanted to step into the room, but he couldn't. As he approached the open door, his arms and legs became lethargic, unable to move forward, just like when he'd first been cast from the house, except this was limited to Peaches's bedroom. He'd never seen nor heard Peaches cry until Jerome was killed. And now. Who was she talking to? And why?

Buster stepped back and headed for the empty living room. The air conditioner groaned off. As it sputtered, the front window rattled as if the entire house ached with great pain. He stood at the front window and touched a shaking pane with his finger. A faint tickle fluttered in his hand as the pane stopped moving and the air conditioner fell silent.

A few hairs pricked on his arm, and he removed his finger. A print marked the spot where he'd touched the glass. *Am I real?* He asked himself.

"Boo?"

Buster turned. "You okay?"

"Thank you," said Peaches as she stood in the hallway.

"For what?"

"The bottle. Everything else." Her hands folded together, holding a tissue. "Why'd you do it?"

He shrugged his shoulders. "Dunno. You got my goat. Didn't want to hear you whine no more."

Peaches nodded. "Okay," she muttered.

"Jasper, you gotta a bunch of kids who look up to you. I don't know if I ever had that. But they need you right now."

Peaches nodded.

"So, that's it?" said Buster.

"You right, boo. That's all I can say right now."

"Who were you callin'?"

"Somebody who helps me."

"When you want a drink?" asked Buster.

"Yeah," said Peaches. "Cause there'd be another that follows it if I started." She walked into the room and stood next to Buster. "So, I called somebody and that made me want to thank you. I'd hug you if I could."

"Nah, it's nothing."

"To you, it's nothing. To me it's what—" she bit her lower lip and continued, "it's just what I needed."

"Sorry I made a mess. I can't mop it up—lost my Midas touch, I guess."

"Don't matter. I'll get it later."

"You got your keys—goin' somewhere?" he asked.

"The church—"

"No, Jasper—don't go back there," said Buster.

Peaches smiled. "You're sweet. I'm not going to that one. Different church. I'm meetin' some people. But you can stay heah if you want to. I'll be back in about an hour or so."

A car honked somewhere outside.

"Don't have much else place to go," he finally added.

"You ain't seen your sister again?"

Buster shook his head. "Wake up and I'm not there. Kinda have trouble remembering how to get back."

"The amnesia?" she asked.

"I guess."

"Maybe it's not amnesia."

"How's that?"

"Just a hunch," she said, as she looked down and smoothed out her skirt. "If Sally really left Earl, not sure what else you can do for her."

"But I'm still here, so—"

"So ya are. Well, don't tear up ma house while I'm out. Be back in a bit." Peaches headed for the door.

"Jasper?"

"Yeah, shuga?"

"How's Carlos?"

Peaches closed her eyes briefly, like a yawn, but without. 'He's alright, Buster. Mopey as usual. But he'll pull through, I think."

"He know it ain't his fault, right?"

"Yeah, he does. Somewhere. He just too young for that kinda pain, so he'll just be angry at the world and shoot arrows real high for awhile. Hopefully none of 'em will land on anyone. Unless it's me aiming at Mr. Harvard."

"Not your fault either," Buster added. "Carlos is gonna, well, he's gonna be alright."

Peaches breathed, then smiled. "See you later, Buster."

CHAPTER TWENTY-TWO

Buster had never really known what he was *supposed* to feel like as a ghost. But something had changed. If he could describe it, he felt like a constipated sneeze: contained, looking for escape, building and on the verge of pain.

He hadn't seen Peaches since the day he'd knocked the glass from her hand, and this pain only grew. After that, Buster obsessed over finding Tinsley. Yet, he struggled finding the farms or the secret shed.

The longer he wandered, the more the pain grew. It started low, not a tickle, but not quite an itch, either. Eventually, it festered beyond the sharp throb of a bee sting to humming and buzzing, as if electrified into a ball of glass and fuzz. His hands flickered like an eye twitch. After hours, maybe days, of following shadows and echoes, he stopped. The bad dream had lifted like a forty-ounce hangover, leaving him with a foul, stale taste. If he had breath, it surely smelled rotten.

The haze dissipated, and Buster realized the metal shed stood twenty feet in front of him. He did not care that he couldn't piece together how he found it; rather, he savored the satisfaction of discovery. Buster walked toward the dark green Range Rover parked in front. He passed the car and noticed a foggy shimmer in the windows like a flash of light. Buster faced the sky and saw a whitewash haze covering the sun as a cloud moved in from the west.

Buster reached for the doorknob and turned.

Nothing.

Buster balled his fist and hit the door with the bottom of his hand. A dull, throbbing pain and a sound that went nowhere.

"If a ghost hears a tree falling in the woods, then God laughs," Buster grumbled.

He clenched both fists until beads of ghost sweat

formed. He pounded as if in a boxing match. The latch turned. Stunned, Buster froze with fists in the air. Professor Tinsley peered from the dark interior behind the door and looked from left to right and back.

Now! thought Buster, as he closed his eyes and ran through the man connected with Buster's existence as a ghost.

Tinsley screamed into a phone, "I will have a product to deliver!"

Buster steadied himself on a table as the door latched behind him. The cool, dark lab helped him tolerate the nausea.

Tinsley turned back after locking the door and paced frantically in front of a table of aquariums. The radio played softly in the background.

"Fuck!" Tinsley yelled as he scratched his head. "Where the fuck did that faggot hide my notebook?" he mumbled.

"Who you callin' names, you sonofabitch?" asked Buster, as he sturdied his legs.

The drone of an air conditioner sputtered between the sounds of classical music.

Buster looked at Tinsley, who faced the wall of maps.

"What the hell did that little boy do to you?" Buster wiped his forehead. Buster's knee quivered. No longer five years old hiding in his Nana's broom closet, no longer trembling because two drunk Klansmen stormed his house, Buster shook with the urgency of a runner heading for the bend of a race.

"I'm talking to you, you low-cotton piece of trash!" Buster yelled as he walked over to Tinsley, who stood rigid. The radio station played clear over the drone of a fan. Buster stood at the Professor's shoulder, whose color had drained.

Buster leaned to whisper into Tinsley's ear. "Can you hear me? *Boy?*"

The professor's eye twitched between shallow breaths.

"ANSWER ME!" Buster yelled.

Tinsley turned and looked at the wall behind Buster. "Wh-who are you?" he stuttered.

Buster stepped back, then blinked at the radio as the music played.

Tinsley backed away toward his desk, with a hand massaging his temple. "I-I- don't- don't. Where are you?" Tinsley then glanced under the lab table, behind the aquariums.

"I'm here," Buster said hoarsely, uncertain. *Am I dreaming?*

"Where?"

Buster waved his hand directly in front of Tinsley.

Tinsley exhaled deep and the color began to return. "Fuck. I'm talking to myself. I gotta get some sleep."

"Side effect of what you cooking in your lab, Mr. Harvard?" asked Buster.

"Good grief, I'm hearing voices. I've really snapped," said Tinsley, as he walked over to his desk and took two pills from a bottle.

"You hadn't snapped yet. But I might just have to do that myself if you don't answer me. Buster Sparkle will make your lily-white ass somebody's prison bitch if you don't—"

The professor stopped and spit water out. "Who?" he muttered.

Buster didn't speak.

"What's that name again?" Tinsley asked himself.

"Buster Sparkle."

Tinsley exhaled a laugh that could skin a snake. "Holy fuck, I need a break. Now I'm talking *aloud* to that black plumber who swiped my notebook at the lab."

Buster didn't move.

Tinsley shook his head and smiled. "Great test case. I couldn't risk that foolish man reading my notes anyway. They all thought it was a heart attack, probably from fried chicken and gizzards, instead of my poison," Tinsley took a swig from a glass on his desk. "Now I gotta finish backing up these files so I don't have more notebooks for prying fingers." He removed a thumb drive from the computer and inserted another.

The radio popped with static, and a saxophone played. Tinsley turned up the volume.

Buster flickered with a burning pain. *The black notebook?* The word charged through him like the snap of a wooden bat meeting a fast pitch over home plate.

I drank poison. He repeated, as the ball flew high and out of the park to a silent stadium. He put his hand over his chest and felt the burn spread from his heart into his throat. *Tinsley killed me. At the university farms.* He thought.

Buster then saw himself alone in an old house in the country, keeping company from the world. The burn continued from his throat back down his spine as he felt his heart stop once again, and he slumped over the steering wheel of his truck at the farms. Professor Tinsley looked left and right over his shoulders again at the quiet lot, and reached into the open window to remove a half-empty water bottle and a black notebook from Buster's hands.

That's the notebook Jasper has, thought Buster.

"So did you write down in your notebook what you did to Mike?" asked Buster. "What about Li'l J? Did killing an eight-year-old prove anything?"

Tinsley took two more pills. "I am not about to let a little misplaced guilt about a plumber, a druggie, and a little rodent affect my work. This was something far bigger than three nobodies."

Buster fumed. The burning electrified and he buzzed. The sound of a heartbeat throbbed and his eyes watered. *That's not Tinsley's heartbeat,* he realized. Buster felt raw. Chaffed. Exposed like a blister in the sun.

This time, Tinsley and Buster made eye contact. Tinsley swaggered from his chair and glared at Buster like a startled deer.

"We done, you an' me," said Buster as he charged Tinsley, who just stood there, in utter disbelief that Buster had manifested beyond a hallucination.

The two connected. Buster's hands grabbed the professor's shirt like loose skin. As the feeling of tangibility, weight, and resistance fueled his anger, Buster shoved as hard as he could. His fingers seared as he squeezed onto flesh for the first time that he could remember.

Remember. Memories. A flood coursed through Buster as he held onto Tinsley for a moment as fireworks of images exploded to light a dark sky. Buster holding a small black notebook that he'd accidentally mistaken for his facilities workbook. Diagrams and drawings that he didn't understand, but something he knew he'd picked up from the lab that wasn't his.

Buster and Tinsley slammed into the desk, knocking papers as the computer monitor slid to the end. Tinsley pushed Buster off and turned to the side to grab a chair. Dazed with the new heaviness, Buster shook his head.

Buster stared out his truck window at a very jittery Art Tinsley, who knocked at Buster's window as if he needed to crack the shell of an egg. Buster looked back at the notebook and remembered seeing something that looked like maps and instructions. He rolled down his window.

"I'm sorry mister, I thought—"

Professor Tinsley held out his hand as the glass lowered.

"I didn't mean to pick up yours—I thought it was my workbook for the physical plant's jobs."

"Here. This is yours." Tinsley handed Buster another small notebook as the two traded.

"Thanks, Professor. Won't get the rest of my jobs done this week without this—"

Tinsley swiftly pulled his small notebook into his hands and thumbed through the pages of graphs and notes and markings and charts, and looked back at Buster.

Buster felt a smack on his back as a chair made contact. He fell to the ground and scrambled to the other side of the lab table, opposite of Tinsley.

"You look like you seen a ghost, Professor Harvard," Buster groaned as he stumbled to his hands and then his feet. His balance felt almost reversed.

Tinsley stared, holding a chair firmly in his hands.

263

"Gonna be kinda hard to kill me given that I'm already dead," snarled Buster.

Tinsley looked at the chair and threw it down, and looked on the table for something to grab.

"Get the fuck away from me, you...freak," sputtered Tinsley, as he grabbed a beaker of liquid and threw it at Buster.

The glass shattered, spraying its contents across the table and on Buster. The smell of alcohol burned as Buster put his hands up to wipe his face.

Buster looked at his notebook, then saw the Professor inspect his own, as if counting money. "Don't worry, Professor, I didn't take nothing. Knew it wasn't mine when I saw all them pictures."

Tinsley's eyes glowered as he grabbed a book, a beaker, anything within arms' reach of Buster.

Buster heard a faint thump and felt warmth as a burner flared on. A trail of alcohol on the lab table ignited, spilling to the floor with a cloud of flame, before burning low.

Buster stepped away before the flames reached him and he charged the Professor.

"Why?" spit Buster as he pushed the Professor against a table.

"What are you doing, spreading ants so you can then sell a fancy poison?" Buster laughed.

Tinsley stopped and looked at Buster, ashen.

"Why did you steal my notebook?" growled Tinsley as he tried to push Buster off.

"I didn't!"

"Don't play dumb with me, plumber. You couldn't just leave well enough alone, could you? Swiping something that wasn't yours? Bet you thought you could bribe me with it, didn't you?"

"What the hell are you talking about?"

"Well, I took care of you, although not as clean as I did a drug addict that nobody would miss.

"Why Li'l J?" Buster pushed back as he grabbed Tinsley

by his neck and pushed back.

Professor swung back, sending Buster into the lab table, knocking it to the ground, glass and flames spreading to the papers now on the floor. "Li'l J is just a casualty of something bigger than his tiny, little life."

Buster landed a punch.

The professor fought back.

"What's bigger?" said Buster. "Your girl? Think your Mary Jane's gonna look up to her daddy when she finds out he's crook and a murderer?"

"Finds out what?" smirked Tinsley, as he kneed Buster in the chest. "Can't point a finger at something you can't find."

Buster grabbed Tinsley by the throat and pulled him to the ground. "What the hell are you talking about?"

"Nobody knew it was poison that killed you."

"Thought you was making fire ant poison?"

Tinsley laughed. "Sure. That's what makes patents, Irish bank accounts, and department heads. But it also can give one mean heart attack. Fortunately for me, no one in Mississippi cared enough about a poor, black plumber to request a toxicology report. Just plain, ol' fashioned heart failure."

The two locked each other and rolled across the lab floor. The fire from the lab table consumed, the flames now burning papers scattered on the floor and on Tinsley's desk.

"Sorry to be short, I've got a grant deadline, and it's a lot of money," said Tinsley, as he handed Buster a bottle of water through the truck window.

Buster held his palm up and he tilted the bottle back. He paused and wiped his mouth, "No problem, brother. Thank you."

Tinsley looked down, then across the empty gravel lot, then back at Buster. "Where you headed next?"

"Across campus. Got a dorm with a leak." Buster finished the bottle. "Thanks, thisheet cake..." he wiped sweat from his forehead. He stretched his mouth, feeling a swollen

tongue roll like a mouth full of gum. He coughed up phlegm and glanced at Tinsley. "Solly..." he felt hot. The words he spoke didn't form accurately.

Tinsley eyed Buster as if inspecting a row of cotton.

"I fear furry..." Buster slurred as a burn rose quickly up his throat and into his nose. He gurgled water back up. The tips of his fingers felt numb. He fumbled for the truck door as he looked up at Tinsley, leaning against the door with his weight on both hands. Tinsley's head tilted, looking curious and inquisitive.

Buster's skin pricked like he'd been stung by a hundred wasps as he leaned out the open window, clear liquid sputtering from his nose and mouth. The smell of fertilizer and burnt matches filled the cab as he grabbed his chest. His heart pounded erratically and then simply stopped.

Buster folded onto the steering wheel, facing a silent, observant Art Tinsley, Professor of Entomology and Toxicology.

"So why you doin' this, for you?"

"Cause I can. Breed an ant that I know how to kill cause I built the poison that just so happens to have a nasty side effect on plumbers. Plus, the money's pretty good when you hedge the black market. Fortunately, the US military isn't the only buyer, and it's not hard to sell down in Mexico. Release a few ants here and there and soon, everyone will need it. But a dead plumber or drug addict wouldn't be able to talk about that sorta thing." Tinsley rolled on top of Buster and pinned him to the ground.

Buster felt dizzy as the professor cut off his air—his real air—supply.

"Well, ain't that a shame? Maybe you're just a cat, cause it seems like I can hurt you again," said Tinsley as he squeezed. "I'll take every fucking life you have. When I'm done, I head over to your fairy friend to get my notebook back."

Lights sparkled in Buster's eyes and the flames swirled in blurry vision, and he couldn't breathe. He turned to see a fire now growing on Tinsley's desk from the papers that spilled to the floor.

"Hope you saved them disks," whispered Buster.

Tinsley turned to his desk, now engulfed. "No!" He jumped up and ran toward the fire.

Buster coughed and grabbed his throat. The professor scrambled to reach the desk, shoving the burning pile of papers to the floor, scattering them. He reached for his computer and removed a thumb drive. He pulled the small, black object from the computer right as it popped with a green light. A trail of blue smoke curled like a beanstalk above the desk. Buster scrambled to his feet and charged him, knocking the drive from his hand. They both turned and watched it hit the leg of the lab table and land in a wet patch of cement by the aquarium tables. Smoke now filled the lab and the radio sparked.

"You are not gonna ruin my work!" said Tinsley, as he broke free from Buster's grasp and ran for the disk as flames reached the pool of alcohol.

Buster rushed the professor, knocking him off-balance. The two of them smacked against another lab table opposite from the professor's desk and hit the floor. A loud crack was followed by the sound of glass hitting the floor.

"Oh, God," muttered the professor. His grip quivered and blood trickled from his temple.

Buster released Tinsley and reached for the disk. His hand flickered and he had to pick it up again. He dropped it in a puddle, where blue and green flames curled around it.

"No! No!" Tinsley shouted, as he tried to hold up a long table that leaned precariously on a broken leg. A cracked aquarium followed by three others had slid for the sloped edge. Tinsley, still on his knees, strained to lift the heavy end of the table. The cracked aquarium slid further onto the professor, and the broken glass split like a bag of potato chips.

"NO!" screamed Tinsley as he shook a hand free from the table. "Off!" Tinsley brushed himself fiercely as he let go of the table corner, sending the cracked aquarium to the floor, spilling its contents at his feet.

"Ow!" the professor twisted and jerked.

Buster stepped back.

Tinsley struggled to stand and jerked again, bumping into the table, which tipped over. Two more aquariums slid into his knees, then onto the floor and cracked open.

"No! No!" he looked at Buster in panic.

Buster flickered once as the fire grew, drowning out the radio, and watched, uncertain of what to do.

"Fuck!" yelled the professor as he stripped off his pants, hitting himself where ants now crawled and bit. He fell to the floor in the dirt and broken glass, cutting himself. The professor vomited. Welts the size of golf balls began to show. Buster felt nauseous, and his hands flickered again.

Tinsley kicked as if he'd fallen on hot grease. He writhed as thousands of ants covered the floor. Half-naked, covered in dirt and blood and ants, the professor pulled himself up a lab table for support.

"Help me," he sputtered, covered in red and pink blotches, as he coughed up phlegm. Covered in crawling red and black dots, the professor's nose bled.

Buster felt light. His hands flickered again as the radio popped in and out as the flames grew. *I don't have much time*, he thought as he debated. At that moment, Buster pictured Li'l J, crushed under the bookcase in Peaches' house, asking Mary Jane's dad for help.

He shook his head and gave Tinsley one last look, "I'll help you like you helped Li'l J. Being dead hasn't been so bad—you get used to the loneliness."

Buster turned his back on the professor as flames engulfed the lab. He closed his eyes and thought of nothing other than Peaches and her group of nuggets on movie night. In a flicker, he stood in Peaches's kitchen. Peaches dropped her coffee mug on the floor.

Buster remembered one thing and blurted, "The notebook!"

CHAPTER TWENTY-THREE

"Shayla, baby, you gonna put the music on? Time to start this Honey Ball Pageant, in honor of Li'l J!"

"Yes, mama, hold on!"

"Lord, I hope it has a beat other than *boom-ch, boom-ch, boom-ch*," muttered Lucy.

Shayla rolled her eyes. "As if—"

"Miss Lucy, this a Vogue Ball, not a white boy circuit party!" said Willie as he stretched his shoulder.

"Would be if Carlos picked the music," muttered Shayla.

"Truth," said Willie, giving a fist bump.

Carlos elbowed him.

Willie elbowed back. "C'mon son, it's all good! Whatcha gotta be that way for?"

"Carlos, you gonna walk the floor?"

"Course he is!" said Willie.

Carlos nodded.

"What you gonna be, baby doll?" asked Lucy.

"Symphonic Realness," said Carlos.

Lucy turned and stared at Stella.

Stella ignored her, "You own that realness, sweetie!"

The stereo kicked on with a static hiss, followed by a boom. Stella covered her ears, and Buster felt dizzy.

"Don't break ma windas, Shay-shay!" shouted Peaches from the kitchen.

"Gonna be real when he get to Julliard! Just you wait an see!" shouted Willie.

"If—"

"When—" shouted Shayla and Willie together as the volume dropped.

Lucy and Stella's heads jerked up together like they'd been pulled by a string, and Mama Peaches walked into the room.

"Whatever. Go ahead and tell 'em, Mama." Carlos said, as if asking a parent to break the family secret about Santa.

"Tell 'em what, sugar?" asked Peaches.

Stella and Lucy rose and walked over behind Carlos.

"I can't go," said Carlos. "I can't afford to go to Julliard for an audition, which means I won't get a chance to go."

Willie squeezed a word through a fake cough.

Shayla punched him, "Rude!"

He shrugged.

"Carlos, you eighteen, right?"

"Yes, Mama," he said, somewhat disarmed, "but what's that got to do with—"

"Sugar, who says *you* got to pay?" asked Stella.

Carlos looked at Stella, "What are you talking about? Of course I got to pay for it. The school won't."

"Oh, would somebody please hurry the hell up?" groaned Lucy.

Everyone looked at her.

"There's always one," muttered Stella.

"Jasper, what are you cookin' up your sleeve?" asked Buster.

Peaches knelt with a soft grunt. "If you could go, would you?"

Carlos stepped back. "Why—but I can't."

"Boy, is that child dense!" said Lucy. "Ow!" she exclaimed.

"I'll do it again if you don't shush," said Stella.

Peaches sighed, "Boo, you keep that negative thinking up, and life is gonna pass right by you." She eyed Buster, then pulled an envelope out of a pocket and handed it to Carlos. "Happy birthday, Carlos."

Carlos stared at the green paper.

"Well, open it, silly!" said Shayla.

Carlos gently fingered the flap, then ripped it open and held the card in front of him. He waited, and then looked at Peaches, and everyone who stood beaming behind her. Then, he opened the card.

Buster saw a slow smile start, then shoot across his face like a bottle rocket.

"Honey, it's a plane ticket with a little bit of cash to get you through the trip."

Carlos looked down, then up, then down, then up.

"Oh, and a number and an address of one of my friends who will let you stay on her couch so you can audition. She lives on the West Side with two dancers, not far from the school."

"Lord that boy been struck mute—ow! Stop hitting me!" exclaimed Lucy, as Peaches popped the back of her head.

Carlos started jumping on his toes.

"That boy hadn't smiled since I met him," said Buster.

Carlos shouted "Thank you, thank you! Holy shit, thank you!"

"Easy," said Peaches as Carlos hugged her. "It's not just me, boo, but we all pitched in. Oscar at the bar passed a tip jar one night, and—"

"Oh my God, this is bitchin'!" shouted Carlos, as he ran circles hugging and giving high fives.

"You welcome, sugar—"

"Go show 'em how it's done—"

"We gonna come visit."

Shayla extended a fist, "Hell yeah, it's bitchin'. You gonna go if I have to throw you on that plane myself."

"And Li'l J helped, too," Stella said, with an inhale as if jumping into a cold pool.

Carlos stopped. "What?"

"That's right," said Peaches. "Li'l J helped, too."

"How?" asked Carlos. "How'd he get money?"

"Chores," said Peaches.

"You paid him?" Carlos asked.

"He helped us," said Stella.

"But—"

"But nothing, Mary!" yelled Lucy. "He begged and pleaded for us to give him somethin' to do, cause he wanted

271

his big brother to go to that school in New York City and play his clarinet. So he came by it honestly and his heart was into it. So, you get your ASS on that fucking plane and NAIL that fucking audition and leave this little hellhole called Clover that we LOVE so dearly, and show that school what gifts God gave a poor, gay, black boy from Mississippi."

Peaches, Stella, Willie, Shayla, and Buster all stared at Lucy, who clacked her tongue and crossed her arms.

No one said a word.

Lucy scanned the room. "Well, are we gonna walk the floor or jus stand and stare like a bunch a mute, white people at a gospel church? Shayla, cut the music back on!"

*****

"Is this gonna work?" asked Buster.

"Buster, you hadn't caught a damn thing since you died. I got you to a gay bar, now you got me to go fishing. We are gonna do this."

Buster shook his head. "Fine."

Peaches barked, "Just try it." She began to sing softly, "*Ooh it's alright, and it's coming.*"

Peaches lowered the cane pole into the pond, near a lily pad.

The two sat on the edge of a forgotten dock and watched the still water, listening to the cool fall breeze in the tops of the trees.

"Seems like that professor's notebook was the X that marked the spot for the police," said Buster.

"Hell, boo, more than that—the feds got involved. They sayin' now some heads is gonna roll at the college because no one was checking up on him," said Peaches.

"He had a daughter, didn't he?" asked Buster. "I kept seeing a teenager when he possessed me."

Peaches nodded. "And a wife. Heard they keepin' to themselves. Someone said Mrs. Tinsley is homeschooling their daughter until the end of the school year. It's all everybody's talking about—the town, the college, the students."

"They never gonna figure out he killed Mike or Li'l J or me, are they?"

Peaches looked at him. "I'm sorry, boo, I don't think so. But seems like he died in the worse possible way somebody like him should. Did you see—well, I haven't asked it and don't know why I should."

"We fought at that shed. I was so angry after the funeral and it was all I could think about. He had on the radio and I was mad as the devil, and then it just happened. He could hear me, then he could see me. He was takin stuff off the computer cause you had that notebook. I might have been able to help him—I don't know, cause I was gettin' invisible again after it caught on fire. Might be somethin' I'll have to answer for later, but at this point, can't change it," Buster stopped. "I feel mostly for Carlos and Li'l J, but I guess people knowing what happened won't bring Li'l J back."

Peaches sighed. "No, it won't. But you stopped him, and that counts, even if people don't know the whole story. They now trying to figure out where all he dumped ants. The farmers in the Delta are getting real fidgety. Some legislators are threatening to cut some of the school's funding. Too bad you didn't meet a ghost ant and you could round up all them critters, too."

"Think my detective days are done," said Buster.

"You did good, Buster Sparkle."

The yellow and orange float bobbed ever-so-gently on the cool surface of the pond.

"Keep your eye on the..."

"Shhh! I know how to fish," she whispered without looking at him.

"Right."

"Shush afore I send you off this dock." She picked up the tune again, "*Do you remember that day-*"

Buster smirked. "This dock ain't yours—you can't cast

me off it."

Peaches smacked her lips. "Mmmm-huh. Just another straight ghost tryin' to keep a girl down."

Flop!

They froze as a large fish jumped, making an arc four feet in the air over from the float.

Neither spoke, and they waited in unison for a fish to take the bait.

A tree frog sang in the distance as the late November sun cooled below the tree line.

"Nothing like late fall in Mississippi to feel human again," said Peaches.

"Jasper?"

"Yeah, Buster?"

"I ain't. Well-" Buster stopped. "*Peaches*, maybe I've never been much of a friend to anybody. I'm we met."

"Ho, baby, that just killed you to say it, din't it?"

"That we're friends?"

"Ha! You know damn well what I mean." She smiled and hummed, *"Love is good, love is strong, we gotta get right back to where we started from."*

"Guess I should call you by the name you like. I'm just sayin' thank you."

"You're mighty welcome, Buster." She paused, then said, "I am really sorry about that day in the school yard. For what I did. For what those kids did. For what our parents did. A lot of us did wrong even when we didn't know it."

"You been like a—well, I guess 'brother' isn't the right word."

"Baby steps, boo."

"I'm sorry people treat you like they do. I wasn't even a brother to Sally until I was dead," said Buster.

"I should have done different that day. It bothered me a long time. But I did different this time. Not sure we can do nothin' bout people that don't like us. 'Cept pray for 'em, as my momma would say."

Buster didn't answer. The edge of a cloud passed and a

faint breeze rippled the water.

"Buster!" Peaches squealed as the float disappeared below the surface of the water.

"Buster, a fish!" she whispered.

The end of the cane pole nearly hit the water as Peaches jerked slightly and leaned back. The float remained under water. "Here, put your hands in mine and see if you can feel it fighting!"

A few moments later, the trees rustled.

The line darted in circles as she leaned back. "Whoo, Lordy, this fellow is putting up a fight!"

The breeze picked up strength and the trees around the pond swayed slightly.

"Buster, I think I got him!" said Peaches as the line circled near the dock. "C'mon now, put your hands by mine and try to take the pole. Sun just went behind them trees, so you in the shade now. I'll keep humming so there's music to help you." Peaches worked the cane pole back to bring the line in closer.

Leaves fluttered and fell to the water.

"Oh, that breeze feels good," Peaches focused on the cane pole as she hummed her melody.

Her thick fingers wrapped around the pole like rope. She slowly leaned toward Buster while watching the line zip through the water like a moth dancing around a light.

"Seriously, Buster, take this. Put your hand right where mine is."

No response.

"Buster?" Peaches turned. She sat alone on the dock.

"Where'd the hell you go?" The fish jerked. Peaches immediately turned and snapped the rod back. A rather large perch held onto the end of the line.

"Ooowee, look at that rainbow on his belly. Almost like glitter."

Peaches lifted the rod until she could reach the fish. She carefully grasped the perch from the head down as it flexed its spiny fins.

Peaches looked around. "Come on, Buster, get back here quick."

A leaf grazed her hand. It tickled as she shook it away, only to realize that a monarch flew in jerky circles just two feet in front of her. It struggled against the breeze, fluttering to a landing on the cane pole that now rested in Peaches's lap. It slowly opened and closed its wings twice, facing her.

"Well look at you, pretty fella. Where's my friend?"

The fish flopped, and a splash marked where the perch fell to freedom. "Damn things. I don't like to clean 'em anyhow."

The butterfly opened and closed its wings, remaining on the pole that slightly trembled.

Peaches eyed the butterfly.

The butterfly opened and closed its wings again.

"Shoo."

The butterfly's wings opened and closed twice.

Peaches looked around the pond, then askance at the butterfly. It flew from the pole as another fish flopped. It circled Peaches's head twice before the breeze brought a flapping cluster of yellow leaves.

Peaches bit her lip. "Boo, I think you passed," she whispered and exhaled a quick breath. "Take care of Li'l J out there. Give him a hug from Mama Peaches." She wiped her cheek and breathed deep before continuing to sing, "*Oh, and it's alright and it's coming 'long... we've gotta get right back to where we started from.*"

Leaves flocked like birds as the butterfly disappeared into the cluster. Treetops swayed in the early dusk.

"*Love is good, love can be strong...*" Peaches watched the leaves swirl in an updraft to join another cluster passing in the wind overhead. She rocked, back alone on the dock, as the leaves swept past the tree line, and sang, "*A love like ours can never fade away, you know it's only just begun.*"

<<<<>>>>

EPILOGUE

Peaches knelt on her blanket covering the cold red clay, and pulled a withered weed.

"You'd think a dead man wouldn't be so hard to find, but here you were, this whole time, just a few blocks from my house," she said to the granite headstone. "Seems like your sister managed to get you a marker. You haven't been gone long, but I sure miss talking to you. Guess you know, but Carlos got accepted. Early decision or something. They wouldn't pay for his audition, but, Buster, they are paying for that boy's entire college tuition!"

She sighed.

"We all excited. Willie is going to Atlanta, and Shayla still deciding."

"Oh, and Earl has himself in a hot mess. He got in a fight with some woman at the liquor store and is wanted on aggravated assault. They haven't found his worthless butt."

"Tell Li'l J I said..." she stopped suddenly. "Somebody's coming. Although, maybe I'm not crazy talking to you here." A woman approached from the hill. She looked at Peaches, paused and looked around, and continued.

Peaches waved, then looked back at the headstone.

The woman approached. "Hi, I—oh," she said as she looked down. "That's my brother," she said, pointing to the marker. "I didn't realize you were at—did you know my brother?"

"Hi, yes, well, a little. From the..." she said, then extended her hand. "My name is Peaches."

"I'm Sally," She shook hands with Peaches as she looked from the grave back to Peaches. "I didn't know he had, well, I didn't know much about Buster. We weren't close. I was the only one at the service—not counting my best friend Martha and the preacher."

"I'm sorry I missed that...I didn't know him very long,

to be honest, but he did talk about you. It's nice to finally meet you," said Peaches.

"Oh," Sally said, as she looked at the headstone.

"Well, I'll let you two have a visit," Peaches offered.

"Oh, that's okay. Honestly, this may sound weird, but, do you mind if I join you?"

"Not at all, honey—

"It's just that...it's almost like death is bringing us—" Sally cut herself short. "Might be nice to meet one of his friends."

Peaches smiled. "Here's, let's have a sit on my blanket for a spell. I wanna hear more about Buster's baby sister."